"Stay with me. Please."

Samantha wasn't sure what she was asking him—to stay the night or forever. But it didn't matter. Right now she knew she couldn't face a night without Caleb, her body tucked against his, his warmth making her feel safe just for a while.

His gaze flickered, a flash of wild, out-of-control hunger, so intense she should have been afraid, but she wasn't. A tremor ran through her—excitement and expectation.

Tomorrow night Samantha would leave, run as fast and far as she could. She'd leave Caleb and the zombies behind. She would have to.

But tonight…

She ran her hands down his chest, the rocklike ripples of his abs, and marveled again at how any man could be built like him, especially one who didn't live in a gym.

And Caleb didn't. He roamed the roads, wild and free, hunting monsters, killing monsters, never settling, never giving up.

She had never met anyone like him.

And tonight he was hers.

Books by Lori Devoti

Harlequin Nocturne

Unbound #18
Guardian's Keep #32
Wild Hunt #41
Holiday with a Vampire II #54
"The Vampire Who Stole Christmas"
Dark Crusade #62
The Hellhound King #82
Zombie Moon #91

*Unbound

LORI DEVOTI

grew up in southern Missouri and attended college at the University of Missouri-Columbia, where she earned a bachelor of journalism. However, she made it clear to anyone who asked, she was not a writer; she worked for the dark side—advertising. Now, twenty years later, she's proud to declare herself a writer and visits her dark side by writing paranormals for Harlequin Nocturne.

Lori lives in Wisconsin with her husband, daughter, son, an extremely patient shepherd mix and the world's pushiest Siberian husky. To learn more about what Lori is working on now, visit her Web site at www.loridevoti.com.

Zombie Moon

LORI DEVOTI

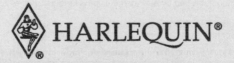

HARLEQUIN®

TORONTO • NEW YORK • LONDON
AMSTERDAM • PARIS • SYDNEY • HAMBURG
STOCKHOLM • ATHENS • TOKYO • MILAN • MADRID
PRAGUE • WARSAW • BUDAPEST • AUCKLAND

PLEASE RECYCLE • THIS PRODUCT IS RECYCLABLE

Recycling programs
for this product may
not exist in your area.

ISBN-13: 978-0-373-61838-5

ZOMBIE MOON

Dear Reader,

Zombie Moon is the story of two people whose lives were changed forever by monsters most people think exist only in B movies.

Caleb Locke and Samantha Wagner both lost people to zombies. Caleb lost his entire family. Samantha lost her best friend.

Caleb chooses to deal with his grief by searching out and killing every zombie he can find. Samantha holds on by hoping she can save her friend by hunting down the world's only known zombie hunter, Caleb.

But once they team up, they both discover the other isn't quite what they thought. Both have secrets. The question is, will those secrets destroy them, or can they overcome their pasts, defeat the zombies and find love together?

Zombie Moon was a lot of fun to write. I hope you enjoy it!

Lori Devoti

Special thanks for this book go to my editor Tara Gavin who called me to see how I felt about zombies…and for liking the idea of a werewolf hunting them.

Thanks also to Shawna Rice for being understanding and a jewel to work with, and of course, to my agent Holly Root for everything she does.

I'd also like to thank a few of my friends who helped get me through some difficult months while writing this book…Eve Silver, Laura Drewry, Kristina Cook, Caroline Linden, Sally MacKenzie and Ann Christopher. I can't tell you how much I appreciate each of you letting me cry on your virtual shoulders.…

Chapter 1

The stench of death hung in the alley like smoke in a bar—so thick Caleb Locke swore he could see it.

He spat. He certainly had no trouble tasting or smelling the evidence of what had been here before him.

Both the benefit and curse of being a werewolf.

Caleb rubbed his hand over his mouth and studied the shadows that lined the narrow passage. Five people had died in this alley in the past week. They'd been found with their skulls cracked and their brains gone. Since then, two more people had gone missing.

Caleb was here to find the killers. He took a few quiet steps forward, deeper into the darkness, then stopped and sniffed.

The alley appeared to be empty, but Caleb knew better. He knew his prey was near. He just had to lure them into the open.

He slung the pack he wore on his back sideways so he could reach into its depths. From inside he pulled a vacuum-sealed metal container.

He paused to double-check his first impression before opening the thermos. Closing his eyes, he took another quick inhalation of the alley's cool, damp air. The scent of death was no stronger. No sound except his own breathing broke the silence. He cursed. He would have to spend his precious bait. The last he had.

He opened the lid. Air hissed free. He paused one last time, but there was still no sign of life—or death—in the alley.

Resolved that this time his prey wouldn't come to him easily, he returned his attention to his task and dumped the contents of the cylinder out onto his bare palm.

Zombie caviar—chunks of human brain. Looking at it, holding it, even stealing it from the recently deceased in hospitals and funeral homes, had stopped bothering him long ago.

Hoping what he held would be enough, he broke off a golf-ball–size bit. Then he glanced around.

The alley was lined with normal human refuse—rolling trash bins, metal garbage cans, broken boxes and the like. No one object or area held any value over another as far as attracting the monsters, but there were definite advantages to luring them to an open space. There he could pick off a few before they realized he was standing in the shadows waiting to attack.

He touched the holster that hung from his belt. An old WWI revolver he'd rechambered to take a more powerful round. One well-aimed shot meant one less zombie. Quick, easy and fairly mess free…as dealing with zombies went. However, if more than a few showed up for the picnic he'd laid out, he'd have to go for bigger, messier ammo. His shotgun.

He had it, too, already tucked inside a Dumpster.

Confident tonight would prove to be an easy evening of zombie killing, he deposited the brains he'd taken from the canister onto a forgotten cardboard box, then scraped his hand over its edge. After one more quick look around, he positioned the bait in the center of the alley, took a step back and surveyed the scene.

Satisfied that his trap was set, he hopped into the Dumpster.

It wouldn't be long now.

Samantha Wagner pulled her coat more tightly around her body. The sun had fallen past the horizon only an hour earlier, but the temperature had quickly plummeted.

The wind cut through the silver faux-fur-lined trench coat she'd bought at a secondhand shop two days earlier. Wisconsin in November bore little resemblance to her home state of Tennessee in the same month. Back home the trees were still changing, exploding in fiery displays of red and yellow. Here the trees were bare; snow littered the ground and rain fell in hard icy pellets. A lovely combination if you were a penguin or a polar bear. Samantha was neither. She might not look it, but she was as southern as sweet tea and fried green tomatoes.

Hoping to block more of the wind, she flipped up her collar and kicked a clump of ice out of her path. It skittered over the wet pavement and lodged under a Dumpster. Still, she jumped at the noise. She bit her lip in annoyance. If she was going to be jumping at every little sound, she had no business embarking on this mission. But even as she chastised herself, she released herself from some of the guilt. The street was empty, dark and cold, and unfortunately she knew what had happened to the last visitors to this place.

She shivered and tried not to think of the pictures she'd seen on the Internet, the image of a teenage prostitute, bite marks clear on her arms and legs, her arms pulled from their sockets.

The girl's brain had been missing, too. At least that's what the local paper had reported.

And there had been others....

Samantha pressed her lips together and tried again to forget the images. She concentrated instead on avoiding the patches of ice that spotted the sidewalk and thinking of why she was here—to find Caleb Locke. Once she did, she could leave.

She reached into her coat pocket with her left hand and felt the tiny metal lump she'd sewn into the lining. A wave of guilt surged through her. She squeezed the metal tube and squelched the unwelcome emotion.

If the stories of Caleb Locke were true, she was doing him a favor, and more importantly, she didn't really have a choice.

To her right, down an alley, something clanged. Already jumpy, she tensed. Her right hand went to the other pocket where she kept a snub-nosed revolver. Touching the grip relaxed her. What the small weapon lacked in firepower, she made up for in accuracy. She'd been practicing with it daily for the last month. *Funny how old skills came back.*

She'd learned to shoot when she was six. Started with cans and moved up to vegetable-thieving rabbits by the time she was twelve. But by twenty she'd left that life behind, and replaced guns and red meat with yoga and tofu.

She'd never planned on going back.

But all that had changed when her best friend, Allison, disappeared.

There was another clang. She pulled the gun from her pocket and stepped sideways into the alley. The breeze caught her coat, flapping it open.

The wind cut through her, but the cold wasn't what froze her in place. It was what she saw. Zombies, six of them, scrabbling and scraping, each trying to get what looked a hell of a lot like human brains into their open maws.

She closed her eyes, briefly blocking out the sight, but not the reality. Zombies were real.

Until now she'd held out some slim hope this was all some horrible mistake or a joke gone wrong. But no, the video, the Internet reports, all of it was real.

She lifted her gun and fired.

A woman—or what used to be a woman—shuffled toward the pile of brains. Her feet were bare, her taffeta dress torn and stained. Her skin was gray and bald patches of scalp shone through hair that at some point in its past had been pulled into an elaborate updo. A strand of pearls hung lopsided from one side of her head.

A man in a stained tux followed.

A wedding party or a couple stuck on a perpetual prom date from hell. Caleb couldn't tell which, and he was twenty years past caring.

He'd seen too many walking corpses, witnessed too many of them lash out at loved ones they had forgotten. They weren't the brothers, sisters and mothers they used to be. They were monsters. Monsters he was determined to exterminate.

He rose a little higher inside the Dumpster and balanced the stock of his shotgun on its metal edge. Four more zombies shuffled behind the first two.

His finger resting lightly on the trigger, he waited. The closer the group gathered together, the easier downing multiples with one shot would be.

The prom pair had reached the bait. They dug their fingers into it like two kids digging into a jar of peanut butter. Their eyes rolled back in their heads, revealing nothing but whites as they sucked their fingers clean. Zombie clean, anyway. Bits of brain fell from their dry mouths, spattering the alley floor. They shrieked at its loss, the girl falling onto her knees to scrabble for the crumbs on the ground.

The four that had lagged behind were close now. Close enough they saw the feast and screamed, too, a dry, heaving noise that in no way resembled words, but that released an odor so intense someone less steeled to the stench of death would have hurled. Caleb, however, embraced it. It meant the hunt was on; his prey was here. Besides, the stench of a zombie still moving was nothing to that of one that had been eviscerated, and ultimately that was his goal.

The zombies scuffled closer, stumbling and staggering as they tried to hurry feet that in at least one case no longer existed. A motorcyclist, Caleb guessed. The zombie wore leather pants, jacket and one boot. The other leg ended in a stump, but the zombie didn't seem to notice. He thumped closer, his body listing back and forth as if at any moment he would fall to the ground.

His arm was missing, too. Probably chopped off in

whatever accident had killed the man. He reached the prom partners first. With his remaining hand, he lashed at the female in taffeta. She roared back at him. Her date, on the ground, too, now, glanced at them. With no recognition of what was happening on his face, he continued to shove brains into his mouth at a furious pace.

The female turned, saw the brains were gone and threw herself onto the tuxedo-outfitted zombie whom Caleb had pegged as her date.

The other three had reached them now. A brawl broke out. The zombies, powered by greed and rage, tore at each other's limbs and clothing. Bits of material and zombie flew from the circle they had formed.

Caleb was immune to their noise and smell, immune to everything except the adrenaline that came with the hunt. It pumped through him, making him eager for the kill.

They were close, close enough he could take out three with one pull of the trigger.

He lowered his cheek to the shotgun's stock, caressed the trigger one last time and whispered the words he whispered each time he downed a zombie—the promise to keep up his hunt, to complete his revenge, no matter the cost. Ready, he prepared to fire.

A shot rang out. Caleb jerked his finger away from the trigger. He hadn't fired. His gaze locked onto the zombies, his zombies, his prey.

The prom queen staggered backward and pressed her hand to her torn and stained bodice. But no blood oozed through her fingers and no yelp of pain left her lips. But then, whether she realized it or not, she was a zombie. She had little blood left to lose and no ability to feel anything, not joy, sorrow or even pain. Those sensations existed with life, and once it was lost, they didn't return, not even if the body was reanimated.

No, now the once pretty prom queen was nothing but a mindless, devouring shell.

A mindless, devouring shell that was no more affected by a bullet to the heart than a bear was by a bee sting.

Caleb cursed and jerked his gaze to the end of the alley from where the shot had come.

What he saw caused him to still. He'd expected police or perhaps a human store owner out to protect his property. What he hadn't expected was an avenging angel dressed in a silver trench coat, tight-fitting black pants and a breast-hugging shirt.

Her hair was damp and dark and clung to her face, but with his werewolf vision Caleb could see the red in it. Just as even from this distance he could see the determination in the set of her jaw and the tinge of fear in her oversize eyes.

She cocked the gun and fired again.

But this bullet, just like the first, did nothing to stop the zombies.

Like the bear with that bee sting, the shot just angered them further.

The zombies rushed toward the shooter.

The zombies flung their heads to the side and smashed against each other like drunks in a mosh pit as they fought to get to Samantha—even the female whom she'd shot in the heart, twice.

The bullet hadn't stopped the demented creature, hadn't even slowed her down. If anything, it had drawn the entire group's attention away from their squabble and focused it onto Samantha.

Her heart beat loudly and sweat broke out over her body, but Samantha stood steady. She had a weapon; she knew how to use it. She would be fine. Besides, she had nowhere to run.

Tightening her jaw, she cocked her gun and fired again. It had to work; it had to stop them.

The zombie in the front, a woman dressed in a housecoat and bare feet, stopped, but only for a second. Her mouth dropped open and her hand rose. She pointed to her forehead and stuck her index finger through the round hole that now lay between her eyes.

Then she shrieked.

The other zombies didn't seem to notice her distress. They kept coming.

Heart? Brain? Where did Samantha have to shoot the creatures to stop them? What the hell was left?

Holding her gun at her side, Samantha hesitated. She'd used three shots. She had three rounds left for five zombies. She was no math genius, but even she knew those odds weren't good.

Three rounds. Two to do what damage she could to the zombies, and the last... Better dead than killed by what staggered toward her.

She lifted the gun and fired again, this time hitting a male in a tuxedo. The round caught him in the eye. He didn't blink, figuratively or literally. Not that he could have. His eyelids appeared to have gone missing long ago.

Without hesitating she fired her fourth bullet, into his throat. It zipped through him to strike a man in leather, as well.

Two for the price of one...but neither fell.

Samantha was down to her last round.

The taffeta-adorned female staggered forward, her hand out, inches from touching Samantha.

She lifted the gun.

What the hell was the woman doing?

With his shotgun gripped in his hands like a club, Caleb sprinted forward. He swung and smashed the heavy butt of the gun into a zombie skull. He didn't pause to see which creature he hit. He just spun and slammed the stock into another.

A bullet whizzed past him. He glanced at the woman firing. Her gaze was on him, her eyes round as she sucked in a breath.

A hand landed on his shoulder. He swung the gun like a bat and caught the prom queen across the forehead.

While the party-going zombie was still on the ground, he flipped the shotgun end over end and with the butt pressed against his shoulder, pumped a round into the chamber. Then he fired, up close and very personal.

Shot roared out of the barrel. The gun recoiled against his shoulder. He held tight and pumped it again. His back to the woman in the silver coat, he raised the gun head height and fired again. He kept firing until he knew there wasn't a zombie standing. Then he fired some more. Smoke and the smell of gunpowder clogged the air, taking the edge off the stench of death and decay at least.

He flipped the gun again so the butt was down, then he roamed the alley, stepping over the fallen zombies, nudging each with his toe. The one in the tux twitched, so Caleb smashed the butt of the shotgun into the mess that had been the zombie's head, until he was sure all brain matter had been destroyed.

Without looking at the woman, he muttered, "Shooting them does no good. Not unless you take out their brain stem." He didn't know who the female was or why she was here, but when she'd seen the zombies she should have run. Any rational human would have. But she hadn't, which meant she was either very stupid or she knew what she was looking at and had thought she could kill it.

There was only one place for amateur zombie hunters. The grave.

Her ignorance could easily have gotten her killed or, worse, it could have gotten her turned into one of the monsters that now lay decomposing on the alley floor.

The prom queen, her face a mass of gore, flicked her fingers. Caleb lifted his foot and smashed his steel-toed boot into what was left of her skull. Then he stomped down one last time, making sure he made contact with her spine.

When her hand had fallen and he was confident none of the others were going to rise, he turned to the woman.

He could see her hair and features clearly now. Dark hair with a hint of red that brushed her shoulders and oversize hazel eyes. Her face was tiny, almost delicate, and her stature matched the gun she carried—petite, not meant for the job she'd put before it.

"You need to get out of here and not come back." He didn't bother softening his tone or asking how she was. She'd walked into this; now she needed to get out…and stay out.

Zombies were pack animals, not for security so much

as the inability to think on their own. If one stumbled in any direction, all those around him would follow. And while the zombies' brains were far from fresh, their combined scent would still be triple the attractant of his small bit of bait.

If six had shown on the first encounter, another ten might come later. At least Caleb could hope. He'd been following a growing trail of zombies for months. After twenty years of searching, he was getting close to their source. He could feel it.

He pulled a rag from his pocket and wiped bits of brain and decayed flesh from the butt of his shotgun.

Then he looked at the woman. She was standing in the same spot, hadn't moved so much as an inch. If he had to guess, she hadn't even blinked, maybe hadn't breathed.

Her face was ashen, as lacking in color as the prom queen's had been, and the revolver she held tumbled from her fingers.

She turned and ran a few stumbling steps, made it all of eight feet before doubling over and puking on the asphalt.

Caleb threw the cloth he'd used onto the ground and growled.

He was no one's nursemaid.

He picked up the pistol she had dropped and shoved it into the back of his jeans. With it secure, he turned, thinking to leave, but as his gaze fell on the pile of zombies, he remembered where he was, and what else would be arriving soon.

With another growl, he strode toward the woman. He was within grabbing range when he heard the shuffling footsteps of more zombies.

He slapped his hand over the woman's mouth and jerked her against him. "Do not say a word. Don't even breathe," he hissed. Then he walked backward, dragging her with him. She didn't struggle—the one smart thing he'd seen from her since her arrival. He took some heart in that, gained hope that she had some sense.

Once they were hidden behind the Dumpster, he whispered another warning in her ear then dropped his hand from her mouth and loosened his hold.

She sank to a squat and rested her forehead against the Dumpster, her fingers twitching at her sides. Her perfume reached out to him, a light floral scent completely out of place in the death-filled alley.

Not a scent he'd associate with someone hunting zombies. Perhaps she was just a thrill seeker, coming armed to an area advertised as dangerous. If so, she'd received quite the lesson.

He doubted she'd repeat the prank soon.

Her coat bunched between her shoulder blades. When he glanced at her she looked away and studied the solid wall of green metal inches from her face.

She didn't trust him.

That was fine. He didn't need or want her trust.

He just wanted her to stay out of his way. Tossing her a warning glance, he peered over the top of the Dumpster.

Four more zombies had gathered in the alley. They bent awkwardly, reaching for the gore that had been their own kind. Their eyes blank, possibly sightless, they shoveled bits of decaying flesh into their mouths.

This batch seemed older than the first, in worse shape, which made sense. The younger zombies, those retaining more of their function and body parts, made it to any scene first. The older ones came along later and were left the role of scavenger.

A male dressed in a stained green leisure suit ripped off the prom queen's arm and chomped down with toothless jaws.

Beside Caleb, the woman grabbed hold of the Dumpster's lip and pulled herself to a stand. Her fingers were white against the green metal. Turned whiter as her grip on the edge tightened.

Ignoring her, he pulled his revolver from its holster. He needed to take out the zombies' brain stems. From this distance the shotgun wouldn't work. Up close it worked great. One blast opened a zombie's brittle skull, made it easy to smash through any important bits left behind. But at this distance, he needed accuracy and the shotgun wasn't built for that. His revolver, however, was.

He rested his hand on the edge of the Dumpster and waited. He needed a clean shot, hopefully from behind.

The woman laid her hand, cool but surprisingly steady, on his arm. "Let me."

He raised a brow. She had wasted five bullets without downing a single zombie. Then she had puked on the pavement.

His faith in her was far from impressive.

He stared at her briefly then turned his attention back to the zombies. Leisure suit was standing sideways, his head cocked as if listening to or smelling something.

It was all the warning Caleb had before the creature turned. With a yowl the zombie staggered toward them.

Joining his cries, his companions followed.

Caleb cocked the gun, fired…and missed the stampeding zombies completely. Habit made him curse, but survival instinct made him focus. He couldn't afford to do as the woman beside him had done and fire wildly. He had to think, to calculate his best move. His ability to do so even while under attack, combined with his werewolf talents, had kept him alive so far.

The monsters stamping and scrambling toward him were facing him. The revolver's round would shoot through their skulls, but with the group turned toward him and moving at the pace they were, taking out their brain stem would be nothing more than luck, and Caleb's luck had run out a long time ago. He didn't believe in it anymore, didn't believe in anything, didn't trust in anything except his own skill.

But his options were few. He shoved the revolver into the woman's hand. "Just don't shoot me," he said before shoving the Dumpster out of their way and charging the zombies, shotgun in hand.

Chapter 2

Samantha stood frozen, unable to move, unable to believe the man who had pulled her behind the Dumpster had then—once the zombies had actually arrived, when she and he were in the most danger—kicked their barricade away and left her standing completely exposed.

What kind of idiot was he?

The man—Caleb Locke, she hoped—raced toward the four new arrivals. Two feet away, he lifted his shotgun and fired. The closest zombie, a man in a leisure suit, crumpled. The shot had annihilated the top third of him, blown his brains out the back of his skull.

She tasted bile, wanted to look away, but couldn't. Shooting zombies was harder than she had imagined, because despite their gruesome appearance and horrendous smell, they still looked human, still carried clues of what they had been in life.

The other zombies, however, didn't seem to share Samantha's qualms. As one, they jumped on the carnage that had been their companion and began fighting over his remains.

Samantha watched, unable to do anything more. At least they were occupied, or so she hoped.

Two of them, women, looked up and sniffed the air like dogs catching wind of a squirrel. Their eyes were hollow—not lacking in emotion, but hollow as in missing. Breath shuddered through Samantha.

A third zombie, who appeared to have at one time been a teenage boy dressed in a torn football jersey, lurched to a stand. He had his eyes and they were both pointed at Samantha.

Caleb's shotgun fired. The noise slammed into Samantha, her body tensed and her ears rang. She was comfortable with guns, but no amount of experience or practice could have readied her for this.

One of the female zombies near Caleb screeched. Had he missed? Or had he hit his target, and the second zombie was objecting?

Samantha had no time to glance in his direction to see. The zombie focused on her was bent over and, like the football star he might have once been, was hurtling toward her.

"Damn it!" Caleb yelled and fired again. This time Samantha saw what he hit, saw the small bits of metal slam into the zombie headed toward her. The shot got the zombie in the side, spun its body so it was pointed toward Caleb, its back to Samantha.

It was her chance to run, to get the hell away from

here and forget she had ever wanted to find Caleb Locke.

But she couldn't. Her loyalty to Allison and a childhood of watching old Westerns where the good guys fought, no matter the odds, wouldn't let her.

One hand felt heavy. A memory of Caleb slipping something into her grip flashed through her mind. She lifted her hand, surprised to see a gun there—a big gun, heavy and capable of bringing down anything, even a zombie.

She'd asked for this gun, and she knew how to use it. Yes, she'd wasted five bullets trying to kill the first group of zombies, but that was before Caleb had told her what she'd done wrong. She could do this now. She had to.

She took two giant steps forward and lifted the gun. Her arm shook. She lifted her other arm, held the weapon with two hands to keep it steady. Ready to pull the trigger, she repeated the crazed zombie hunter's lecture. "Take out the brain stem—it's the only way to stop them."

She pulled in a breath and forgot where she was, forced herself not to hear Caleb's yells or the zombies' screams. Just focused on the indented spot where the zombie's head met his neck.

Then she fired.

His shotgun held to his shoulder, Caleb froze. The woman stood behind the zombie he'd been about to blast back to the coffin. Only his werewolf reflexes saved her from being blasted along with him.

He bit the inside of his cheek to keep from pulling the trigger anyway. There was no room for stupidity when hunting zombies. Better the woman die by shotgun spray than be turned by a zombie. He'd given her the gun because he'd had to, because he couldn't leave her standing there unarmed, but he hadn't expected her to jump into the battle with it, not after she had failed so miserably before.

But then thrill seekers weren't usually listed at the top of the dean's list. They weren't listed at all, because usually they were dead.

The zombie seemed to sense someone was behind him. He lifted one hand and listed to one side as if preparing to turn.

The muzzle flashed and a shot exploded in the night. Caleb tensed, sure the zombie would stagger the foot or so that separated him from the woman. He was too close. Caleb wouldn't get there in time to stop his bite. And then Caleb would have one more zombie to kill— the thrill-seeking woman who didn't have the sense to stay out of an alley filled with the living dead.

The bullet sped through the zombie's neck and came out his mouth. It kept going until it hit a fourth zombie, this one dressed in pants and a silk blouse. The bit of metal lodged in her shoulder. She jerked and stepped to one side, knocking into the second half of the old woman pair that Caleb had been sighting with his shotgun. This new pair staggered forward, their arms out like something out of a cut-rate Frankenstein flick.

The teen zombie, the one the woman had shot, crumpled. Behind him, the woman in silver still stood. She looked calm now, in control. She lifted her gun again.

"Get down," she yelled. Then she fired.

Granny number two flopped forward.

Caleb glared at the woman who was downing his zombies with his gun, interrupting his hunt. "You get down," he yelled back.

The remaining zombie, the one in silk, oblivious to their disagreement, stepped over her fallen companion.

Caleb pumped his shotgun and lifted it to his cheek. Then without knowing if the woman had listened to him or not, he fired.

Samantha dropped to the ground seconds before the psycho hunter discharged his shotgun.

While the blast still echoed down the alley, she hopped back to her feet. She was barely upright before two more explosions told her he was repeating the manic shooting he'd done before.

Her hands shaking, she strode toward him.

"They're dead already," she yelled. She knew she shouldn't care, but she couldn't help it.

Caleb turned to face her. His eyes were unlike any man's she'd seen before, golden, wild, but not insane; intriguing, she realized.

"They're zombies. Being dead doesn't stop them," he said.

He lifted his foot and smashed his heavy boot into what was left of an older woman's skull. Samantha turned her face to the side.

He continued smashing and kicking, giving no sign he noticed the ungodly gore and its stench.

Finally, he looked up at her. "Fair shot. Was it luck?"

Fighting to keep from losing what little remained of her lunch, Samantha took a minute to reply. When she had focused enough to understand his question, she bristled. "Luck and guns don't mix." Her father had pounded that into her, that knowing how to fire a gun wasn't enough. You had to have the skill to use it well, or you shouldn't even pick one up. Anything less would just get you killed.

Caleb stared at her for a second as if waiting for some further answer, then he grunted and held out his hand.

His fingertips were square, as were his hands. There was strength in them, too. She'd never noticed a man's hands before; it made her uncomfortable that she did now, while surrounded by death.

She shifted her weight from one foot to the other.

"My revolver," he prompted.

"Oh." Carefully keeping her gaze from his hands, or any part of him, she removed the remaining ammunition, and handed him the weapon.

He lifted a brow. Ruffled, she dumped the bullets into his hand, too.

With a shake of his head, he immediately reloaded the weapon and slipped it into a leather holster that hung from his belt.

Then he turned and walked away.

Confused, she stood there for a second. Then she held up her hand and called, "Wait." She might not like him, she might not trust him, he might, in fact, intimidate the hell out of her, but he was the only chance she had to save Allison.

He kept walking.

She glanced at the carnage. Swallowing to keep from throwing up again, she yelled, "There could be more."

He turned slowly and let out a breath laden with

strained patience. "If there are they aren't worth fighting. That last batch could barely stay upright."

She fought the need to squirm. She'd been proud of what she had done, that she hadn't panicked, that she'd downed two of the four. And now he was telling her they hadn't counted, had been no real challenge at all.

"You're welcome, by the way," she murmured.

He studied her for a second. She thought he was going to say something, ask her how she got here, why she hadn't freaked when she'd seen the zombies, ask any number of reasonable questions in this unreasonable situation, but he didn't. He just reached to the small of his back, pulled out her snub-nose revolver and set it on one of the few remaining clean patches of asphalt.

Then he strode out of the alley.

The woman still stood behind him surrounded by massacred zombies. Caleb would be lying to himself if he didn't admit he was intrigued by her. Why was she here and how had she found the strength of mind to sneak up on that zombie and plug him in the brain pan? But regardless of his interest, Caleb didn't mingle. Not with anyone.

Sure, he had hookups with the occasional female. He wasn't a zombie himself. But he didn't get close, not emotionally.

And somehow he guessed this woman wouldn't be easy to set aside, wouldn't be easy to forget, not if he let her get close.

He could see her in his mind, standing ankle deep in zombie gore, his oversize pistol hanging at her side, and her silver coat pushed back to reveal her body-hugging black outfit. He had never seen anyone—in person, on a billboard, or in a pinup magazine—look even half as sexy.

She was a strange mix, polite and angry, scared and fearless. She hadn't been shocked when she had first seen the zombies in the alley. She had been shaken, not completely prepared perhaps, but not shocked. And despite the quiver he'd seen run through her, she'd pulled out her little gun and shot. Then later when he was sure she would realize she was in over her head, she had not only shot the zombies with his gun, but she'd followed his instructions and destroyed them. Pulled off a shot very few could, blasting through their brain stem with a single bullet.

He had to admire a woman like that. He didn't want to, but he couldn't help himself.

Which meant he needed to get away from her and fast, and that was exactly what he was going to do. Right now.

Damn the man. He didn't stop.

Samantha watched as the elusive Caleb Locke strode from the alley without so much as a "thank you very kindly." With a gun strapped to his hip and a shotgun at his side, he looked like a character from some old Western. She had never met anyone as confident of their power as Caleb Locke, never realized someone like him could really exist.

He was every action hero of every movie she had ever seen, ever secretly fantasized of meeting. And now she had and he had just walked away, left her standing in an alley filled with decomposing corpses.

What did she do now? She needed a hero. She needed

Caleb Locke. Fighting a sense of failure and loss, she walked to her revolver.

The stench of death intensified. Gagging, she retrieved the weapon and turned.

A shadow darker than the growing night loomed before her. She looked up, into the face of a six-foot-tall black man or what had at one time been a six-foot-tall black man. Now he was the walking dead.

Cold wrapped around her. She'd thought this stage of her nightmare was over, but as she stared at the zombie dressed all in black—black suit, shirt and tie—she couldn't deny it wasn't. Not by a long shot.

Funny, she'd made a joke. Long shot, just like her odds of surviving this alone.

The zombie slung his body sideways, using inertia to move his arm, to send it swinging toward her. He was old, older and more decayed than the others, even the last four. But that just made looking at him, realizing what he was and what he used to be, all the more horrifying.

Her brain shut down. She was done, couldn't think, didn't want to think.

Operating on pure gut reflex, she lifted the gun and fired. The bullet hit the creature right between his sunken eyes. He stared back at her stupidly, didn't fall or bleed or—

She remembered Caleb's words.

Shooting a zombie anywhere but the brain stem didn't stop them. It just made them angry.

And she'd just used her last bullet.

Caleb smelled the zombie seconds before the gun fired. He'd already turned and was racing back to where he'd left the woman in the body-hugging outfit and space-worthy silver coat when it did.

She stood in the alley surrounded by the fallen zombies, her body perfectly still. For a moment he thought the zombie had already struck, that he was seeing the poison of its bite work its way through her system. Then her fingers opened and the pistol fell to the ground.

He realized then she was out of bullets. Realized then he couldn't reach her, not before the zombie did.

But his gun could.

He jerked the heavy pistol from its holster and slid it across the icy pavement like an Olympic curling champion. It knocked into her foot. She blinked, then dropped to a squat, grabbed the hefty revolver as if she'd practiced the move for a lifetime and fired again.

The bullet hit the zombie lurking over her in the base of the throat.

Despite Caleb's annoyance with her and his resolve that he wouldn't engage her in any way, a sliver of pride sliced through him. She'd stayed cool, picked up his gun and fired. And she'd aimed. Come damn close to hitting the target, too.

But the bullet had missed its mark.

The zombie jerked so his right arm flung up and out, deadweight like a man flinging a fifty-pound sack of flour. And like that sack of flour it hit the woman hard… knocked her in the head with a thud.

She fell backward, the gun tumbling out of her fingers and discharging wildly as the grips bounced off the asphalt. Then she landed, too, unconscious from the zombie's blow before her skull collided with the ground.

Her head bounced up and landed again; she didn't wince. She didn't move at all.

Caleb cursed, running and sliding now. He still held his shotgun, but instinct had taken over. He couldn't stop the urge to rush toward the monster, just like he couldn't stop his own monster, his wolf, from jumping forward, forcing his body to shift.

Even filled with adrenaline, he felt the pain as his body morphed. Bones bent; skin stretched. The change was always excruciating, his punishment for the choice he had made, but he couldn't stop running, had to leap actually, grit his teeth and push himself through the pain. He left the ground human, but landed on the creature's back one hundred percent wolf.

One hundred percent pissed-off, hungry-for-revenge wolf.

The hunger and the drive to kill were always intense, too intense, when he attacked in wolf form. All logic left him for a while. Like the old tales of lore, he would go berserk, tear into the walking dead's necks and sever their heads from their spines in a few ravaging snaps.

This time was no different. The zombie stumbled, an accidental move that proved defensive. Caleb fell onto the pavement, but immediately hopped back onto his feet. Facing the zombie, he growled. The creature was old; it had been dead for years. It smelled of mold and rot.

The zombie bent and swung its arm toward Caleb in the same erratic motion it had used to down the woman. Caleb jumped back and the monster's fingers brushed his fur. He bristled and the wolf in him took over.

He leaped and hit the zombie square in the chest, forcing it backward. Then he lunged upward to grab ahold of the decaying flesh of the zombie's neck. The creature flailed at him, but it was a hideously unfair fight. The zombie was too old; it had long lost any real use of its arms. They hung at its sides lifeless unless the creature used the entirety of its body weight to fling them haphazardly at its chosen target.

Somewhere buried, Caleb the man processed this, but on the surface, in control of his body, Caleb the wolf didn't care. The wolf only wanted to destroy.

And he did. He tore and pulled. Chomped into the zombie's neck again and again, through dried flesh and decayed muscle and finally through bone.

In seconds the zombie was nothing but a quivering corpse, just enough of his brain stem left to allow him to twitch and jerk like a snake with its head removed.

Caleb padded around the remains, sniffing, his lip curled. He was coming down from the animalistic high, waiting for his human half to regain control. It took four rounds, four circular trips.

With each pass, more gore found its way onto his fur and feet, until his pads were caked with it.

The wolf didn't mind, but the man hated it.

Still a wolf, but finally under control, Caleb sat. He needed to leave. He should have left before. There had been gunshots. The neighborhood might be deserted, but someone had to have heard. At some point someone would come to investigate.

He glanced at the woman lying five feet away. Her coat was open, revealing a lithe, toned body. Her outfit was fully visible now, some kind of workout pants and top, not the kick-ass jumpsuit he'd first imagined.

Despite knowing that time was running out, he trotted

toward her; he couldn't resist running his nose over her face.

Somehow as a wolf this felt safer, less personal than it would have been as a human. Her perfume reached out to him again. Jasmine. As a teen, before his world had collapsed, he'd had a girlfriend who used jasmine-scented soaps. The smell brought back memories, made him long for something he could never have.

His ears slipped low against his head. He took three steps back.

The woman was okay. She was breathing. She would come to and be fine. Yes, she'd wake to the massacred zombies, but that couldn't be helped. He couldn't hang around to clean up; he couldn't risk being caught when the police inevitably arrived.

Deciding to leave his clothing and escape as a wolf, he loped ten feet down the alley.

The woman moaned, rolled over and threw up again.

He paused, closed his eyes and willed himself not to weaken.

She wasn't his problem…would be nothing *but* a problem.

A siren wailed in the distance. His head jerked toward the sound. It was time to run.

He lifted one paw…he had to go.

He stopped and turned back. Her wet hair blended with the rain-dampened asphalt, but he knew it was red. Knew she was strong, too. And he knew she needed him.

Why else would she have come to this alley? Why else would she have stayed and fought the zombies when she could have run?

He sighed.

And he knew, damn everything, he couldn't leave her.

The siren wailed again, closer but not here yet.

Already moving toward her, he shifted form. He paused briefly to gather his boots and clothing. Still naked, he scooped her up and flung her over his shoulder.

Then as the sirens grew louder, he did what he should have done before. He disappeared into the shadows.

Chapter 3

Samantha stretched out her arm to slap at her alarm clock. Her hand hit a phone and sent it tumbling onto the ground. With a moan she rolled over, wondering when she'd moved the clock. Maybe Allison—

Her eyes flying open, she stiffened. No, not Allison. Her best friend and roommate had moved away over two months ago, taken a new job out of state and then disappeared altogether.

It was why Samantha had traveled north, why she had been looking for... Her mind latched on to something. Caleb Locke.

The events of the previous day flooded back to her. Caleb, strong and confident, with a sense of power that made her forget exploding guns and screeching zombies.

Zombies.

A cold sweat sprang from her pores.

She rolled onto her stomach and pressed her face into the pillow. Then she remembered where she was… or wasn't. She wasn't at home. She was in Wisconsin… cold, dreary Wisconsin.

Which meant she wasn't in her snug little house, safe in her room. Her fingers dug into the pillow. And she wasn't in the damp alley she remembered from last night.

So, where was she and who had brought her here? Caleb Locke? Her heart fluttered.

No, she remembered him walking away, leaving her. The disappointment she'd felt in the alley returned.

She only knew one other person in Wisconsin, and he wasn't someone she wanted to be with.

She jerked to a sitting position and gathered the thin blankets around her. The room was small and dingy. The furnishings consisted of the double bed she sat on, a small round laminate-topped table, a TV and two shelves that were mounted to the wall on either side of the bed, forming side tables.

By the looks and smell of the place, she knew immediately she was in a cheap motel, closely reminiscent of Norman Bates's, and she was alone.

Her gaze crawled to the two visible doors, one flanked by heavily curtained windows, and one off a tiny alcove. The bathroom, she guessed.

The sound of water running emanated from behind the closed door. A shower. Images of plastic curtains, giant knives and zombies laying in wait zipped through her brain. She rose on her knees to run but was stopped by the surprising realization that she wore only her bra and panties.

She hadn't stripped down to her underwear, not recently and not here. Which meant someone had done it for her.

Her heart battered against her ribs as if intent on escaping her body. Blood roared through her veins. She patted the covers, searching for her gun, her clothes, something to make her feel safe and in control.

Coming up empty, she leaped from the bed and raced to the door. A padlock hung from a hasp, making it impossible to open. She flung open the curtains, but bars covered the windows on her side, making even just breaking the glass a more difficult task.

But that didn't mean she wouldn't try. She spun and searched the small space for something to jam through the metal grid. Her gaze lit on the table. She surged forward and jerked at it. The top cut into her hands, but the table didn't budge. It was bolted to the floor.

For a second she stared stupidly at its base, wondering why anyone would bolt down a table.

No reason, except this, to keep someone from using it to escape or fight.

Serial killers did things like that.

She hurried back to the windows and the open curtains. The world outside was dark, with not even the cliché Vacancy sign all such motels should have. There were no sounds, either, no people coming and going, and no TVs blaring.

Absolutely no sign of life.

She realized then she wasn't in a motel, not a working one anyway. Whatever this place was, it had been deserted. There was no one here, except her and whoever stood behind that bathroom door.

The door suddenly looked bigger, ominous.

She grabbed the lone lamp from one of the makeshift side tables and jerked its cord from the wall. Then with it held against her chest, she crept toward the bathroom door.

When whoever—or whatever—was inside came out, she would have one chance, one brief moment, to smash the lamp onto his head.

That was it.

It would have to do.

Hours had gone by, or what felt like hours. Samantha's arm ached from the intensity of her grip on the lamp. Her thighs and back ached, too. Her body was taut, ready to spring, but the person or thing moving around on the other side of the cheap motel door refused to reveal himself.

She had started feeling silly ten minutes earlier.

Zombies didn't shower, or she couldn't imagine they did, but that didn't mean whoever was in the bathroom was safe, either. Safe people didn't take your clothing and padlock you into a room.

She mumbled that truth to herself, reminding herself that manners had no place in survival. Back home in Tennessee, while Allison had been teaching meditation and deep breathing at her yoga classes next door, Samantha had been pounding the basics of self-defense into her students.

If Allison had listened to her and been a little less trusting, maybe neither of them would be in the situations they were in now. But no, despite Allison's past, she had been trusting, had been the perfect Zen yoga instructor.

And truthfully, Samantha had envied her friend's

balance, her ability to put aside the wrongs done to her before and still look at others with trust and faith.

She had since Allison's disappearance tried to capture just a bit of that Zen for herself.

She definitely could use some now.

Keeping her eyes open, she lowered her arms and pulled in one smooth continuous breath. Holding the air in her lungs, she paused to do as Allison had taught her, to appreciate it. Already feeling calmer, she exhaled in the same smooth continuous manner she had inhaled. Then she paused again.

With a smile she realized it was working. Feeling stronger, she repeated the process four more times, and relaxed more with each repetition.

At the end of her fifth breath, the bathroom door flew open, and every particle of Zen she'd accumulated dissolved like sugar in sweet tea.

The knob knocked into the wall and a man, one-hundred-percent naked, stepped out of the steam-filled space.

Samantha opened her mouth to scream, then snapped her jaws shut. She was locked into the small room with her captor; the time for screaming was past. Now was the time to fight.

As he stepped into the main room, Caleb's gaze shot to the bed. He'd left the mysterious female there before going into the bathroom to shower. If she didn't come to on her own, he knew he would have to get her to a doctor. He would have taken her before showering, but showing up at an emergency room coated in blood tended to complicate an already complicated life.

And the female hadn't looked any better.

He had peeled off both of their clothes with plans of washing them along with his body in the shower.

As he'd pulled the tight material from her lean, but muscular form, images of her standing under the shower's stream with him, of water beading on her breasts, running down her cleavage, across her flat belly and finally getting lost in the thatch of curls that would hide her sex had almost overwhelmed him.

And he'd come close to taking not only her clothing, but her into the shower with him, as well.

But he didn't know her. Didn't know if she was the type to consider a no-commitment, no-previous-introduction hookup. So, he'd pushed aside his imaginings and left her lying in her undergarments on the motel bed's stained comforter.

He hadn't, however, stopped thinking of her, and hoping he would turn around in the tiny shower to find she had joined him under the pounding water.

She hadn't, of course, but as he stepped into the room, his gaze still shot to the bed.

Because, despite the certainty that extending their time together would be foolhardy, his body ached for her.

The bed was empty.

Immediately, he tensed. Alert, but not quickly enough. Something flashed in the darkness beside him—the downward movement of a weapon racing toward his skull.

Cursing his preoccupation with the female, he dropped to a crouch.

An object crashed onto the floor beside him. He leaped, rushing who or whatever had attacked. Sharp shards of pottery bit into his bare feet. He growled and kept going.

His shoulder collided with a body. He drove his assailant backward six feet into the main room, stopping only after both of them had landed on the bed. Fists pummeled the side of his head and his back. A knee jammed into his thigh, aiming, he knew, for a much more sensitive part. He growled again and grappled for control. One wrist contained in his hand, he stared down into the raging hazel eyes of the woman he'd fantasized about while standing alone in the shower.

She pulled back her free fist and punched him in the eye. With one last curse, he grabbed that wrist, too, and held her pinned to the bed.

"I should have left you," he muttered. But his body betrayed his words. His sex, fully exposed if she cared to look, hardened, and his heart rate sped.

Her eyes widened and her lips parted, surprised either by his presence or his words. He didn't know which and didn't for the moment care to find out. He lowered his mouth to hers and captured whatever questions had been about to escape.

Shock at realizing she lay trapped under the naked hunter quelled the adrenaline that had raced through Samantha, but once his lips touched hers it was back in full force.

His lips were soft but strong. His kiss patient but dominant, as if he could take his time because he knew she wouldn't fight him. She knew he shouldn't be kissing her, that she should fight him, but power and confidence emanated from him. Reminded her of those fantasies, the ones she had never really believed would come true, hadn't even thought she wanted to come true.

Her fingers relaxed, curled so their tips brushed over the tops of his hands. He softened his hold, but didn't release her.

It didn't matter; she didn't want to be released. It had been months since she had been this close to a man, a lifetime since she had felt this safe.

His lips moved from her mouth to her neck. The stubble on his chin was rough against her skin. He smelled of soap.

She arched her back and moaned. His tongue darted out, tasted her.

His teeth nibbled at her neck and she squirmed beneath him. His thigh moved between hers, and suddenly everything became very real. What she was doing became very real.

She jerked back, freeing her hands with one quick movement, and shoved them against his chest.

He rolled off of her without complaint, without comment or apology. He just landed on his feet and stared down at her, his gaze hooded and steady. His hair, long for a man, was still wet from the shower. It clung to his face. It reminded her of where they were and how little she knew of him. Or for that matter, how little he knew of her.

Feeling even more exposed than she was, she scrambled to a sitting position and pulled the bedcovers around her.

"Who are you?" he asked.

She studied a cigarette hole in the comforter. This wasn't how she had planned this conversation, not after she'd almost… She'd never… One-night stands were not something she did. She took care of her health and body and was training to be a nurse. She knew all too well the dangers of unguarded sex in the modern world.

She felt a strange need to tell him that, but she swallowed the words. She didn't owe him an explanation, and based on how he was staring at her, unemotional, almost detached, she doubted he'd even listen.

But his stance also made her reluctant to talk to him at all. He had just lain naked on her mostly undressed body, a body she had to guess he had undressed. He could at least look apologetic, embarrassed...something.

She lifted her chin and stared him down. "Caleb Locke?" At the flicker in his eyes, she inclined her head. "I've been looking for you."

Damn, the woman put up a good act. The problem was, Caleb couldn't tell which of her reactions was the act—the passion she'd exhibited seconds earlier or the toughness she was throwing at him now.

He angled his head and studied her a bit more, let her see that he was analyzing the truth behind her calm facade.

"You weren't surprised by the zombies." It was one of the things that had been gnawing at him. In the twenty years since he had discovered the existence of the monsters, he'd only encountered face-to-face a handful of other people who believed in them, even fewer who had actually seen or battled them.

Zombies didn't tend to leave witnesses behind, or if they did, those witnesses didn't stay human for long. A zombie's bite was highly contagious. In fact, it turned everyone except those already infected with lycanthropy into the walking dead, too. That little fact was why Caleb had become a werewolf.

She grabbed a lock of her hair and twirled it around her finger—a telltale sign that she wasn't as in control of her emotions as she wanted him to believe.

He pushed his advantage, taking a step closer. "How'd you learn about the zombies? Not from a hunter, that's clear. Or if you did, he's probably not around to teach you anymore." Anyone who shot at zombies like she had, without knowing their Achilles' heel, wound up dead or turned. Just like she would have if he hadn't been around to save her.

Her gaze flicked to the side. She swallowed. Finally, her voice hard, but with vulnerability showing in her eyes, she said, "Would you mind giving me my clothes? I'm not used to having a business conversation in my underwear."

Business. So that's what this was. He suppressed a smile. If only all his business could start like this had. He looked at her again, planning to taunt her a bit more. Her hand was fully entangled in her hair now. She was nervous; beyond that, she was scared.

He twisted his lips to the side. It was easy to forget women, people, still had those emotions. He'd killed them off so long ago.

He turned and stalked to the bathroom. After pulling on his still wet pants, he tossed her her clothes and her coat. The coat was made of some kind of stain-resistant fabric that he had simply wiped down, but the rest of her outfit he'd had to actually wash.

The thin material of her top and leggings were almost dry, but still it took her a bit of time and maneuvering to get her body into them. He turned his back to her, but watched her in the bathroom mirror as she hopped in place and jerked at the cloth. Finally dressed, she walked to the door and grabbed ahold of the padlock.

"And this."

In her clothing, thin and damp as they were, she was more confident. He felt more comfortable dealing with this persona than the nervous kitten, but still, he didn't take orders.

"And that?" he replied without moving.

"Unlock the door," she said.

He walked to the round table and leaned against it. Bolted to the floor, the piece didn't shift with the pressure of his weight. "Who are you and why were you in that alley?" he asked.

Her jaw jutted out. He could see she was weighing whether to answer him or not. He waited. He had nowhere to go, not until some blogger or tabloid Web site posted a new "rumored zombie attack." And even when they did, he didn't expect to have to travel far. Wisconsin and western Michigan had been laden with zombie activity lately.

This last one, five hours north of Chicago, had been the farthest he'd gone in six months. Zombie attacks frequently happened in clusters, but this was the longest time he'd ever spent in one part of the country. And these clusters were bigger. Not one or two zombies, which was the norm. No, here he'd been seeing groups, just like he'd seen last night.

He glanced at the laptop he'd stashed under the bed. It was still there; his guest apparently hadn't noticed it. Not that she would have learned anything from the computer. She wouldn't even be able to log on. His password was a string of numbers, letters and symbols that only had meaning to him—his blood type and the date he was turned into a were.

She closed her eyes briefly, but he saw the resignation in the gesture. She'd decided to be straight with him.

"My name is Samantha Wagner. I wasn't surprised by the zombies because I've seen them before. My best friend, Allison, is being held by them. I want you to help me rescue her."

He kept his face void of expression. Zombies didn't "hold" people. Zombies ate people or turned them into zombies. "Your friend was kidnapped by zombies?" His skepticism was real, but he guessed she didn't realize the reason for it.

He knew he'd guessed right when she replied.

"Don't play with me. You won't convince me those things today weren't real. I'm not crazy." Her tone was harsh, but something in her face said she didn't completely believe her own words.

She'd told other people then, been shot down, counseled, maybe even received the suggestions of medication. He knew the routine; he'd been through it.

"Are you sure?" he asked. It wasn't his job to reassure her. Besides, if she didn't believe, if she thought herself crazy, she'd be easier to get rid of. He didn't need a sidekick and he didn't need a job. He had his own mission to fulfill, his own revenge to seek. And with the activity he'd seen lately, he suspected he was closer to doing so than he had ever been before.

She met his gaze. "I know I've seen zombies, if that's what you mean."

So something else made her doubt her sanity.

She glanced at the bed. He got it then. Lying with

him, kissing him—that had been crazy. If he'd been in his wolf form, his fur would have ruffled, but he wasn't and his human brain had a chance to smooth out his instinctive reaction. She was right. Kissing him was crazy. Getting mixed up with him in any way would be even crazier.

He pushed himself away from the table. "I can't help you." He pulled a key from his pocket and walked to the door. "This neighborhood is deserted. May make it scary, but also makes it safe. Walk to the first cross street. I'll get a cab to pick you up."

He would log on to the Internet as soon as she was gone, call her a cab and check the blogs.

It was time to get back to the hunt. If he was lucky there'd be another report already. With each confirmed sighting in the region, he narrowed down the possible source of these zombies a bit more.

He shoved the door open with one hand and turned toward the bed. She didn't move.

He scowled. "Leave."

She lowered her hand, leaving one side of her hair bunched a bit around her ear. It should have looked silly, but it didn't; it looked endearing instead, like a child waking from a nap.

Caleb growled. He didn't have the time or patience for this. "Leave now. I said it was safe out there. I can't make any guarantees if you stay here." He let just a shade of the anger and pain that he lived with every day shine from his eyes, and raised one side of his upper lip in a snarl. It was an expression that had sent more than one testosterone-filled pup scurrying away.

She shuddered and walked to the door. Confident he'd made his point, he bent to retrieve the laptop. The door banged closed. He sighed, deflating a bit. Being Caleb Locke the man was tiring enough without having to play up his zombie-hunter reality for an audience.

He was meant to be alone. Enjoyed being alone. Still, he glanced over his shoulder as if he could catch one last glimpse of her.

She stared back at him, her spine pressed against the door, and her arms crossed over her chest. The laptop slipped from his fingers.

"I told you, I need your help." The fear was still apparent in her eyes, but her posture was pure determination. She didn't mean to leave. Of course, it wasn't really her choice. Stubborn, strong, whatever her traits, she would be no match for him. He wouldn't even have to lay a hand on her. One simple shift, one little peek at his secret, and she'd go running.

The reminder of what he'd given up to destroy his family's killers angered him. He pulled back his shoulders and lowered his head.

She held out one hand. "Don't. Intimidation isn't going to work. I've faced monsters I never dreamed existed. I've seen what they do to people. They have my friend. I'd do anything to save her. Anything." She dropped her gaze as she whispered the last.

He clenched his jaw. Little did she know there were not only monsters out there, but one in here with her. If he shifted, she'd run. He had no doubt of that, but would she come back? Would she share what she'd seen with others? Would he be featured on the blogs he frequented for news of zombies? Zombie-hunter werewolf!

Of course he would. The hunter would become the hunted. If he shifted in front of her, revealed what he was, he would have to kill her or accept being stalked forever.

Apparently, seeing acceptance in his hesitation, she walked to the other side of the room. There she turned and looked around for a place to sit, he realized. The room had no chairs. The bed and the table were the only flat surfaces, and he was next to both.

Looking uncomfortable, she pressed both of her palms flat against the wall behind her and leaned back so her hands were tucked in the small of her back.

"Will you at least listen to me? It won't cost you anything to do that, will it?" she asked.

It wouldn't and since he'd decided he wasn't going to scare her out of his room, listening to her and then rejecting her proposal was probably the fastest way to be rid of her.

He sat on the bed and opened his laptop. He might as well log on and get updated on any new sightings while she talked.

"Two months ago, my best friend and roommate, Allison Samuels, got a job offer in Texas. We've known each other since middle school." Her voice wavered, but Caleb didn't look up. After a second, she continued, "Allison graduated last fall. I'm supposed to graduate in May, not that…" Her lips formed a line. She seemed to be sorting something out, something she apparently didn't want to say out loud.

Not really interested in whatever internal demons she was fighting, Caleb powered up the laptop and logged on to the Internet. He went directly to his RSS feed.

While he was scrolling down the list of blogs, his visitor, Samantha, got over her moment of uncertainty and continued. "Allison got a job at a lab. It was a huge break—most labs require a lot more experience and training than she had.

"She didn't tell me much about it, she couldn't. She had to sign all kinds of privacy agreements. They were doing research—top-secret stuff—and Allison was excited. She said it could change everything we thought we knew about life and death."

Caleb looked up. Life and death. A chill passed over his body.

Samantha's gaze was on him. Her eyes looked pale in this light, almost silvery like her coat. There were circles under them, too. "She called daily. At first she was the same old Allison, excited by what she was doing, amazed at the things she had seen. Then a week went by with no calls, no e-mails, no updates on Twitter or Facebook. Nothing. I didn't have an address. I didn't know what to do. All I knew was that the lab was in Texas."

"Texas is a big state," he replied, more to let her know he was listening than to add to the conversation.

She nodded. "And I've never been there."

"What about her family? They have an address? Someone had to know where she went."

Samantha shook her head. "Allison grew up in foster care. She had no one, no one but me. When we met, she was at her fifth home in four years. By high school her foster brother was beating on her, working up to other things. I convinced her she didn't have to put up with it and got her to a shelter. She was almost eighteen. We worked it so she didn't have to go back after that, didn't have to go anywhere. We moved in together and have been together ever since.

"I'm all she has. She needs me." The words were low, an admittance of sorts.

Caleb set the computer onto the mattress beside him. "She moved away without giving you an address. Maybe you thought she needed you more than she did. Maybe she wanted to make it on her own for a while."

Her head snapped up. "No. It wasn't like that. She didn't give me an address because the job included room and board. She was living at the lab. If she'd revealed her location, she would have lost her job."

"Still…" he began.

"I did hear from her, though, one last time." She picked up her coat from where he'd dropped it on the bed earlier and fussed with the lining. Realizing there was some kind of hidden pocket there, he waited. In a few seconds she pulled out a folded piece of paper. "Here." She held out the note and tilted her head toward his laptop.

The paper was stained and worn, making it obvious it had been folded and unfolded numerous times, left on a table where someone had been eating and drinking, too.

Caleb ignored all that and read the one line of type—a Web address to one of the upload-your-own-video sites. Feeling unnaturally uneasy he plugged the address into his browser.

Chapter 4

Samantha waited as Caleb entered the Web address into his computer. She'd watched the video over and over, had the damned thing memorized. Each time panic rose in her throat, each time she cursed herself for not being there to help her friend and each time she felt more and more like a failure.

But once the images started moving, she couldn't stop herself from stepping close and watching the thing one more time.

The video opened on a close-up of Allison's face. The jostling picture made it apparent Samantha's friend had set up the recording. After a few seconds, there was a noise behind her. She stepped back, turned and said something about looking for a file she couldn't find. A man stood in front of her, but he was backlit, making it impossible to make out his face. You could, however, from his silhouette, tell he was wearing a lab coat.

"I heard you tried to contact your friend," he said.

Allison's hand, held at her side, moved, making a signal only she and Samantha understood. It was their distress signal. They'd devised the simple tapping of thumb and two fingers together when Allison had lived at her last foster home so Samantha would know if Allison was in trouble, even when she didn't feel like she could say the words.

Seeing it now, Samantha's stomach clenched. She curled her fingers into her palms, stopping herself from reaching for the screen. The video was old...had happened a month ago...at least.

In the video Allison replied. She knew that, but she had to remind herself every time.

"I wouldn't do that. You told me to stop."

"I did." The man moved closer. One arm was behind his back. "I'd hoped you'd respect the need for secrecy."

"I do." Allison's hand moved again, faster.

"What are you doing?" he asked. "Are you hiding something?"

"Me? No." Allison held out her empty hands.

He angled his head, seemed to be studying her.

"It's just...well, Mrs. Granville...she seemed okay yesterday," Allison said.

"And she's okay today. Didn't you see her?" he asked.

"I...I did. A few hours ago. She...she looked like the others."

"And how, Allison, is that?" His voice laden with

warning, he shoved his visible hand into his coat pocket.

"Not well."

"The patients who come here, they are very sick. You know that. If we didn't take them in, offer them our treatment, they'd be dead. We give them an alternative. One they agree to in writing." He gestured behind her, to where Samantha guessed a filing cabinet stood.

"But her vital signs…" Her voice quavering at the end, Allison paused. Samantha recognized the tone, knew her friend was afraid. Impotent rage surged inside her just like it did each time she saw the recording. She glanced at Caleb. He sat quietly watching the video with no expression visible on his face or in his posture.

"Vital signs? What are they? Just some human-created symbol of life." The man stepped closer. It was here, this split second where Samantha, on every single viewing, thought he would move just an inch to the side, just enough that she could make out his face. As always she tensed in anticipation and as always he didn't. He stayed cast in shadows. "Mrs. Granville is walking, isn't she? Eating? Talking? Isn't that life?"

"She isn't breathing."

He shrugged. "What does it matter?"

"Humans need oxygen." The words were low, like Allison was saying them to herself, reassuring herself of their truth.

"Mrs. Granville doesn't. You should be celebrating that fact, not worrying over it." He sighed. "You watched her eat breakfast. She had a good appetite, didn't she? That fits into your standard definition as a sign of good health, doesn't it?"

"Yes." Allison reached for something on a table

beside her, a clipboard. She shuffled through the papers attached to it, her posture stiff and her movements harried. Her hands were shaking. Samantha couldn't see it in the video, but she knew her friend, knew they were.

Apparently, finding the record she'd been searching for, Allison looked up. Her finger pressed against the paper clipped to the board, she asked, "But did you see what she ate? She doesn't stop eating, and Marie's cat… She left it with Mrs. Granville after breakfast. She thought it would soothe her, and now it's missing."

"Are you accusing Mrs. Granville of eating Marie's cat?" The man chuckled. "Come on now. She's an eighty-year-old librarian who served on the local animal shelter's board for twenty-two years. She is hardly the cat-eating type." He laughed again.

But Allison didn't seem ruffled by his scoffs. "She attacked Jack."

The man in the video made a huffing noise. It was obvious now he was losing patience. "She's been through a lot. As you have pointed out ad nauseam, she flatlined. When she came back—when they all come back—they are confused."

Allison moved the clipboard so it wasn't visible to the camera. By the way she was standing, Samantha could tell she was holding it over her chest, like a shield. "Where is Jack? I haven't seen him today."

The man leaned back on his heels. "He's…recovering. Another side effect of the treatment. A good one. People come back stronger than they've ever been, even at their healthiest. Mrs. Granville did a little damage to him, completely unintentional, of course."

"What about looking for the others who esc—"

Allison bit off the word. "Who disappeared. Jack was doing that. He was worried they might be…"

The doctor moved closer. Allison let her words fade.

"We have never lost a patient. If Jack said we had, he was wrong."

Allison was quiet for a moment, then murmured, "I'd like to see him."

"Would you?"

The tiny depiction of the room on Caleb's computer screen went silent again. Samantha had to fight the need to scream into the laptop, to tell Allison to shut up, to tell the man whatever he wanted to hear and just get the hell out of that room.

"Maybe that's a good idea after all." The man turned and stepped out the door.

While he was gone, Allison stared back at the camera. It looked as if she was going to whisper something, but then the door opened and another man shuffled into the room. She turned to face him.

He was dressed in scrubs, green ones that accentuated the gray cast of his skin, and he was wearing a collar— the kind dogs wear when their owners have invested in underground fencing.

The man Allison had spoken with before waited for this new man to enter, then stepped back into the room. The first man held a square electronic device. "Jack was getting a treatment. You don't mind being part of it, do you, Allison?" He twisted a knob.

The man called Jack bent at the waist and touched his toes. Another twist of the knob and he stood.

"Jack, tell Allison how you are doing," the first man ordered.

Jack turned and stared at Allison. In the background the first man lifted the box to his lips and whispered something into it. Allison took a step back, but there was nowhere to go and no time. Jack, his hands held out in front of him, charged toward her.

Allison screamed and darted to the side, but Jack leaped into her path. Allison moved to the side, but the man did, too. They lunged back and forth like two kids playing a game of keep-away around a couch. Then Jack surged forward, too fast for any human. The camera seemed to zero in on him, on his gray face and the uncontrolled hunger in his eyes. It was that glimpse that had first put the word *zombie* into Samantha's unbelieving mind.

With a crash the screen went black.

Samantha stared at it, afraid the video would start up again, that she'd be forced to watch her friend's fate again.

"That's your proof?" Caleb asked, startling her.

Samantha pulled her gaze away from the screen. Her heart was pounding and sweat had gathered on her upper lip and inside her bra, but Caleb sat there as if she'd just shown him a report on weed control. Bored and not the tiniest bit disturbed.

"She was attacked by a zombie, and that man, her boss, was controlling him," she said.

"She was attacked, yes, but by a zombie? You have no proof of that. The guy could have been wearing makeup. The Internet is filled with frauds. Maybe your friend thought it would be funny to play a prank on you. When did you get it?" He glanced at the screen. "Uploaded the beginning of October. Perfect time for some Halloween fun at your expense."

Samantha didn't bother answering the insulting suggestion. Allison wouldn't even think to pull such a prank on her. Instead, she asked, "Were the zombies last night wearing makeup?"

He shifted his jaw to the side. "That's different. I saw them in person. There's no missing a zombie in person."

Samantha didn't bother arguing the point. She grabbed the computer and entered another address. "Here. How about this one? Proof enough?"

It was another video, without Allison in it.

This video was shorter with no sound, but it was clear that it had been filmed inside the same building. The room had the same cinderblock walls and institutional paint job. The video opened on a man wearing a Texas college sweatshirt. He was sitting at a table next to two other gray-skinned men. All three had trays in front of them loaded with what appeared to be brains.

"Cow," Caleb offered. "People do eat calf brains."

Samantha didn't acknowledge his interruption. He'd see soon enough.

One of the men picked up his pile of brains and shoved it into his mouth. His plate empty, he reached for sweatshirt-wearing Mr. Texas's serving. Texas objected, throwing his body over his plate.

The second man stared at him for a second then picked up his metal tray and whacked Texas over the head. Texas didn't fight back, didn't object at all, and his attacker whacked him over and over until Samantha thought he would never stop. Finally there was a cracking noise. The attacker stopped and stared as if surprised. Then he reached down and tugged at Texas's ear, jerked at it until it came off in his hand. He stared at it, flipped it back and forth as if he had no idea what it was. Then he popped it into his mouth and with his mouth open began to chew.

From somewhere off screen a fourth man, wearing what looked like a padded beekeeper outfit, rushed into the room. He held the same type of box the man in the first video had carried. He twisted its knob, right then left, but the man chomping on the ear didn't respond.

Instead, he shoved Texas out of his chair and onto the floor. Then he jumped on him. His hands around Texas's neck, he smashed the comatose man's skull into the ground over and over, kept going until blood spattered everything in view.

The beekeeper dropped the box and sprinted out of the room.

Still on the floor, the zombie slammed Texas's head one last time into the floor. Then he shoved the dead man's brains into his mouth.

At the table, the third man picked up his plate and threw it like a Frisbee into the camera.

Again, the screen went black.

There was silence for a second. Samantha pulled back. It was just as ugly every time she watched it.

"How about that? That happen at your family get-togethers?" she asked, her voice cold.

Caleb tapped his index finger on the keyboard. For a moment Samantha thought she'd said too much, that he wouldn't reply, but finally, he lowered the laptop onto the mattress.

"There was nothing connecting the two clips."

"The *One Flew Over the Cuckoo's Nest* decor?" She ticked off one finger. "The Texas sweatshirt?" She ticked off another. "The zombies?" She held up three fingers.

When he didn't reply, she closed her eyes and counted to herself. Calm, or at least calmer, she opened them. "That was Allison in the first video and before you ask, I know it wasn't an act because she gave me a sign." Samantha repeated the hand signal she and Allison had shared. "It's special. She would only use that to tell me what I was seeing was real, that she needed my help…" Her words trailed off to nothing. She was tired, exhausted actually. She'd never fought for anything as she'd fought for this, never wanted—no, needed—anything as much as she needed Caleb Locke to look up at her and say, "Yes, I'll come with you."

He stared at her through golden-brown eyes. They weren't dark enough to be so cold; it made her wonder if he wore contacts that somehow hid his emotions.

He sighed and suddenly looked every bit as tired as she felt. "How'd you find me?" he asked.

Caleb still wasn't convinced by the videos. As he'd told Samantha, it was impossible to tell from a recording if what you were looking at were zombies or well made-up actors.

In fact, while he sought out blogs for written tales of sightings, he had never acted on a video report. They were just too easy to fake for the amount of attention they created for the producer. It brought out the glory hounds, the charlatans.

But Samantha's video was different. Whoever had uploaded it had kept it quiet, hadn't posted links to it on every paranormal social network site that existed.

Didn't even have a cute name like Office Zombie or I'm Zombie Damn It.

No, just a name. Allison.

He pointed to the tiny two-point type that indicated who had uploaded the video. "Your friend?"

Samantha nodded, but her gaze dropped.

His suspicions were instantly alerted. "How'd she do it?" he asked.

Samantha's eyes darted back to his face. "Do what?"

"Upload the video. If what we saw was real..." At the stricken expression on Samantha's face, he let his explanation die off. But it didn't change his question. If the video was real, her friend had been attacked by a zombie. So, who uploaded the video?

Samantha shook her head as if shaking off a bad dream. "I don't know. I guess she uploaded the video after... Maybe they left her alone, didn't realize what she was doing."

Caleb stared at her for a second, hard. She was lying to herself. If the video was real, the woman shown on it was dead, or worse, undead.

When she didn't waver, didn't seem willing to admit to that truth, he shrugged. What she believed didn't matter. What he believed did. And if he believed these videos were real, it meant somewhere in Texas there was a zombie manufacturing plant.

He'd often wondered where the zombies came from. He'd guessed they were like werewolves, some rare DNA-mutating virus or bacterial infection that was passed from person to person. But if Samantha's video was real, there was more to it than that. There was a person behind the zombies, creating them, a person he could blame for his parents' deaths, a person he could kill.

Which meant he really couldn't send Samantha away—not until he knew for sure.

Still, though, he wanted to know how she had found him. Her appearance, her perfectly created video, it was all just too perfect. Too much of a zombie hunter's dream.

He nodded as if accepting her answer and repeated his earlier question. "So, how did you find me?"

"The Internet."

A quick answer, too quick, and it wasn't a complete answer, wasn't even the beginning of a complete answer.

"I've been hanging out on blogs and bulletin boards where they talk about zombies. Your name was mentioned. In fact, it was the only name mentioned—at least in a way that made me think you might be real."

"And how is that?"

"Understated. You weren't online telling everyone how many zombies you have slaughtered, posting pictures and stats."

He grunted. Posers. There were a lot of them. A lot more than there were legitimate hunters.

"Then I e-mailed one of the bloggers and asked about you." She hesitated. "I may have acted like I already knew you." She glanced at him, unsure. He ignored the unspoken apology. He didn't care what lies people told about him, as long as they left him alone.

Licking her lips, she continued, "He was all over it, wanted me to get you to make a guest appearance. I told him I would, but I needed to locate you first...that I'd lost my cell phone with your number during an attack.

He gave me the tip on what was happening here. Said you'd show for sure. And you did."

Her story nagged at Caleb. He hadn't considered before now that the same bloggers who tracked the zombies might also track him.

But it also rang true.

He snapped his laptop shut and shoved it back into its bag. Time to get moving.

"Aren't you going to help me?" she asked. "I can pay. I have money with me." She reached for her coat.

He turned to look at her, a "no" forming in his throat. He'd slipped up, been too comfortable. If this woman could find him, a thousand other zombie groupies could, too. And that was the best case scenario. Worst, she was an actress, hired to lure him out. Hell, some blogger might be lurking outside the motel right now, salivating over the footage he'd already given them back at the alley. He glanced at her, sure of his answer now.

Her eyes glimmered. She held on to her silver coat like a child clutching her teddy bear during a storm.

She looked desperate. Damn her.

Chapter 5

Caleb stalked around the side of the dark motel, Samantha dogging his steps. If she was legit, he couldn't leave her here, and if she wasn't, what better way to find out than by keeping her with him and tricking her into revealing the truth? Then he would scare the Internet rankings out of her and whoever had hired her.

Scanning the area for any bloggers bearing cameras, he stopped next to the beater he'd stolen in Milwaukee before heading north to this town. The undeveloped lot next to the motel seemed empty.

He motioned for Samantha to climb in and retrieved the screwdriver that served as his key from under the seat. Then he joined her in the vehicle.

Her eyes widened as he wiggled the ignition.

"Lost my key," he offered with zero intention of her believing him.

He could tell by the way she shifted in her seat she didn't, but she didn't object, either. But then if she truly needed his services as a zombie hunter, she couldn't be splitting hairs about his morality.

He didn't say anything else, not until he'd steered the vehicle onto the state highway and felt confident no one was following.

"Tell me what you know," he said, glancing at her and considering where if anywhere she could have hidden a recorder. He'd washed both her clothes and her coat. Of course he'd only rinsed the outside of the coat, and he hadn't noticed the paper hidden inside its thick lining. He could have missed a recorder, too.

She twisted the coat's belt and started talking. "The lab is in Texas. Somewhere near Waco, I think."

"Your friend tell you that?" he asked.

She stared down at the strip of silver cloth in her hand. "No, we shared a computer. I went into the history. She'd researched Waco a lot. Either her job was there or she was planning a trip there."

"And who plans a trip to Waco?" he added.

Samantha relaxed a bit against the upholstery; perhaps she took his light response as a sign he had relaxed, too. If she had, she was wrong.

"It isn't the first place that would pop to mind for a vacation—even if Allison would have had time for a vacation, which she didn't. She was supposed to start the job immediately. That was one of the conditions of getting the position. She was hired one day and had to start three days later."

"Didn't leave her much time to tie things up." It started to rain. Caleb turned on the wipers.

"Like I said, she was supposed to live at the lab

and since she was in research, she didn't even need much clothing. They provided scrubs and lab coats. She packed a few things in the trunk of her car and left with maybe four suitcases. The job paid well. She said if she needed more clothing, she'd buy it there."

The mention of clothing made Caleb remember that his passenger didn't have any—at least none that wasn't on her back. A sign she wasn't who she said she was? His gaze on the road, he kept his voice neutral and asked, "How about you? If we're driving to Texas, do you need to stop somewhere to get anything?"

Her eyebrows rose. "Oh. I completely forgot." She laughed. "I had a bag with me when I left Tennessee, but it got stolen—not long after I got here. Right after I bought this coat, actually."

"Really?" He tapped his finger against the steering wheel. "Well, at least you have that. And money...?"

She fiddled with her belt again, ran it through her fingers. "Money...yes, I have money. How else would I pay you?" She licked her lips.

He forced himself not to stare as her tongue darted out to moisten her lips. "I don't know. I'm sure we could come up with some kind of...trade."

Her gaze jumped to him. She stiffened.

Still thinking of the many ways she could repay him, he smiled, but he covered his thoughts with words. "You did handle my gun well."

A bit of air left her lungs. She relaxed again. "My father," she said. "I grew up with firearms. They don't scare me."

He wanted to ask her what did, but he suspected she didn't completely know the answer to that herself. Most people didn't, not until they had to stare that fear right in the eyeball. Instead, he changed the subject.

"So, Waco." He only knew one thing about Waco: that it had been home to the Branch Davidians. Probably after that mess, a quiet research institute wouldn't raise many eyebrows in the area. It added weight to her tale, but, of course, if the video was a fake, its producer would have created a good story to go with it, one designed with him and his probable suspicions in mind.

"Open the glove box," he instructed.

She looked at him questioningly, but did as he asked. Inside were two stiletto knives and a PDA. "You ever dissect a frog in high school biology?" he asked.

She stared at the glove box's contents, but didn't reach inside.

"Take one of the knives and keep it on you. A zombie gets close to you, pith him, just like that frog."

"And if I can't?" she asked.

He took his eyes off the road long enough to stare back at her. "Then jam it through your heart."

Her hand shaking, she reached for one of the blades. He waited for her to make her selection, then added in a softer voice, "Just get him first." Because if she didn't, she wouldn't have to worry about turning the knife on herself. Caleb would do it for her.

After she slipped the blade into her coat pocket, he told her to take out the PDA, too. "It has Internet. While I drive you might as well look for attacks. The sites are bookmarked." He talked her through maneuvering his PDA. Then while she clicked and typed, they rode in silence for a few minutes.

After a while, she looked up. "I found some. What now?"

"Write down anything in Texas. We'll drive a little then we'll stop and chart it." Charting was one of his methods of sorting the real from the fake. Where there was one zombie sighting there tended to be more. Clusters of attacks or sightings always took top priority. If the video was real, odds were there would be sightings around the place. Charted properly with the right software, which he owned, he might even be able to pin the place down within a thirty-mile radius or so.

He pulled a stenographer's pad from under his seat. There was a pencil jammed into its wire coil. While she scribbled, he drove. For now he was just heading south. Once she had some data, they would stop, he'd enter it into his computer and they'd see what popped out. Then he'd plug the area into the GPS he kept in his laptop bag when he wasn't using it and they'd settle in for the drive.

And along the way, he'd watch for any sign they were being followed or that she was recording him. He glanced at her. He'd focused on the possibility of a video being made of them, but perhaps he was thinking too high-tech. She could also just be planning an article or a blog piece on him.

Of course, that would be a lot easier to fake. Why waste the time it was going to take riding around with him? Unless of course she was a blogger with morals.

He snorted.

She glanced at him, but he just made a dismissive motion with his hand and she went back to reading. A comfortable silence fell between them. It was nice, he realized, to have someone in the car with him, even if they weren't talking. Maybe *because* they weren't talking.

Fighting zombies was lonely. Not only because of the killing itself, but because he couldn't share what he did with anyone. He had to eke out an existence just beneath the radar. And loner though he was, every now and then it would be a relief to tell someone what he'd seen that day, to know someone else understood. So, he sank against his seat and enjoyed riding in silence, but not alone.

It was an hour before Samantha looked up again. She had written down three promising sightings in the past three months.

One a month. That was a lot—unless one person was responsible for faking them, or some town was trying to pull in the tourists. But that happened more in the ghost arena. Some overmortgaged inn owner would get the bright idea to seed the Internet with sightings of a pair of dead lovers. It happened with almost all paranormal phenomena, but not quite as much with zombies as ghosts. The heyday of zombies was fifty years past; ghosts were the new supernatural black.

So, Caleb's interest was definitely piqued by the data. He started watching for an exit.

Ten minutes later they were parked in front of a truck stop with a sign out front that bragged of wireless. He grabbed his laptop bag and they strolled inside. Two truckers turned to look at them. Samantha's coat flapped open as they came through the door and the pair's gazes lingered on her revealing tight outfit a little longer than Caleb liked.

He slipped his arm around her waist and tugged her to his side. She moved as if to break away. He leaned closer, so he could whisper in her ear. "You might want to pick up some new clothes, after all."

She glanced at him from the corner of her eye, then following his gaze, looked at the truckers. One of them, a bearded man wearing suspenders over his double-wide gut, took a sip of coffee and tipped his cap.

She stepped closer to Caleb. His hand cupped her hip as if the two had been molded to fit together. He moved his fingers, swirled them over the smooth, stretchy material of her pants. She jumped, but under the trucker's watchful gaze quickly settled back down.

Caleb turned his attention to the two men, stared at them until they fidgeted in their seats and dropped their eyes.

Once he was sure they had gotten the message, he gestured to a booth in the back and pulled Samantha along with him. His gaze still on the truckers, he waited for her to slide in.

A full sixty seconds later he realized she hadn't moved and scowled at her.

She pointed at a Restroom sign. There was an arrow under it that pointed down a hallway nowhere near the truckers.

He grunted and slid into the booth without her. He watched to make sure she turned down the hallway, even considered following her for a second, but he couldn't follow her inside the restroom, not without upsetting a few bystanders and alerting Samantha that he was watching her a little more carefully than she might like. So, he made do with watching her disappear in the right direction and then focused on doing what he did best—hunting zombies.

Within seconds he'd powered up his computer and

was lost in the world of online zombies. He'd never worked with anyone before. So, while in the car he'd asked her to make the list, he couldn't leave it to her judgment alone. He had to check the sites himself, too. Plus, if she wasn't what she said she was, her sighting would most likely be fake, too, or all posted at the same site.

And that was exactly what he discovered. All three of the sightings she had listed came from BrainHungry.com BrainHungry was a fairly new blog that had already developed a rather passionate if misguided following. Flame wars frequently broke out in the comments, arguments over everything from the best way to kill a zombie to whether they preferred brains from a certain ethnic or age group.

Caleb didn't bother dropping into the fight to educate the uneducated masses. It wasn't his job. Besides, if they were busy fighting amongst themselves they weren't getting in his way—or so he had thought.

He glanced back at the hallway where Samantha had disappeared. Could she be working with the owners of BrainHungry? He would have to research the site a bit, see what he could learn about the owners. But not now. Now he needed to see if there were any other hits she had missed.

He had just discovered an entry claiming two zombies in hospital gowns had been spotted staggering through a Wisconsin mall parking lot, less than twenty miles from where he had met Samantha, when someone cleared his throat.

Caleb looked up to see the suspender-wearing trucker staring down at him.

"Take it you're fond of that girl?" He waggled a hairy

eyebrow. Caleb lifted his lip in response. Fondness didn't matter. She'd come in with him; if the guy had thoughts she might not leave with him, too, he had some hurting in his future.

The man held up his hands and took a step back. "Hey, just trying to help. Thought you'd want to know…" He shook his head and turned as if to leave.

Unease crept over Caleb. He grabbed the man by his fleshy upper arm. "I'd want to know what?"

The man ran his tongue over his teeth, like he was picking part of his lunch out of them. "Nothing much. Just that she left without you." He shoved his hands into his front pockets, pushing his pants a little lower under his stomach, and jerked his head toward the front windows.

Through the dingy glass, Caleb caught a flash of Samantha's silver coat disappearing behind a full-size van with blacked-out windows.

He shoved his laptop into the trucker's hands. "Anything happens to this I'll kill you."

The trucker opened his mouth, but Caleb pulled a knife from his bag and poked the tip of the blade into the man's gut. "Do you believe me?"

The man's eyes shifted to the side. Caleb poked him again. "I don't have time for you to act brave, or think about calling for help. Just know if when I come back, my laptop isn't safe or there's some other unpleasant surprise waiting for me, I'll track you down and leave you in such little bits even the zombies won't bother with you." Then he slipped the knife into his sleeve and sprinted from the restaurant.

The van was parked two rows back, fifty feet from the door Caleb had exited. Black smoke chugged out of its exhaust pipe as it coughed to life. A man carrying a six-pack of beer stepped in front of him. The van was already moving, was going to pass where Caleb stood any second. He ripped the cans out of the man's hand and hurled them one after the other at the vehicle.

The first hit the windshield, the second the passenger window. Glass cracked and beer exploded onto the van. Caleb jogged toward it, tossing cans as he went.

As one smashed into the side of the vehicle, the van stopped. Caleb rushed forward and jerked open the driver's door. An older man in a round-brimmed hat adorned with fishing flies shrank against the seat. He glanced to the passenger seat where a woman wearing a visor and wraparound sunglasses clung to her door. "Run," he yelled at her. "There ain't nothing here worth dying over."

The woman threw open the door and tumbled out of the van. Caleb grabbed the driver by the front of the shirt. "Where is she?"

The man stared and sputtered, then jerked his keys from the ignition and tried to shove them into Caleb's hand. Caleb leaned past him and stared into the back of the vehicle. Then he cursed. It was empty. He sniffed. The van smelled of peanuts and beef jerky. Not a single hint of Samantha's fresh jasmine scent—nor of decaying zombie flesh.

He dropped the remaining can of beer into the man's lap and whirled around. Two men wearing tight T-shirts that bunched up on their biceps to reveal barbed wire tattoos strode toward him. Their arms folded over their chests, they stepped into his space.

"What's happening here, friend?" one asked.

Caleb let the knife he'd shown the trucker slip into his

hand, while still keeping it hidden from their view. "My wife was abducted. I saw the van—" he gestured to the blacked-out windows "—and jumped to conclusions."

The men glanced at each other. "Abducted? Here?"

From behind the building there came a scream. Caleb barreled past the two men, sending both staggering in circles.

A car pulled into the lot, heading straight for him, not bothering to slow or dash to the side. He jumped, landed on the front bumper and then ran up the hood, over the roof and back down the trunk. Then he leaped and kept running.

Knife in hand now, he turned the corner.

Her legs braced wide, Samantha stood on top of a rolling Dumpster. The stiletto blade he'd given her was in her hand and the tip was inches from her heart. Below her on the ground, arms reaching toward her was a zombie. A fresh one. It smelled of death, but the decay was still slight.

"Samantha," Caleb yelled.

Her gaze shot to him; it looked hollow and haunted but still alive. She hadn't been bitten, not yet.

The zombie turned, too. It was a man, or had been. He was wearing a polo shirt and shorts, like he'd been on his way to the golf course, but it wasn't his clothing that drew Caleb's attention. It was the collar clamped around his neck.

Texas.

Wishing he had his thermos of brains, Caleb waved his hands and yelled again. "Come and get me, you brain-hungry bastard."

The zombie wavered, leaned on his right foot as if

preparing to do as Caleb said and then jerked and looked back at Samantha.

Caleb yelled again, but the zombie didn't react. Apparently, whoever was controlling the monster had too strong of a hold, or had imprinted his assignment too completely into the undead creature's head.

Caleb stared up at Samantha. "Remember what I told you. We'll only get one shot." He held up his blade, telling her to be ready with hers. Then he charged.

Hitting the zombie was easy. Holding the creature pinned against the Dumpster on which Samantha stood was much harder.

Caleb believed with his werewolf-altered blood he was immune to a zombie's bite, but he had never actually tested the theory. Even immune, getting bitten was something to be avoided at all cost—except perhaps the cost of saving someone else from the bite. Samantha. With that in mind, he put all of his preternatural strength into holding the zombie's arms pinned against its sides and shoving its back against the Dumpster.

As the monster lurched forward with its head, trying to make contact with Caleb's face or neck, Caleb yelled, "Now!"

He didn't have to worry about Samantha's response. She scuttled to the edge of the Dumpster, the knife held ready in her hand. Then when she was barely less than an arm's length away, she thrust down, driving the blade into the indented space at the base of the zombie's skull and pithing the creature just like Caleb had instructed.

He had never been more proud or relieved.

The false life drained from the zombie. Caleb let the

creature crumple onto the ground, then he held up his arms and waited for Samantha to fall down against him.

Samantha placed her hands on Caleb's shoulders and slid off the Dumpster, letting her body slide down his as she did. Then she stood pressed against him, feeling his heartbeat, feeling her own, and knowing while it was wrong to allow herself to be this close to someone she barely knew, to trust someone she barely knew, there wasn't a damned thing she could do about. Caleb was warm, strong and alive.

"What happened?" he asked.

She leaned her forehead against his chest and breathed for a second. He smelled good, like licorice. The scent, or maybe it was his warmth, calmed her, or she thought it did until she stared at her hands. They were shaking. Then she remembered what she had done with them... and what she had been about to do.

Caleb reached up and stroked her hair, whispered in her ear, "You did good. Really good." He glanced to the side, where the zombie had fallen.

The sounds of horns honking and people yelling echoed from the front of the building. He caught her fingers in his hands. "We need to get moving, but first..." He jerked the stiletto blade from the back of the zombie's skull and dropped it onto the ground. Then he grabbed the corpse under the arms and slung it into the Dumpster.

Samantha stepped back, shaken by the ease with which he'd moved, as if the zombie's body weighed no more than a good-size bag of mulch.

Unaware of her surprise, Caleb wiped the stiletto clean on a rag and slipped the blade into his boot. After throwing the rag into the Dumpster, too, he looked up. Catching her stare, he angled his head.

Realizing her nerves were showing, she laughed. "Sorry. It's just…" She gestured to the Dumpster. "This… I… It's hard to take it all in."

He grabbed her by the arm and tugged her back around the building, so they would come around the front from the opposite side she had left. "Yeah, well, hopefully you won't have to get used to it."

Stumbling over her own feet to keep up, Samantha swallowed the lump that had been lodged in her throat since she'd realized what had grabbed her. She had never agreed with anything anyone had said quite as much as she agreed with Caleb right then.

But if as she suspected this wasn't destined to be her last encounter with a zombie, she had to do better. She had to be stronger. There was no sugarcoating what had happened. She had chickened out.

The zombie had almost had her. It would have had her if Caleb hadn't appeared. She'd been standing on that Dumpster telling herself she could do it, that she could drive the blade into her own heart. But it had been a lie. She couldn't.

Now she had to wonder what Caleb would have done if she hadn't used the blade to spear the zombie's brain, if the zombie had reached her first and bitten her.

She shivered and walked faster to keep up with the man she knew in her heart would kill her with zero hesitation.

Chapter 6

Getting away from the truck stop was easier than Caleb could have hoped. While he and Samantha had been occupied near the Dumpster, a second zombie had apparently staggered out of nowhere and into the path of a semi.

With random zombie parts scattered over the parking lot, Caleb's attack on the van seemed to have fled all memory. In fact, thanks to the smell there weren't even many onlookers. The few there were had shirts or some other cloth tied around their faces. Taking their cue, Caleb jerked off his shirt and followed suit. With his face hidden, he'd be a lot less likely to jog any memories of his earlier run-in with the van.

As they came around the corner to the front entrance, a policeman stopped them. "You see anything?"

He glanced from Caleb to Samantha, who looked appropriately green.

Caleb grabbed her hand and pulled her toward the restaurant's door. "We were in our car…uh…looking for something." He ran his hand down Samantha's backside, cluing the officer into exactly what kind of search they had been conducting.

The policeman frowned, but waved them on. "A nice guy would give the lady the shirt."

Caleb smiled even though the other man couldn't see it. "But I'm not a nice guy. That's why she loves me." He glanced at Samantha. "Ain't that right, sweetie?" Then he shoved open the door and hustled her inside.

Samantha stumbled into the restaurant feeling sick and shaken.

Caleb glanced over his shoulder as the door closed behind them, then grabbed her by the elbow. "Are you okay?"

She wasn't sure how to answer. Was she? "The smell…why is it so bad?" She coughed into her hand, struggling to keep from throwing up. She'd already done so once in front of the hunter; she didn't want to repeat the act.

"I'm not sure. Might have something to do with its age, but I'm guessing it has more to do with how it died…the last time. Smashed by a semi. More organs exposed means more rot exposed." He shook his head. "Guess that's another way to rid the world of a zombie although I don't often have a semi sitting by waiting on me." His voice was dry, as if truly considering the idea of adding a semi to his arsenal of weapons.

Samantha shivered. Caleb pulled her against him,

against his bare chest. She placed her hand on his skin, and again reveled in how warm he could be when it was so cold outside. Wanting to see if the scent of licorice was still there, still as soothing, she leaned closer until her nose brushed his neck. It was. All bad memories of zombies fled. She edged closer still, until her entire body was flush against him, until his heat seemed to be hers.

She stared into his golden eyes, and he stared back at her. He was going to kiss her; she could feel it. She parted her lips and rose ever so slightly onto her toes, waited for him to pull down the shirt that covered his lower face and capture her lips with his.

The door behind them flew open. Cold air rushed in, followed closely by two women in sweatpants and parkas. One fell; the other raced to a nearby trash can, gagging.

Samantha jumped away from Caleb, flushing as she did. The hunter made her forget where she was, what was going on around them and that she barely knew him. She had never been this susceptible to anyone before.

"What was...?" the one who had fallen began, but Caleb turned away, placed his hand on the small of Samantha's back and steered her toward the booth where they had sat when they had first entered.

"I'm not... I couldn't eat," she mumbled. Now that she wasn't pressed against Caleb, she realized the stench had followed them inside. It seemed to cling to her hair like cigarette smoke. Everything she ate would taste of it—not just now, maybe forever. She grabbed a napkin from the table and spat into it, then grabbed another to keep pressed to her mouth and nose.

A waitress strode toward them. "Did you see the sign?

No shirt, no—" Her nose curled. She paled then turned and jogged back to the kitchen.

Caleb didn't seem to notice her. He left Samantha standing next to the booth then redirected his path to the lunch bar at the back of the restaurant, next to the kitchen. One of the truckers they'd encountered on their first visit sat sprawled over one of the tiny stools. Caleb stepped close to him, lifted his shirt briefly from his face, then leaned even closer, apparently to mumble in the man's ear.

The trucker glanced from Caleb to the scene outside the window where emergency workers dressed in gas masks and white biohazard suits stood around the grill of a semi. They stood in a half circle, shaking their heads and gesturing wildly. The trucker pressed his lips into a line, then without saying a word handed Caleb a bag. Caleb's laptop bag, Samantha realized. Caleb slapped the man on the back and strolled back to her.

"Time to roll," he said. "But we need to talk and soon."

Still bare-chested, he jerked the shirt from his face and walked back out into the stench and cold. And Samantha, idiot that she was, followed him.

They drove ten miles before Samantha's curiosity beat down her shock. "Where are we going?" She glanced at Caleb out of the corner of her eye. He hadn't bothered to put his shirt back on. As he reached for the stereo the muscles in his shoulders bulged. He punched a few buttons, scanning radio stations, then apparently not finding anything of interest, flipped the radio off.

She fidgeted in her seat, trying not to stare, trying not to notice the lines of definition in his arms, even down his neck and over his ribs. He was solid sinewy muscle. She doubted there was an ounce of fat on him.

"Texas," he replied, startling her out of her thoughts. She moved her gaze away from his naked chest.

"Waco for now. When we get a chance I'll stop and finish charting the sightings." He paused. His hand lay on his camo-covered thigh. He tapped his middle finger up and down. "I found another one, one you missed."

"Really?" She turned back to the door, trying to hide her surprise. After a moment, she looked back at him. More zombie sightings. The nightmare she was caught in got bigger and bigger. "Where did they come from?" she asked.

He glanced at her.

Realizing she had messed up, she waved her hands and tried to cover her stumble. "Not the ones in Texas. The others. The ones you were fighting when I first found you and the one..." She shuddered. "The one who attacked me at the truck stop."

His finger moved again, slower. "Tell me what happened. You headed to the bathroom. What happened next?"

Samantha closed her eyes, not wanting to live through it again. "I made it to the bathroom and finished what I had to do. It was a one-seater and someone was rattling the knob. I yelled at them that I was almost done, but they kept jerking on the door so hard I thought the lock would break. It made me angry."

She huffed, a half laugh at how stupid she had been. "I jerked open the door ready to glare at whoever it was and came face-to-face with that zombie."

"Face-to-face and it didn't get you?" Caleb asked. His tone was neutral, but the question made Samantha suspect he didn't believe her. It annoyed her, but it also made her realize he was right. The zombie had been right there. Yes, she had moved quickly. But quick enough to evade the undead if the creature had been intent on catching her?

Beside her, Caleb cleared his throat, waiting for an answer.

Glancing back at him, she blurted, "I've taught and trained in self-defense for years. My judgment may not always be sound, but my reflexes are."

Her tone must have been harsh. His eyebrow twitched.

She swallowed both her ire and her unease—the first because he'd doubted her and the second because she suspected there was more to the encounter with the zombie than she had assumed. She placed her hands on her lap and continued. "He lunged at the doorway. His arm hit the actual door, keeping me from shutting it—not that that would have been the best move. He probably would have just come in after me, trapping me...." She was quiet for a second, thinking of the horror of being trapped in that tiny space with a flesh-hungry monster.

"You had your knife," Caleb offered, as if that would have saved her. She'd had it out in the open too and had almost been forced to use it on herself.

"Anyway, I dropped to the floor and shimmied between his legs. By the time he realized what I had done, I was back on my feet and running."

"He ran after you."

It was an obvious truth, one she didn't bother acknowledging. She did, however, take a moment to study the hunter. His attitude had changed. There was something off about it.

"The parking lot was crowded…there were a lot of people coming and going. I didn't want him to get any of them so I ran behind the building."

"You could have run into the restaurant, to me."

She stiffened. She could have. She should have. Running off alone had been insane, but she hadn't thought. She had just reacted and her first instinct had been to get out of the building where she knew the zombie was. Her second had been to get him away from all the people milling around outside. There had been children there—a family with twin toddlers. The little girls had been squabbling over a bag of jelly beans when she'd raced by. The sight had sent an icy thrust of terror through her core.

Caleb put on the blinker before changing lanes, then glanced at her. "Why didn't you come to me?"

She stared at him, thinking, analyzing him. His finger had stilled, but there was a shadow in his eyes. A suspicion. "I guess I wasn't sure if push came to shove that you would save me."

The skin around his mouth hardened. "You didn't think I'd kill the zombie?"

"No, I knew you would do that. I just wasn't sure you wouldn't kill me and anyone else who got in your way while you were doing so." Like those toddlers. Would Caleb have worried about them? Or would he have mowed them down with his shotgun as he fired on the zombie? He had done it to Samantha, fired when she was well within striking range.

He turned to look at her. A part of her tensed, waiting,

hoping for his denial. Then he turned back to the road. "Next time come to me."

She sighed and leaned her head back against the seat. "You're right. I should trust you."

His eyes still focused straight ahead, he murmured, "No, I wouldn't do that."

She closed her eyes and wondered what the hell she was doing in this car with him and why, despite his words and her actions, she suspected that at another time in another place, she would have run to him.

Caleb forced himself not to look at Samantha. The quiet peace that had existed between them before the truck stop had disappeared. She didn't trust him. That was good. She shouldn't. No one should. But even as he reminded himself of that fact, a tiny piece of him objected, wished that it wasn't a fact, that it didn't have to be.

They rode in silence a few more miles, her staring out the window and him lost in disquieting memories of who he used to be. Finally, unable to take the quiet any longer, he said, "So, the zombie came after you while you were in the bathroom."

Apparently as lost in her thoughts as he had been in his, she jumped. "Yes," she replied.

The zombie's appearance and targeting of Samantha couldn't be coincidence. Either she was a fraud and the attack had been staged or whoever was behind the lab in Texas was having her followed. Except, he realized, the zombies had been real. Which left only one possibility. The lab in Texas was behind the attack.

"He was wearing a collar," she murmured.

Her statement was so close to what Caleb was thinking, his suspicions rose anew. They were almost to Minneapolis and neither had eaten yet today. He glanced at her. "You up for another stop?"

Her hand moved to her stomach. She nodded. "After what I saw and smelled, I'd say I'll never eat again. But I'm studying to be a nurse and I know whether I feel like it or not, I need food. I didn't eat yesterday, either."

Twenty-four hours with no food. Caleb watched for the first highway sign advertising restaurants, then flipped on his blinker. In no time they were sitting in a fast food joint's parking lot mowing through bags of burgers. At least Caleb was mowing through burgers; Samantha was picking through her garden salad.

She forked one piece of unnaturally green lettuce from the plastic box it was served in and twirled it around. Caleb lifted his gaze from his laptop, which he had fired up as soon as they'd pulled into a parking spot, after getting their food at the drive-through.

Seeing him watching her, she put the lettuce into her mouth and smiled. He shifted his gaze back to the computer and reached for a third burger.

"That meat is factory farmed, you know," she said.

He paused, expecting her to say more, like why the hell he cared, but she only stared at him expectantly. Turning back to his computer screen, he chomped into the meat and chewed slowly.

He felt her shudder. He took another bite. "Have you seen the conditions—"

He set the burger down. "Have you seen what I do?" Had she seen what zombies did? After living with that for twenty years, no amount of animal misfortune could move him and it certainly couldn't stop him from enjoying his favorite burger.

At least he didn't think it could. But Samantha apparently had a different opinion. She began a twenty-minute lecture on the entire life cycle of a factory-farmed cow. On and on she droned, until he couldn't stand to hear another word.

"Enough," he said, tossing a grease-stained napkin onto the floor. "I bought eight burgers. I'm going to eat eight burgers and then tomorrow I will buy eight more. I don't care about the fate of some cow. I don't care about the fate of anyone or anything as long as every day I survive and a number of zombies don't."

He stared at her. "If you can't live with that, you need to find another ride."

Her fork hovered halfway between her mouth and the plastic plate. Slowly she placed it onto her half-eaten salad and slid what remained of the meal onto the floor.

Then she opened the passenger door and got out.

Caleb closed his eyes and cursed, loudly.

His burger slipped from his fingers and fell onto his pants. The sandwich fell open, its contents landing on his lap. Ketchup smeared his pants.

With another curse, he hopped out of the car and brushed the debris onto the ground. Samantha stood with her back to him, her arms wrapped around her body.

He glanced into the car at her salad and his bag full of burgers. Then he reached inside and grabbed both. He walked to her and held out her lunch. She eyed him with suspicion, but took the salad.

He stood beside her holding the warm bag for a second, then he walked to a trash can and shoved it inside.

Without looking at her, he stalked back to the car. "Get in. We have fourteen hours to go and I still need lunch."

Five minutes later they were back on the road.

Chapter 7

Caleb hadn't said anything since he'd pulled out of the last fast food place. Mexican. He'd listed off his options and she'd shaken her head at each. Finally he'd ordered six bean burritos, no dairy, and peeled out.

She stopped herself from telling him what else, besides beans, were in the things, or that white flour tortillas really weren't the healthiest choice.

She shouldn't have said anything about the burgers, either. She'd never done that before. Allison was the radical vegetarian. Samantha had given up meat years ago, too, but until today had never harassed anyone else about it. That was more what Allison would have done.

Maybe that was why she had stormed at Caleb. Doing what Allison would have done made her mission feel less futile. As if she were preparing for her friend's return.

Caleb, however, hadn't seen it that way.

But he had dumped the burgers.

The edges of her lips turned up. He'd done that for her. A small, unimportant gesture perhaps, but she didn't think so. She doubted Caleb Locke had ever altered himself to please another person before.

The fact that he had done so for her warmed every inch of her.

As he munched on burrito number five, she leaned her head against the window and drowsed off. Maybe she'd misjudged him. Maybe he wouldn't sacrifice her or anyone to kill a zombie.

It had been dark four hours when Caleb saw the lights ahead. As they got closer, he could see a semi was jack-knifed across the interstate.

Samantha was sound asleep in the passenger seat. They'd driven steady with only stops for gas and food. After the scene over the burgers, he had steered clear of any meat and settled on peanut butter crackers and trail mix. If there was any problem with his choices, Samantha didn't offer a comment.

He'd only eaten half of the crackers, though. He placed his hand on his stomach. Apparently, even a werewolf's digestive system took issue with six fast food bean burritos. There was a lesson there somewhere, but what?

Not to let a woman's irrational demands get to him? To stay true to what he was? Werewolves ate meat and a lot of it. Samantha was lucky he hadn't decided to shift and find his own lunch in one of the fields they had driven by.

He slanted a glance her direction, wondering how the sight of him tearing into a freshly killed rabbit would have affected her. Of course, at least the rabbit would have had the benefit of free range before becoming dinner. Maybe that would have appeased her.

He grunted. The werewolf zombie hunter and the yoga instructing nurse. A match made in heaven…or hell. Zombie hell, to be exact.

As he followed the example of the cars in front of him and slowed to get around the semi, he let himself think about her a bit more. Why had he thrown away his lunch? Why had seeing her upset made him want to make her happy?

Why did he care?

His mind snapped down like a trap around the last thought. Care? He didn't care about anyone, even himself. He couldn't afford to. He had just been alone too long, was unused to dealing with others, and he'd let that get to him.

It wouldn't happen again.

He grabbed a handful of the trail mix and shoved it into his mouth.

The traffic was slowed almost to a stop now. A trooper stood next to the grill of the truck waving an illuminated wand, telling each car to keep moving. But, of course, each one slowed to rubberneck the scene.

Then some smart-ass in an oversize truck tried to bump his way past on the shoulder just as the car in front of Caleb veered to the left to avoid something that had fallen from the semi's window.

Brakes shrieked. Metal crunched against metal, but

Caleb barely noticed. He was too focused on the object that had fallen from the semi. An arm. A human arm.

He looked up.

A gray-faced zombie, a woman who'd probably been in her twenties when she died, grinned down at him. In her hand was another arm. She dropped it and lunged out the window.

The arm landed six feet from the first one, right on the hood of the compact in front of him. This time the trooper and the driver of the car noticed it and recognized exactly what it was.

The trooper jerked free the radio that had been clipped to his shirt pocket and began yelling into it. Then, reaching for his gun, he took a step back.

The zombie was out of the window now. It had landed not that far from the arm onto the roof of the compact. Inside the vehicle the driver panicked. He hit the gas, ramming into the oversize truck that he'd already struck once.

The zombie slid, then stretched out its arms and grabbed on to the luggage rack attached to the top of the car. It looked over its shoulder. Its nose and lip were pierced and there were tattoos around its neck. And it was fresh. Probably hadn't been dead more than a few days. Caleb cracked the window and inhaled. The creature barely smelled of rot. It *was* fresh. It hadn't been days since her death; it had been hours.

And it looked almost happy about it. It let go of the luggage rack and landed with a thump onto the hood of Caleb's stolen car.

The semi was on one side of them. The truck that had tried to squeeze past the line was on the other. In front and behind them were other cars.

He and Samantha were trapped.

Samantha.

He grabbed his laptop case and her arm at the same time. "Wake up."

She jerked awake, her eyes wide and wild immediately.

"Zombie," he said and pointed to their hood.

The female monster stood, legs braced and hands on its hips. It looked down at them and chuckled.

He had never seen a zombie this animated, didn't know exactly what to expect.

It strode forward and kicked out their windshield. Caleb grabbed it by the boot. "Run," he yelled at Samantha.

She opened her door, and placed one foot on the ground outside. Caleb twisted the zombie's leg. Something popped. The zombie didn't react; they never did. That at least was the same, fresh or old.

And killing them would be the same, too.

Still holding on to the zombie, he reached for the stiletto blade he'd placed in his boot.

As the passenger-side door slammed shut, the zombie roared and jerked at its leg. It seemed determined now to get free.

The knife in his hand, Caleb considered his next move. He had to get to the zombie's brain stem. There was only one way to do that from here. He was going to have to pull the creature into the car with him.

He jerked, hard. The zombie plunged toward him, but just when he thought he had it, the undead monster reached up and grabbed hold of the roof.

To Caleb's left something clicked.

His gun pointed at Caleb, the trooper yelled, "Raise your hands. Now!"

The zombie pulled back its free leg and kicked Caleb in the face. Blood streamed from his nose. The zombie stilled. There was a loud, disturbing sniffing noise.

It smelled the blood. Controlling the creature was about to get a hell of a lot harder.

Caleb grabbed at its other foot, but with a new strength, the thing curled its knees inward and pulled its body out of the car.

Caleb slammed his fist into the dashboard. He'd lost it. With the trooper standing to his left, blocking the driver's-side door, there was only one other quick exit option.

He leaned back and smashed the remaining mosaic of broken safety glass out of the windshield with his boot.

The trooper fired. The bullet grazed Caleb's shoulder. He winced. Unlike zombies, werewolves did feel pain; lycanthropy didn't change that little biological lesson of survival one bit. The lycanthropy virus would make him heal faster, but first he had to survive this attack.

Covered in blood now, he crawled through the windshield. Bits of glass gouged into his bare stomach and back, adding to his wounds.

The trooper fired again, or someone did. Caleb couldn't see the officer and didn't feel the bite of the bullet. Not wanting to give the officer a chance to better his aim, he surged to his feet.

The trooper, he realized, had quit worrying about him. A new worry had him fully occupied.

The zombie stood on the ground five feet from the

trooper. It raised its arm as if to reach for him. The officer was talking to it, warning it to step back.

The zombie, of course, didn't. It hopped forward on two feet, like a child jumping into a mud puddle. Shock at the creature's move was clear on the trooper's face.

Caleb felt it, too. Zombies didn't hop; they lurched and staggered. Just how fresh was the damned thing?

The trooper's gun wavered. Caleb could see the indecision on his face as he wrestled with the thought of killing what appeared to be a young unarmed woman. An almost impossible call for an officer of the law, but not for Caleb.

His knife held overhead, ready to plunge into the base of the zombie's neck, Caleb leaped.

The trooper fired and the zombie spun. The errant bullet slammed into Caleb's wounded shoulder. He gritted his teeth against the pain and concentrated on his target. With the zombie facing him, however, his target was lost.

And then the zombie did the impossible. It danced to the side, flinging its arm out behind it as it did and crashing it into Caleb. He landed on the asphalt, the impact jolting his body. He didn't drop his blade, didn't lose sight of the zombie, didn't even pause before surging forward after it. But none of that mattered. Not to the trooper.

The zombie, without even turning its head to look, had grabbed the officer around the throat and was cutting off all his access to air.

"Where's the girl?" it asked, coolly, casually. "Wanna save this?" It shook the trooper. "Come closer." Then it grinned.

The thing seemed to be enjoying itself, and for the

first time in a long time, Caleb wondered what kind of person this tattooed, pierced girl had been before she became a zombie.

Then he saw the collar.

"Nice necklace," he said.

The zombie jerked its head. The fingers of its free hand went to its throat.

"Pick that up recently?" he asked.

A crease formed between the zombie's brows. Then without warning, its head shook, a quick violent motion as if it were trying to shake something free. Its eyes focused back on Caleb. "The girl. Where is the—"

"Right here."

There was a flash of movement behind the dangling trooper, and the crunch of metal hitting bone.

The zombie took a step, the lurching type of step Caleb expected from its kind, and then another. Then with no other warning the thing crumpled.

The trooper fell to the ground and didn't move, but neither did the zombie.

Standing behind them, the stiletto blade from Caleb's glove compartment in her hand, was Samantha.

She stared down at her handiwork. Her head and hand were shaking. "I pithed her," she said. Then she looked up.

Not knowing how else to reply, Caleb grabbed Samantha by the hand and tugged her away from the scene. "And you are getting damn good at it," he muttered.

"Wait!" She tried to twist away. "The highway patrol officer. We have to help him."

Caleb tightened his grip. "Remember the first rule of a zombie attack?"

Still looking over her shoulder at the unconscious trooper, she didn't reply.

"If there was one, more may follow." He glanced around. People were out of their cars now, screaming into cell phones. More police and emergency workers would be here as soon as they could make it past the giant snarl of traffic that had formed behind them.

"There are people," Samantha argued. "Besides the officer. There may be children…"

"And every one of them saw you jam a blade into the back of some woman's neck. Not a zombie's neck, a woman. She's dead and you are her killer."

"I'm not. I didn't."

He jerked her closer. "You planning to tell them she was a zombie? That someone else got to her first? You think they'll say, 'Sure. Okay. Thanks for helping'?"

Samantha's gaze drifted over the people staring at her through their car windshields, horror, anger and fear clear on their faces. "But I… What about…?"

"You want to save them? Get in the truck." He shoved her toward the 4x4 that had tried to squeeze by the traffic earlier. The driver was still behind the wheel, but he wouldn't be for long, not once Caleb made him another offer.

While Samantha stared at the congregated vehicles, processing what he had said, he reached into his car for his laptop bag and a duffel he kept packed with the rest of his minimal belongings. Then he rammed her in the butt with the duffel and herded her toward the truck.

As he had suspected, given the option of hauling ass out of his truck or riding along with a gun pressed to his temple, the truck's driver chose to haul.

Caleb wrenched the wheel to the left to disengage it from the compact's bumper then smashed on the gas.

The vehicle was hot, white-hot. They couldn't stay in it for long. First order of business had to be dumping it and finding something a lot less conspicuous.

His foot pressed to the floorboard, Caleb couldn't glance at Samantha, but he didn't need to. He could feel her withdrawing, going into some kind of shock, either from what she had done or what she had left behind, or both.

She had killed the zombie with professional ease. Too professional for the short lessons Caleb had provided her.

And what about the zombie? It had asked about Samantha, seemed to know who she was. He had never known of a zombie being aware of anything except its next meal.

What the hell was happening in Texas and how were the damned zombies finding them here?

Chapter 8

Caleb got off the highway at the next exit. Three minutes after leaving the interstate while they were traveling on the state highway that intersected it, two sheriff's vehicles passed them going the other way.

"Reinforcements," he murmured. He had slowed their speed under the limit as soon as they had exited. A fast pace would only draw attention to them. But it was just a matter of time till someone recognized their vehicle.

With that in mind he pulled off at a road with a sign indicating a state park and killed the lights. With only the almost full moon for light, he wove through the winding pathways of the park.

"How can you see?" Samantha spoke her first words since they had left the accident scene.

"Good genetics," he replied. Not his natural ones, of course.

When he saw an opening in the brush, he maneuvered the truck into the space and then jumped out. Without waiting for Samantha to follow his example, he began covering the back of the vehicle with branches. His shoulder ached as did his nose. He shook off both pains.

When he was finished with the camouflage, he stepped back to analyze his work. It wouldn't hold up in broad daylight, but it should work till then.

Satisfied, he grabbed his bags, wincing from the resulting throb in his wounded shoulder, and motioned for Samantha to follow him.

"We're miles from anywhere," she said.

It was dark, as only the wilderness could be. It had to feel deserted to her, but Caleb knew better.

"Not many," he replied. They were actually only about twenty miles from the next town, but Caleb had no intention of walking there.

He wanted a vehicle that wouldn't be connected to them, at least not immediately. Which meant he had to go past the circle the human authorities would expect once they found this vehicle. Or steal a vehicle no one would report missing.

Or better yet, both.

He had to run, fast and far. He had to shift into a wolf.

But first he had to hide Samantha and convince her not to move from the spot—no matter what happened.

He headed toward the woods, not a path through the trees, but the actual woods. His feet crunched through fallen leaves.

He could feel Samantha's gaze on his back, but she followed without objecting to the main entrance, near an oversize sign mounted on a concrete base. Weeds and brush had grown up around the sign. The front was clear and readable during the day or under the blaze of headlights to any vehicle entering the park, but the back was crowded with brambles. He tossed his bags over the front, then pulled back a handful of thorn-covered branches and pointed.

"Wait for me here. I'll return within an hour. I'll signal you with three flashes of the headlights. Come running and don't forget my bags, or my clothes." He began jerking off his pants.

Her gaze had been locked on to the dark space behind the sign. Now she swiveled to face him. He didn't think she could see him. If she could have, he guessed she would have commented on his bloodied appearance by now. But she could feel and hear his movements and she must have sensed what he was doing.

"I… What…" she started.

Tossing his clothes in after the bags, he gave her a nudge. "Just do what I said. An hour. And don't come out."

He didn't wait for her to hide; he didn't have time. He just took off in a run. Two hundred feet down the highway, when he was sure she couldn't see him in the dark, he shifted. Pain ripped through him, as always, but he forced his body to keep moving, stumbling forward. One of the bullets was still lodged in his muscle; the other had thankfully only winged him. When he changed, the bullet still lodged in his shoulder moved closer to the surface. He stopped and took five minutes to dig it out of his own flesh with his teeth. It hurt like hell, even in his wolf form, but it had to be done.

Once he'd spit the offending hunk of metal onto the

grass, he ran as if a hunter with a long scope was chasing him and a herd of antelope was in front of him. He forgot the burning pain in his shoulder and the throb of his nose. He forgot about zombies and Samantha. He forgot about the lab and every question he'd had about the woman who had told him about it.

He just ran.

Samantha sat shivering on the cold concrete. Her coat provided only a slight barrier between her butt and the sign's icy concrete base. But it wasn't just the frigid temperature that chilled her. It was what she had done, what had almost happened back on the interstate.

Two zombies had attacked her now.

It wasn't part of her bargain, but it couldn't be coincidence, either.

And the last zombie had asked about her. Why?

Samantha leaned her head back and closed her eyes, wishing she could close out her reality as easily. Her father had always told her that sacrifices had to be made, that war wasn't clean or easy. But this—what she was doing, what almost happened, what still might be happening if there were more zombies behind the last two she and Caleb had battled—felt wrong.

She laughed. Felt? It was wrong. It was everything she hated about her father, everything Allison had helped her to stop being.

But it was also the only way to save her friend.

Her father was right; sacrifices had to be made. Samantha just needed to decide what and who she was willing to throw on that grenade.

Another chill passed through her. She shuffled her feet

in the dead leaves bunched around the base of the sign and tried to think of something else. Anything else.

It took Caleb forty minutes of running to locate a vehicle he thought could go missing for a few days without being reported. It was a boat of a car parked behind a residential care center. He could tell by the dust inside no one had driven it for months. His guess was the owner had moved into the group home, but hadn't been ready to give up the symbol of independence the car provided.

So, he didn't think the owner would notice its disappearance anytime soon. He just had to hope no one else did, either.

It was the best he could do.

Twenty minutes later he was back at the park.

He pulled up to the sign and flashed the headlights three times. At first there was no movement, then Samantha's head appeared over the top of the sign.

He put the car in Park and went to meet her.

"Here." She handed him his pants.

He pulled them on along with his shirt and boots. He had enough reasons for the police to pull him over; he didn't need to add nudity to the list.

Samantha watched him, her face guarded. He could see the question on her face, but she didn't mention his nudity. Obviously uncomfortable, she glanced at the car instead. "Where'd you…"

He didn't bother answering. He could tell by her expression she didn't want to hear the answer. He picked up his bags instead and carried them to their new ride. "Get in."

She hesitated. "We shouldn't have left," she said after

a moment. "There may have been more zombies. Those people..." She bit her lower lip. "They had no idea what they were dealing with."

He wasn't a charity or a white knight. He had his own reasons for hunting zombies and not a one was to save humanity. To be honest, he wasn't all that sure humanity deserved to be saved.

He opened the passenger door and tossed his bags into the backseat. The light inside came on when he did.

She glanced at the giant bloodstain that spread across his shirt, then moved her gaze to his face. She took a step forward, her hand rising. "You're hurt."

He shook his head. "It's not my blood." A lie, but he didn't have time for care he didn't need.

Her face hardened. "Those people had no idea what they were dealing with, but we did," she said.

He placed both hands on the door opening and took a breath. He wasn't arguing this. There was no reason to. Instead, he pushed himself away from the car and spun. "You don't want to come with me, that's fine. I don't need you anymore. You gave me your tip. I can find the lab without you. Probably easier without you." He crossed his arms over his chest and stared at her.

"I've never had zombies chasing me before. But you arrive and zombies pop up like dead fish in a lake. Why do you think that is, Samantha?"

She straightened her shoulders. "What do you mean?"

"You know what I mean. You heard that last zombie. It was looking for you. Tell me why."

Samantha stared off into space. Her hand rose to

her throat. "She wasn't looking for me. She just...asked about me."

"Asked about you? That wasn't someone's granny enquiring after your health. Zombies don't *ask* about people. Zombies can't ask about people. They aren't human, not anymore."

"But she did," Samantha murmured. "And I...I don't know why." She lifted her gaze. Her eyes were hard now, steely, determined.

"It, not she. It," he replied, but it wasn't Samantha's misguided use of pronouns that nagged at him. It was her change in demeanor, as if she'd made some decision in front of his eyes. He called on every bit of wolf instinct he could, analyzed how she was standing, the angle of her head, any subtle sign that would tell him what she was thinking.

"You know more about this lab than you're telling me, don't you? You aren't some innocent out to save her friend." As he said the words, he realized how true they had to be. He strode the ten feet between them in three steps, grabbed her by the wrist and held it up.

"I'm nobody's patsy. I'm not a tool for you to point and twirl. Tell me who the hell you are and what your connection to this lab is, or I'm leaving you here and the next zombie I meet I'm directing right to you."

She watched him, her eyes huge and scared.

Of him or the fact that he wasn't believing her lies anymore?

Caleb loomed over Samantha. His fingers were tight around her arm. She could feel each of them digging into her flesh. And it wasn't just the physical contact she found intimidating. It was him.

His eyes sparkled and his muscles were coiled, as if he was holding back some anger or energy, something that once set free could never be reined back in.

She would have run if she could have. No, that was a lie. She wouldn't have because Allison's survival depended on her being here, on her convincing Caleb to stay with her.

She lowered her chin and stared him in the eyes. "I told you, my friend works at the lab. You saw the videos. You know everything I know." She jabbed her fingernails into her palms, forced her face to stay calm, not to show the lie, forced her hand not to drift to the metal tube hidden in her coat lining, either.

Caleb's eyes narrowed. He didn't believe her.

If he did what he threatened, if he left her here, Allison would be lost.

Sacrifices had to be made. The words rang through her head. She closed her eyes and thought of Allison, thought of her father, thought of why she had to lie to this man.

Then she opened them and let the tears of frustration roll down her cheeks. "I'm sorry if you think I look at you as a tool, but I need you. You saw the video. They are making zombies. The place has to be filled with them. Somehow, I've managed to take down one or two, but a lab full? I wouldn't stand a chance. Allison wouldn't stand a chance."

His grip softened, but only slightly. The anger in his eyes shifted...he wasn't sure. She could use that doubt, had to use that doubt.

"My friend is missing." She stepped closer to him and placed her free hand on his chest. "I swear to you that is true." She let him see the truth of her statement in her face, let him see how desperate she was. "And my only hope of saving her is you."

He glanced at her hand, fingers spread wide and pale against his dark shirt.

He looked back at her face; his gaze flickered. "But there's something you aren't telling me, too."

A battle broke out inside her. She wanted to tell him everything, wanted to believe she could toss aside the deal she had already made and put her trust in Caleb instead. But she couldn't. She knew if she told him everything, he would see her as the enemy. He'd leave her or kill her, but he certainly wouldn't help her.

She swallowed every word that tried to bubble up to her lips—both lies and truth—and settled instead on a question.

"If you don't trust me, why would you let me go?" There was an obvious answer to this. He wouldn't.

But it didn't mean he'd keep her alive, either. She'd seen him handle his weapons, seen the cold mantle of a killer that he wore so easily. How much harder would it be for him to kill her here, alone in these woods, than it was for him to blow the head off a zombie that still looked so human?

He seemed to ponder the question, too, and for one loud thump of her heart she thought he was going to leave her behind, dead and deserted in the park's overgrown grass.

Then he dropped her wrist and stalked back to the car. "Good point. Get in."

Her knees bent and her forehead sank to her thighs. She'd thought… But he hadn't.

Then she forced herself to stand and walk to the car.

It wasn't over. She still had a chance of saving Allison.

* * *

They drove another hundred miles without incident or conversation. It was close to sunrise now and not that much farther to the Iowa border. Deciding it was time to switch the vehicle, Caleb took a detour down a county road.

Samantha jerked her gaze from the endless farm scenes. "Where are we going?" She glanced at the GPS device he'd stuck to the dashboard.

"Nowhere you need to know about," he replied. Let her think he was looking for some deserted barn in which to dump her body.

There were circles under her eyes; the dark smudges made her irises look more green than hazel. She looked thinner, too, which he knew was impossible. Humans didn't lose enough weight in one day for it to show. But she was stressed and she didn't hide it well.

"We need to get a new ride," he muttered, his voice gruff. "Maybe get some sleep." He slid a quick look at her. The last was for her, but he could use it, too. Spending time in his wolf form had helped his gunshot wound heal, but he needed sleep to really speed the process.

He could feel her staring at him. "You lied to me," she murmured.

Surprised, he looked at her. He couldn't think of a lie he'd told. She was the one pulling or trying to pull some kind of deception.

"That is your blood. I couldn't see it well last night, but I can now." She opened the glove compartment and began digging inside.

"What are you looking for?" he asked, annoyed.

"First-aid kit. I'm guessing you won't agree to go to a doctor." She glanced at him.

He didn't bother answering.

She dumped an owner's manual, a foil envelope of pipe tobacco and about a dozen pens onto the floor.

"I'm fine," he muttered.

"That's a lot of blood," she answered. Her eyes were clouded with concern.

Something in Caleb warmed. He twisted his gaze back to the road.

"When we stop I want you to take your shirt off. I'm training to be a nurse. If you won't go to a doctor, I'll have to do."

A new warmth sprang to life inside him. Images assailed him…her cool hands on his fevered skin, her face drawing closer as she bent toward him, him lying stretched out on a bed, her hair brushing his chest…

He shivered.

She tensed and leaned toward him. Her hand outstretched, she placed it on his forehead. "Do you have a chill? We may need to get some aspirin when we stop for food. It will help take the edge off the pain, too." Her forehead creased. "I hope it isn't infected."

Her hands twisted in her coat. She dropped back against her seat and fell silent. But every few seconds she glanced at him.

He kept his eyes on the road, kept his lips closed and fought the impulse to tell her she had no hope of curing any fever he might have. Quite the contrary.

Just thinking about her caring for him, touching him, was stoking a fire he wasn't sure he could put out.

Chapter 9

Samantha waited at the motel while Caleb ditched their car. She didn't know if he would return with a new one, or if he planned to pick one up in the morning.

Pick one up in the morning... As if they were out of milk or coffee.

She fell back on the bed and stared at the ceiling. This was becoming too normal—killing zombies, stealing cars, lying to Caleb.

Well, not lying. She hadn't lied yet. She had just carefully omitted information.

Her gaze drifted to her coat strewn across the chair.

But it was very important information.

She walked to her coat. When the doctor had given her the metal tube and told her to keep it with her, she hadn't analyzed what it was, hadn't wanted to think about it too much.

Because, she had to admit, she'd known what it was. Known it would tell them where she was.

But that was all she'd thought there was to the thing— that the doctor had simply wanted to know where she was so he would know she was fulfilling her part of their deal.

Now, though, it was getting harder and harder to ignore exactly what she had agreed to do...the repercussions of what she had agreed to do. Two zombies, both wearing collars, had found her in less than that many days.

The doctor was having her followed. Just to keep track of her movements, as a reminder that he was watching? She prayed that was all, but the twisting guilt in her stomach said there was more to it. The sick pain she hadn't been able to shake since spotting the second zombie holding that trooper said there was more to it.

She reached for her coat, ready to throw the garment on the floor and stomp on it until the doctor's little metal tube was nothing but electrodes and bits.

An image of Allison's face flashed through her mind.

Her fingers curled back in toward her palms and she dropped her hand.

So, the doctor was having her followed? She'd been a fool to think he wouldn't. How else would he know she was doing her part...luring Caleb away from Wisconsin just as he'd asked.

Maybe instead of killing the next zombie she needed to give the thing a message for the good doctor. Make a demand of her own.

She and Caleb were out of the state. That deserved something—an assurance that Allison was okay.

The idea gave her strength. Yes. The next zombie that wandered into her path she was giving a job—to tell the doctor she wanted to hear from Allison. A phone call, anything to let her know her friend was okay.

Or she was telling Caleb that Waco was a lie, that as far as she knew there were no zombies there and never had been.

Caleb left the car parked outside a residential care center not all that different from the one where he had found it. Once the car was ditched, he made his way back to the hotel where he had left Samantha. It was growing dark, but not wanting to leave his clothing behind he was forced to jog the three miles from the care center to the hotel as a man.

Running as a human was never as calming as running as a wolf. As a human he felt his pains and remembered his worries. As a wolf he left all of that behind. It was for him the best part of being a werewolf. Alone, it wasn't enough of a trade for becoming a monster out of a midnight horror flick, but then the peace that came from running in wolf form wasn't why he'd sought out the alpha werewolf two decades earlier.

He had wanted revenge. He had wanted to kill zombies. And not only did legend have it that lycanthropy made a human immune to a zombie's bite, but it also gave him an increased sensitivity with all of his senses, quadrupled his strength and speed and gave him the preternatural ability to heal quickly.

In other words, it made him the perfect zombie hunter.

And at the time it was all he had wanted.

No, not *had* wanted. It was all he wanted then, now, forever.

Nothing had changed.

He looked up. He was outside the motel. It looked just like every motel he'd stayed at for the past twenty years. Outside entrance, dark parking lot, flimsy doors...

But behind this flimsy door was something new.

Samantha.

He couldn't trust her.

He knew somehow she had attracted the zombies that had found them since leaving that alley.

Knowingly? Intentionally?

Or was she a victim, too?

Did it matter? He knew the answer, knew it didn't. She had given him enough information—assuming it was true—that he could find the lab alone now.

He knew he should turn around and leave her, find a car and drive away alone.

Except there was room number 22, right in front of him. The dark blue paint had peeled in strips, as if someone had scraped their nails down its length. A light shone from behind the closed curtains.

She was inside, waiting.

He slipped the key into the lock, then placed his hand on the knob and walked inside.

The rattle of the lock only gave Samantha seconds to prepare for Caleb's return. She grabbed her coat off the room's lone chair, folded it in half and shoved it into a drawer. She was standing with her back to the dresser when he entered.

He was dressed. She let out a nervous breath. She

hadn't been sure if he would be; she couldn't imagine why he'd removed his clothes last night before going to find a new car.

But then she couldn't have imagined a lot of things that now seemed routine if not mundane.

Caleb hunted zombies; that eclipsed almost any behavior others might see as strange.

Past just noticing he was clothed, she studied the state of what he wore. His shirt was blood-covered and crusty. His face and neck were still mottled with the brown remnants of last night's attack, too.

He was a disgusting mess and despite it all sexy as hell.

"You're back," she said like an idiot.

He nodded and glanced around the room. Not sure what he was looking for, she took a step back, covertly making sure the drawer behind her was fully closed.

His gaze locked onto his bags and he strode toward them.

She sagged against the dresser. He'd forgotten, or at least decided not to pursue his earlier questions for a while.

Not sure how long she could hold up to his questioning, she was glad for any reprieve.

After tossing his duffel onto the bed and jerking a clean shirt out of it, he pulled the stained one from his body.

His muscles were sleek and firm, like a racehorse's. She had never seen muscles like this on a man. She wanted to place her palm over them, follow them from beginning to end. And, like a horse after a long run, a sheen of sweat covered his body. She wondered if his muscles would twitch under her touch, if she would be able to feel the contained power inside them.

Her palms began to perspire.

Then she saw his wound. Guilt instantly lanced through her. "Oh. Let me get towels." Jerking her gaze away from the temptation of his bare chest, she hurried into the bathroom to retrieve the towels she'd set out earlier. There was soap, too, but not much more. She could make a temporary bandage out of the materials, but that was it. If the bullet was still inside, Caleb would need to see a doctor. He should see a doctor no matter which.

She knew the zombie hunter wouldn't agree to that, but she couldn't obsess about his inevitable resistance now. She would worry over that battle after she had seen just how bad his wounds were. Holding the wet towels out so they didn't soak her one and only outfit, she hurried back into the room.

He was sitting on the bed waiting for her when she returned. His compliance surprised her, but she knew better than to make a comment.

She pressed the steaming towel to his shoulder to loosen the dried blood and handed him another to place on his face. She held hers steady but gentle. He scrubbed with his as if trying to slough off his own skin.

Startled by his violent scrubbing, she grabbed the towel from his hand and held it out to the side. As it dangled from her fingertips, water dripping onto the worn carpeting, his eyes met hers.

Desire, dark and intense, shone from their depths.

Her breath caught in her chest. Her heart thumped... once, twice, three times. She could hear her own blood moving through her veins. The world seemed to narrow until there was nothing except the two of them in it.

Without meaning to, without even realizing she had done it, she dropped the towel she had taken from him.

Another minute dragged by, then he grabbed her other hand, the one still holding a towel to his shoulder.

His skin was darker than hers; his hand dwarfed hers. She squeezed the towel and water dribbled down his chest. Flustered, she moved to wipe it away.

He grabbed her wrists and tugged her into the V of his legs. "It's fine. I'm fine." He pulled her hand away. There were still bits of blood stuck to his chest, but the gaping wound she had expected wasn't there.

It *had* been there. She could see where the edges of a hole had knitted together. The center was still angry and red, but it looked nothing like what it should have looked.

She pressed her palm over the spot. "How...? Is...?" Shaking her head, she stared at it and murmured, "I thought you were shot."

He captured her hand and rubbed his thumb over her palm. "I heal fast."

Samantha's gaze riveted onto what should have been a gory, bleeding mess. Heal fast? No one healed that fast.

Her heart jumped. Something wasn't right...couldn't be right. She inched away from him, but couldn't seem to get her body to move as she knew she should. Couldn't gather up the strength to dash out the door.

He stared down at her palm. "Your hands are tiny and your bones are so fine," he murmured. "Is that why you picked a gun so small?"

Gun. Her gun. She couldn't concentrate on what he was asking. His touch and the doubt that had bubbled up when she had seen his wound warred for her attention. She had nothing left to answer his questions.

Nothing left to do anything.

He found her other hand and rubbed it against his cheek.

His face was rough with stubble.

She stared at the growth. It circled his lips, made them stand out, look smooth and tempting. She wanted to press hers against his, to slip her tongue in between them.

Moisture formed between her legs. She shifted in place, tried to hide the desire that was flaming to life inside her.

She didn't know him. She was lying to him. Sleeping with him...that would just be wrong.

With no warning, he grabbed her by the base of her neck and pulled her face down to meet his. Then his lips touching hers, his tongue slipping into her mouth, he pulled her body down, too, until she was lying flush against him.

All thought of right and wrong, natural and unnatural, fled from her mind.

Caleb could feel every inch of Samantha's curves through her thin clothing. But he still wanted that clothing off.

He reached for the bottom of her shirt and tugged the tight material off of her in one smooth, sweeping motion.

She didn't object. In fact, she helped him, throwing

the unwanted garment to the side before settling back down on top of him.

He ran his hands down her sides. She was thin but muscular, sleek like a dancer or a female werewolf. He paused, wondering, then pushed the errant thought from his head. That would be too easy.

And Caleb's life was never easy.

Accepting that Samantha would be like every other one-stop hookup he'd ever had, he leaned up and nuzzled his lips between her breasts.

She still wore her bra—a simple thing that like her shirt pulled on, and off, over her head. He slid his hands under its bottom band and ran his thumbs over the tips of her breasts.

She arched her back and moved her body so she straddled him.

His erection pulsed against his pants as her sex rubbed over him. He ached to be free, but feared, despite her seemingly eager acceptance of what was about to happen, too quick of a move would scare her away.

Like any prey, she had to be stalked, watched, coaxed.

And like with any hunt, that extra effort would make the outcome all that much sweeter.

He slipped her bra up, releasing her breasts.

They were small, but round and perfect. He teased the tips with his thumbs while nibbling along her neck. She placed her hands on his shoulders and shifted her weight again, rubbing against him again.

His groin tightened. He wanted to yank her remaining clothing from her body and thrust himself inside of her.

But he wouldn't. Not yet.

She moaned and he moved his lips from her throat to her breast. He twirled his tongue around one perfect nipple.

Nothing had ever tasted so good.

She leaned down and blew into his ear.

He shivered and clutched at her backside. Her butt was like the rest of her, the muscles firm and round where they should be. No skinny model here. She ate and used her body, built it into something that made the wolf in him want to snap and howl.

She made *him* want to snap and howl, to leave his mark on her so all others would know she was his.

His. The word vibrated through his mind. *His...*

He pulled her lips to his and lost himself in her kiss. He tried to forget that he wasn't what she thought. The beauty that she was could never accept him, the beast.

Wrong. Stupid. Liar.

The words pecked at Samantha's conscience.

Caleb's hands were gentle on her skin, stroked her back and buttocks as if she were made of spun sugar and might dissolve under his touch.

And she right. She had never felt a fire like what grew inside her with each of his kisses, each of his touches.

How could she so desperately want a man she knew so little about, a man she was about to betray...had betrayed?

And how could she have so little control over her own body and mind that at this moment she didn't care about anything but having him?

She closed her eyes and let the war wage in silence inside her.

Caleb's lips trailed down her neck; his hand found her breast.

Her fingernails scraped over his chest.

She couldn't stop herself, wouldn't stop herself.

Whatever this was, whatever the reason she was driven to do this, she had no intention of stopping.

Decision made, she jerked her workout bra off and over her head then rolled onto her side. Facing him she slipped her thumb under the waist of her yoga pants and inched them down her hips.

As she did, she watched him, appreciated the admiration she saw in his eyes. She reveled in the power his enjoyment of each of her moves gave her.

Then fully naked she trailed her fingers down his chest and let them dance over the skin of his lower abdomen. His pants had come unsnapped, making it clear he wore no underwear. She wanted to grab the opening in both hands and rip his zipper open like a crazed dieter tearing into a bag of chocolates. She wanted to lick and nibble and explore every inch of him.

She wanted to stroke him and feel him stroke her. Then when she knew his body as well as she knew her own, she wanted to sling her leg over his hip, guide his erection into her core and thrust herself down until he was trapped deep inside of her. Then she would move and scream and come and do everything her manner-schooled southern self told her she shouldn't do.

Then she wanted to do all of it over and over again.

Chapter 10

Caleb curled his fingers into the quilt beneath him to keep from jerking Samantha back on top of him. Her fingers danced inches from where he ached to feel her touch, but he held still, let her have the moment and the control.

His body shook with desire. His muscles clenched. His mind screamed and he just lay there dying for the torture to go on and on.

She leaned over him and pressed her lips to his stomach. Her hair brushed his skin; her breath warmed him.

Her tongue lapped at him. She drew tiny, excruciating circles of moisture where seconds earlier her fingers had teased.

Then slowly her hand drifted to the closure of his pants. As she pulled the zipper down, he knew he couldn't contain himself anymore, couldn't fight off the need to touch her anymore.

He rolled onto his side and jerked his pants from his body. As his erection sprang free, he looped his arm around her waist and pulled her body against his.

Then he kissed her, deep and hard, let every bit of pent-up desire free. He growled and nibbled at her lips, murmured things he knew she couldn't hear, that he didn't want her to hear, but that he couldn't stop himself from saying. Words of love and desire and lifetime mates. Words that came from some part of his brain he'd never realized existed, but his wolf had. His wolf knew what was happening. His wolf knew what it wanted.

And for right now, Caleb was going to give that want to the beast.

He rolled again so she was under him, slipped his leg between hers and nudged her with his sex. She opened for him, not shy but eager, grabbed him and guided him inside her. Then she lifted her hips and met each of his thrusts with a need and vigor he'd thought only he could feel.

She moaned and scraped her nails over his back. She arched and threw back her head.

And then as he thrust inside her, harder and faster, she grabbed at him and bit his shoulder.

Her teeth sank into his skin and a roar escaped his throat. He bit her back, holding on to her neck with his teeth as he thrust one last time and exploded inside her.

Then as tiny puffs of air and release left her lips he held her, clung to her and wished like hell he didn't ever have to let her go.

* * *

Samantha awoke to droning buzz.

Her eyelids flew open. She was in a dark room, lying on a hard bed. Beneath her, rough cloth scratched at her naked skin. And draped over her stomach was a warm, masculine arm. Caleb Locke's arm.

As her awareness of her reality grew, the buzzing continued. It was low, but annoying, like a malfunctioning speaker set heavy on the bass.

She glanced at the dresser. The sound was coming from there, from where she had stashed her coat.

A lump formed in her throat. Her hands went to Caleb's arm. He didn't move. He seemed completely oblivious to the hideous noise.

She edged his arm off of her body. He stirred. She stilled, and his eyes flickered open. Sleep had softened them. Seemed to have softened all of him. His hair was ruffled and his lips curved into a tiny half-moon of a smile. "Sam," he murmured.

"Caleb," she replied, her gaze darting to the dresser and back.

"You're still here," he added.

The buzz grew louder and more insistent.

Her fingers on his arms tensed. "Of course."

His brows drew together. "What's wrong?" He made a move to get up.

He didn't hear the noise, she realized. Swallowing, she placed her hand on his chest. Like his arm, it was warm and smooth and hard. Touching him reminded her of what they had done the night before, and that made her swallow again. She curled her fingers into her palm and pulled back her hand.

She couldn't stand to touch him, not with the monotonous buzz sounding in the background.

"Nothing," she replied, tentative, still not sure that he couldn't hear the noise, too, that he wasn't laying some trap for her. "I...I just need to use the bathroom." She swung her legs over the side of the bed.

She could feel his gaze on her bare back. She glanced over her shoulder at him. His eyes were filled with invitation.

She turned to stare at the wall. "I...I just need to get something." She scooped her clothes from the floor and hurried to the dresser and her coat. With the coat in her grasp, she turned toward the bathroom.

Caleb stood in front of her, naked and one hundred percent alert. "Your coat? You need it for the bathroom?"

Outside of the insulating wood of the drawer, the buzz was even louder. Samantha could feel the vibrations in her teeth.

She jerked the coat on. "I...I don't have any other clothes. I thought I'd wash what I do have." She held up the yoga outfit she'd worn through two zombie attacks and an hour squatting behind a sign in the woods. The state of the material spoke for itself. "I thought I'd wear this while they dried." She fingered the belt of the coat.

Caleb angled his head to study her.

The buzzing was so loud now Samantha was beginning to wonder if it was real or if she had stepped into her own personal Edgar Allan Poe-inspired nightmare with a modern buzzing cylinder replacing the beating heart.

Finally, when she thought she couldn't stand the noise any longer, when she was seconds from ripping off her coat and slamming the offending metal object into the wall, Caleb replied. "We'll have to fix that."

She waited, sure it wouldn't be that simple, sure once she started to move away he would stop her again, but as she nodded and took a step toward the bathroom, he did nothing, just watched her go.

Forcing her steps to stay measured, she walked into the bathroom and clicked the door closed behind her. Then she twisted on the shower and with the water pounding into the tiny tub behind her, she ripped off her coat and clawed at the lining where the cylinder was hidden.

Red letters flashed at her from a black strip on the cylinder's side. Ten digits separated into three groups. A phone number.

The doctor wanted her to call.

She wrapped her hand around the thing. A tiny spike of metal had popped out of one end. She moved her thumb over it, but hesitated. She didn't know what would happen if she pressed it. The buzzing might stop, but the number might disappear, too. Or the entire cylinder could blow up.

Deciding she was willing to risk the latter to get rid of the buzzing, she set to work memorizing the number. Once she was confident she had it stored in her mind, she pressed her thumb against the knob.

There was a click, like pressing the end of a ballpoint pen, and the buzzing stopped. No explosion. No smoke. Just blessed silence.

She lowered her head and murmured a prayer of relief. Then she stored the cylinder back into the lining of her coat and hurried into the shower. After quickly cleansing her body and clothes, she left the yoga pants and shirt hanging in the shower, slipped on her coat and walked back into the room.

Caleb was waiting for her, fully dressed and leaning against the motel room's door. His arms were crossed over his chest and she knew with zero doubt that he was onto her.

"Better?" he asked.

She nodded.

He stalked forward.

Her fingers twitched. She could feel the cylinder hanging heavy in her coat's lining and wondered if he could see the bulge.

He ran the backs of his fingers down her cheek. "I'm sorry," he murmured.

"Sorry?" She breathed the word. Standing this close to him, knowing under her coat she was naked, she had a hard time forming a thought much less replying coherently. But she had to. She had to think of something to say that would buy her time away from him, enough time to dial the damn number that had flashed at her in the bathroom.

If she didn't, there was no telling what would happen next. How many zombies would be pounding on their door?

He leaned closer. His breath tickled her skin. She shivered and swayed toward him. She realized what she was doing and what continuing on this track would bring—pleasure, warmth, hours in his arms.

But that was time she didn't have. Not if she wanted to keep the cylinder from buzzing or doing whatever it would do next to get her attention.

She jerked away.

Caleb's hand hung in midair where he'd been millimeters from touching her. The soft, luring expression of his face hardened. His eyes shuttered. He pulled back and dropped his hand to his side.

"You need clothing," he said.

Surprised, Samantha only blinked in response. Then realizing it was a way to get time to make her call, she fingered the collar of her coat. "I do, but I can't go out like this."

He glanced at the bathroom then back at her coat. "I'll get them," he replied.

Easy. Too easy, but Samantha didn't have time to question her luck. She also didn't have time to remove the money she had tucked inside the coat's lining. "I can pay you," she started.

With a shrug, Caleb cut her off. "I don't need money." He stalked toward the door.

Samantha opened her mouth to say she wouldn't wear stolen clothes, that the thought of it made her stomach ache, but then she remembered where she was and what she had already done.

Shoplifting was far from her greatest sin lately.

Plus, she needed Caleb to leave now.

She pressed her lips together and swallowed her objection.

Then with the door closed behind him, she went to get dressed.

Caleb stood outside the motel door, feeling cold and alone. This morning when he woke next to Samantha, it had felt right. He had felt right. At peace. A hunger, the gnawing need to roam that had engulfed him since his family had been killed and he'd become a werewolf had disappeared.

It was the first time since that day that he hadn't awoken with revenge at the forefront of his mind.

He had been...happy.

But then Samantha had stepped away and he'd realized how stupid he was, how easily he had fallen for the seductive trap that she had set.

He'd thought he was hardened to hurt, couldn't feel such emotions anymore, but he had been wrong.

He had felt that single step back as painfully as if she'd had her fingers dug into his heart when she made it.

He clenched his fists and cursed his own stupidity.

His wolf had been wrong, and he had been a fool for listening to the beast.

Not only couldn't Samantha accept what he was, the secret she didn't know, but she didn't even care for the man she did know.

Her tender touches and blazing responses were lies.

And he had fallen for them.

But not again. Never again. After today, he knew her game, or at least her methods. Now he had to discover what she was playing for.

With that in mind he pressed his ear to the cool glass of their room's window and listened. There were noises inside...a door opening and closing, soft murmurs of annoyance and finally footsteps coming toward the door.

Realizing she was leaving the room, he leaped backward, securing a place in the shadows, near a broken ice machine, seconds before the door to their room opened and Samantha stepped out into the wintry air.

Samantha shivered as she stepped into the chilly morning air. Her yoga pants seemed to instantly freeze to her skin. She grabbed the collar of her coat and slipped one side under the other, trying to cover as much of her skin as possible, but with her clothes and hair still wet it did little good.

She was sure she would be blue by the time she was done with this errand. Her hands shoved deep into her pockets, she scurried down the sidewalk toward the office. She had no cell phone and knowing any long-distance calls she placed from the room would be billed to Caleb, she couldn't call from there. So she had to find another phone.

After a quick stop in the office for directions to a pay phone, she headed back out onto the street. The desk clerk had directed her to a grocery store three blocks away. He had first offered to loan her his phone, but she hadn't like the way he'd looked her up and down as he'd gestured to the tiny room behind his desk.

She'd thanked him and hurried out of the office.

She kept up her rapid pace as she made her way to the grocery. The buildings she passed were boarded over and weeds seemed to be choking out the concrete walks. The few people she saw looked harmless enough, but after her time with the zombies she was afraid her ability to judge between safe and dangerous was shot.

How ironic would it be for her to survive three zombie attacks only to be taken out by a common mugger?

With the thought scratching through her mind, she picked up her pace even more. She was almost jogging by the time a building with neon-colored paper signs advertising Canned Goods Four For A Dollar came into view.

Letting out a relieved breath, she shoved her way

through the broken automatic doors and scurried to the pay phone.

The buttons and handset both showed the gray-brown residue of other grocery patron's use. She cringed a little then pressed Zero for the operator.

Collect call for doctor zombie. Will doctor zombie accept the charges? A hysterical giggle bubbled up inside her. An older woman pushing a cart loaded with two cardboard flats of canned goods frowned in disapproval.

With a sigh, Samantha leaned against the wall and waited for her call to go through.

The woman was right. She shouldn't be laughing. There was absolutely nothing amusing about what she was doing.

On the other end of the line a woman answered, using the cover name of the lab, Lifeline Industries. The operator announced she had a collect call for Dr. Allen, the name Samantha had been given. She had no idea if it was the doctor's real name; she had no idea if the man she'd seen on the video and spoken to briefly on the phone even was a doctor. However, she suspected the answer to both was no.

In seconds the baritone voice of the doctor echoed into her ear. After accepting the charges, he addressed Samantha. "Good to hear from you."

As if the call had been her idea. But while it hadn't, she had wanted to talk to him. She clutched the receiver and prepared herself to make the demands she'd practiced back at the motel. She wanted to talk to Allison; if not, she would tell Caleb everything.

"How is your trip progressing?" he asked.

"Fine," she replied. She wasn't sure what else to say,

wasn't sure why the man she hated more than anyone or anything had called her. She suspected the cylinder told him exactly how her trip was progressing, distance wise at least, but if it didn't, if by some chance he didn't know where she was, she wasn't going to tell him.

"Glad to hear that. I was concerned something might have gone wrong. I'd sent some of our patients out to keep an eye on you, for your own safety of course, and I seem to have lost track of them."

His patients, the zombies.

"That's too bad," she answered. He was playing coy; she could, too. Hatred and distaste bubbled like magma inside her. The man talked a good game. He might have convinced her he was some kind of philanthropist if she hadn't seen the video, if she didn't know his life-enhancing lab was actually a factory for monsters. But she had seen it and no amount of concerned words or sympathetic noises would make her forget those images.

He was silent for a second. There was a clicking noise. His tongue snapping against his teeth, she realized. She shuddered, imagining him standing in his white lab coat surrounded by whatever tools he used to turn living human beings into flesh-hungry zombies.

"Did you see them?" he asked.

She considered lying, but then remembered how the first zombie at the truck stop had angled his head like a dog listening to a signal. She suspected that signal had been the doctor or one of his minions giving the creature directions, that the doctor knew all too well what had happened to his "patients."

"I did." She stared at a phone number that had been gouged out on the side of the phone with a key or other metal object. She wished she had such an object and was next to the doctor right now, gouging out his eyes, his throat, his life.

"And how were they when you saw them last?" he prompted.

Her tone dry, she replied, "They were dead, their brains scrambled."

Air hissed into the phone. The doctor was not pleased.

For the first time in days, Samantha smiled.

"And Caleb Locke?" he asked.

Samantha stiffened. "What about Caleb?"

"Are you two getting friendly? Not a bad tack for you to take."

Her stomach clenched. She wanted to scream that it wasn't like that, that she hadn't slept with Caleb to trick him, that the feelings he created inside her were the only good things to happen to her since Allison had left for the damned job with this zombie-making maniac.

She squeezed her eyes shut and swallowed the words, tried to swallow her guilt as well, but that was impossible. It burned through her like a gasoline cocktail.

"How did he react this morning?"

Caught up in her misery, his question caught her off guard. "What?" Did the doctor know what they had done last night? Had zombies watched them? Had the cylinder recorded them?

The sick feeling she'd felt before returned. She wobbled on her feet.

"When I notified you, how did he react? Were you able to get away without him knowing?"

"When you…?" The buzzing. He was asking about the buzzing. "Uh, yes. There wasn't a problem."

"No problem? He didn't seem suspicious? Did he hear the signal?"

She hesitated. It felt as though she was betraying Caleb somehow by answering, but then she'd already done that, hadn't she? "No, he didn't."

"He didn't!" There was no missing the excitement in the doctor's voice.

And there was no missing that somehow Samantha had just made her previous betrayal all that much worse.

"So, it's true. This changes everything."

Samantha didn't ask what was true; she didn't have the heart for it, didn't have the heart for anything. The doctor rambled on, directing her to change their course, to get Caleb to take her to some address in Iowa.

Bile rose in her throat. He was planning a trap. He wanted Caleb, but for what?

Her hand rose of its own accord, reached for the lever that would disconnect the call. Her other instinct—the one that told her to tell Caleb everything—was the right one.

"Allison will be there."

Inches from the lever, her fingers froze.

"Allison? Is she all right? I want to talk to her. If I can't talk to her I won't do it. I won't do anything. No, that's wrong. I'll talk to Caleb, tell him everything I know—that the lab isn't in Texas at all. That it's in Wisconsin and you wanted me to lure him away."

A chill passed through the line. "That would be a very stupid thing to do. You've met my patients, but only a few. Do you really think your new friend, Caleb Locke, would stand a chance against ten of them? Twenty? How about fifty or one hundred? I can do that. I can unleash a village on him."

A village of zombies. A chill passed over Samantha's skin, bored inside her.

"And what about your old friend Allison? Have you forgotten her? I've told her you are working for us. I'd hate to have to tell her I was wrong. She would be so distressed. I doubt she'd ever trust you again. She might even choose to undergo my therapies herself. She has shown an interest in them. So much, that I've been considering—"

"No!" Samantha yelled into the phone.

Another grocery store patron, this time a teenage boy shuffling by with his black hoodie all but hiding his face, stopped and stared.

Samantha stared back, bared her teeth.

He scurried on. She returned to the phone, her expression and mood grim.

"So, I can plan on your arrival?" the doctor asked.

Samantha's palms filmed over with sweat. Allison, who had depended on her since childhood or Caleb? There really wasn't a choice to be made.

"What's the address?"

She scribbled his reply onto her wrist with a pen that dangled from the phone by a piece of twine.

"Good, then. We will look for you there."

We? Samantha closed her eyes and tried not to think of what that meant. Then as she sensed he was getting ready to hang up, she remembered what she'd planned on saying to him, demanding of him.

"Wait! Allison. I need to talk to her."

There was silence and for a second she thought

he'd already disconnected the call. Then he said, "Do you?"

She did; she really did. Her knees buckled. She was beaten down, lost. She'd done so many things she'd never imagined doing, gotten so far from the peaceful Zen person Allison had encouraged her to be.

She had failed her friend in that way. It couldn't be for nothing.

"I do," she whispered. The soft plea was miles from the barked order she'd imagined giving, from how the words would have sounded from her father's lips, but it was all she had left.

She could feel the smile on the other end of the phone, slimy and self-satisfied. The bastard knew he had beaten her. She hated him for it, but she hated herself more.

"Well?" Another pause.

Samantha gripped the receiver until her hands ached.

"I think that can be arranged." He held the phone away from his mouth, or muffled it somehow. Samantha could tell he was talking to someone, but she couldn't make out his words.

Then a new voice came onto the phone. "Sammie?"

Samantha sagged against the wall. "Allison?" She breathed the name. She hadn't realized until right now how little hope she'd really had that her friend was still alive...still herself. Yes, she had been forging forward as if she believed it, but that had been an act to keep herself from facing what she had feared was the truth.

"Yes?" Her friend's voice was colored with confusion.

"Are you…are you…" Alive? A zombie? Samantha didn't know how to ask the question. "Are you okay?"

There was a pause, like their connection wasn't quite in synch, then Allison replied, "Of course. I'm fine. How are you?"

Samantha laughed. Relief washed over her, and tears escaped from the corners of her eyes.

"Fine, great." She didn't know what to say next. The doctor was listening, she had no doubt of that. Reality struck. Nothing had changed. Even if Allison was all right at this moment in time, it didn't mean she would stay that way.

"Happy?" the doctor asked.

Samantha's smile disappeared. "If you hurt her…"

"Hurt her? Why would I do that?" He murmured something and Samantha had the feeling someone was walking away. Allison. Or was she led away? How was the doctor holding her?

"If you make her into one of your patients, I'll—"

"My patients ask for my services. I give them new life and it doesn't come cheaply. You think I'd waste my research and time on someone who didn't beg for my help?" he scoffed.

Allison didn't buy it. Yes, maybe some of those people had asked for some crazy idea of life after death, but if they did, they'd had no idea what that would mean.

"But then, as I said, Allison has shown an interest."

Samantha stiffened, but before she could form a reply, he continued.

"Just do your part by bringing Caleb Locke to the address I gave you and I'll do mine. Allison will be there to meet you. After that it's up to her whether she goes with you or not. I'm not forcing her."

Of course not. That would be inhumane. Samantha gritted her teeth.

Again, there was the sound of the doctor preparing to disconnect and again, Samantha stopped him.

"Wait."

"Yes?"

"Caleb. Why do you want him? What are you going to do to him?" She knew better than to ask the question, knew if the doctor gave an innocent answer she wouldn't believe it, and if he gave a dark one, it would just make trading Caleb for Allison all the more gut-wrenching.

But she had to ask. Some twisted part of her had to hear the doctor's reply.

"Do to him? My, you do have ugly opinions of us, don't you? I, Miss Wagner, am a scientist. I have no interest in hurting your self-proclaimed hunter. I simply want to learn from him, to study him. That, my dear, is what I do."

Then he hung up.

Leaving a new line of questions queued up in Samantha's head. What the hell did the zombie doctor think to learn from Caleb? Why in the world would he want to study him? And how exactly would he do it?

With questions or a scalpel?

Chapter 11

Caleb had slipped a kid in a hoodie five bucks to spy on Samantha while she was in the store. Now he leaned against the sign-covered window waiting for his recruit to come out with a report.

The once-automatic doors crept open and the kid slouched out. Holding the folded five-dollar bill between two fingers, Caleb gestured for the kid to come closer.

The boy reached for his pay. Caleb jerked it back.

The kid cursed and Caleb lifted a bored brow. "What do you have to tell?"

"She's on the phone." He made another move to grab the bill.

He was slow. Even a thirty-year-old zombie could have outsnatched him.

"What's she saying?"

The kid shoved his hands into his pockets and lifted

his shoulders in a disinterested shrug. "Dude, she's at the pay phone. There's nothing but a broken gumball machine near her. It's not like I can load up on jaw breakers—or just stand there staring at her. People around here get jumpy when you do that."

Caleb flicked the five back toward his wrist, dropped it down his sleeve.

"Hey!" The kid grabbed for the disappearing bill.

Caleb shoved his other hand up under the kid's hoodie and dug his thumb into the kid's solar plexus.

"Ever hear stories about the Aztecs?" he murmured.

The kid stared at him, his eyes wide and unsure.

"It's said they sacrificed people by ripping their still-beating hearts out of their chests. I've always wondered if that was true." He squeezed; the kid gagged.

He released his hold, but only slightly. He kept the kid close enough he could grab him again if necessary.

It wasn't.

"She was all emotional—angry then scared then happy. It was like watching some card commercial on TV."

Caleb processed that. "What did she say? Any names?"

"Yeah, Dr. something."

The lab. A chill shot through Caleb. She was talking with someone at the lab.

"A girl's name, too. Alicia, Alice…something like that."

"Allison?"

"Yeah, that was it. She seemed happy when she was talking to her."

Caleb dropped his hold on the kid and stepped away.

Then he held out the folded bill. The kid grabbed it and, hood pulled back over his dirty blond hair, he scurried away.

Caleb ignored him.

Allison was alive and well. And Samantha had been speaking with her.

It was all a lie. Targeted at whom? Him?

The zombies, it appeared, had finally turned the tables. The hunter was now the hunted, and the head dog rounding him up was Samantha.

He had never felt more betrayed in his life. But the need for revenge…that was achingly familiar.

The motel room was still empty when Samantha returned. She let out a sigh of relief. She'd worked out a story to tell Caleb if he noticed she was missing, but she knew he'd see through it. Better if he never suspected she had left at all.

As she scrubbed the now-memorized address off of her arm, she worked on how to get Caleb to the doctor's new address. She couldn't just announce a change in direction. She needed a reason for the new route. And at the moment, she couldn't think of one.

With no other choice except to wait and hope something came to her, she paced around the room.

It took Caleb one trip through the women's section of the closest department store to nab a full wardrobe for Samantha. He had a feeling she wouldn't be thrilled with wearing stolen clothing, but then what did or didn't thrill her was hardly his concern.

His only concern regarding the lying Southern beauty was keeping her alive long enough to figure out what her game was and to use her to draw out whoever was behind the lab.

If there was a lab.

He realized now he didn't even know if he could trust that.

He only knew he couldn't trust Samantha.

Samantha stared silently out the windshield. Caleb had returned to the motel with new clothing about an hour after she had gotten back. She had changed and they'd immediately hit the road again.

There had been no discussion as to what had happened between them; there had been no discussion of anything.

It was unsettling.

Samantha tugged at the stiff cotton shirt Caleb had provided. He'd given her matching stiff denim jeans, too.

She crunched when she sat.

She toyed with the idea of undoing one button on the blouse for breathing room. As it was, her breasts felt smashed and uncomfortable. But as her hand drifted to the button, Caleb's gaze slid toward her.

Suddenly all too aware how he might interpret such a move, she slowly lowered her hand.

She glanced at the GPS on the dash instead. She'd checked the thing earlier and discovered the address the doctor had given her was only a few miles off the highway they were currently traveling. At their current pace, they would pass the turnoff within the hour.

But she had yet to mention the detour and she was running out of time.

* * *

Caleb fidgeted in his seat. They had been driving for three hours; they were almost into Missouri. Samantha hadn't said or done anything to raise his suspicions, but then she really hadn't done anything at all except twiddle with the damned top button of her shirt.

Each time her hand hovered there, his body tensed. He was like a man left days in the desert waiting for a bit of water to drop from a pipe he couldn't quite reach.

It was disconcerting and annoying as hell.

He growled and gripped the steering wheel harder.

She glanced at him nervously with those damned innocent eyes of hers.

He growled again.

He was tired of sitting in this car, tired of being trapped. His skin itched and his bones ached. He jammed his fingers up into his hair.

The full moon was a little over a day away and he was getting antsy. He could feel every tick of the clock as the time to change edged closer.

He twisted his neck to the right and then the left, hoping it would relieve the ever building need to shift.

God, if he felt like this now, how would he feel tonight when the gibbous moon so close to full shone down on him?

It had never been this bad before, never.

He glanced at his passenger. Could she be causing this?

"I need to stop," she blurted, pointing at a sign that advertised a gas station. She pressed her legs together. The button she had been fiddling with popped out of its hole. As she moved, the material parted, revealing the round curve of her breast.

His teeth ground together. He wanted to jump on her, pin her to the side of the car and bite each tiny blue button that remained off her shirt. Then he wanted to start at her neck and nuzzle his way down her throat, her chest, her—

"Caleb, please." She tapped the passenger-side window. Urgent, needy.

Well, so was he.

He growled out a response, or what he hoped passed as a response, and put on his blinker.

Stopping would be good. Walking around would be good.

Jumping her would be sublime.

After thirty minutes in the gas station bathroom trying to think of a way to steer Caleb in the new direction, Samantha walked out of the quick shop and into drizzle.

The car was where she and Caleb had left it, but the zombie hunter was nowhere to be seen. She studied their ride for a second, wondering if she had the skill or the guts to sabotage it.

After only a bit of consideration, she conceded she didn't. Stopping the vehicle from starting wouldn't be that hard—jerking a few wires loose would most likely do that—but not getting caught…that's where she was afraid she'd fall short. Besides, even if she did manage to damage the vehicle and get away with it, Caleb would just steal another one.

And here at a gas station only a few feet off the interstate there would be no shortage of replacements.

She needed another plan.

What would make Caleb change direction and think it was his idea?

The answer was simple. Zombies.

With her plan firm if not completely thought out, she surveyed the parking lot. It held the usual ragtag mix of customers: truckers, families on their way to some relative or another's and salesmen. She ticked each off as being unusable.

Then her eyes lit upon a dark-clothed pair hunkered on the concrete beneath the gas station's short overhang. From here she couldn't tell their gender or age, but she could tell they were desperate.

Desperate enough to play along with what she was about to propose? She hoped so.

She hurried toward them, her hand wrapped around a ten-dollar bill Caleb had given her before entering the quick shop. It seemed wrong to use his own money against him, but then nothing she was doing seemed right.

One more sin to add to her bill. She doubted it weighed down her already soiled wings too much.

"Excuse me." She stopped in front of them.

Neither looked up.

She nudged the closest with her toe. The person, a female probably in her early twenties, slumped to the right onto her companion and squinted up. There were tattoos covering the side of her face, what appeared to be the moon and nine stars.

"Are you one of us?" she asked.

"One...?" Samantha shook her head. It was obvious the woman was on something. Her eyes were dilated and her lids heavy.

"We're gathering for the choosing. Angie got picked last month. She promised she'd put a word in for me."

The choosing? Images of group weddings with special Kool-Aid punch flowed through Samantha's brain. Deciding the pair was crazier than she cared to take on, she turned and ran right into a solid warm chest.

Caleb.

He wasn't looking at Samantha; he was looking at the two people on the ground. "The choosing?" he asked.

"Yeah, you been there?" The woman leaned back her head until Samantha thought it might roll off of her shoulders. "You look familiar. You know Angie?"

"No." He grabbed Samantha by the arm and dragged her toward their car.

"Wait," she called, knowing once she was in the car her plan would be lost. She'd have no way of convincing him to change directions, not without confessing everything.

At the car Caleb jerked open the door and waited for her to climb in. She glanced back at the drugged-out duo.

They hadn't moved, but the female was watching them. She seemed to have found some life somewhere.

"I think they know something," Samantha stuttered.

He glanced back at them. "Meth would be my guess," he muttered, then gestured to the passenger seat.

"No. Zombies. Before you came out she said something about zombies."

He cocked his head. "Zombies? What did she say?"

Samantha swallowed. "She'd seen some, near here,

or not too far." She told him the address the doctor had given her.

He stilled and his mouth pulled tight.

Already in too deep to back out, she forged ahead. "Should we check it out?"

He lifted his chin. "What about Waco? Don't you want to get to your friend as quickly as possible?"

"Of course...but I know you have other responsibilities. If zombies are loose here, might kill people here, I wouldn't want to be what kept you from stopping them."

His eyebrow twitched and for a second she thought he didn't believe her, then he motioned toward the car. "Get in. You're right. We should check it out. It's what I do—check out zombie sightings."

While he walked around to the driver's side of the car, she settled into her seat.

It was going to be okay. He was going to go to the address the doctor had given her. Allison would be there, Caleb would be there and somehow all three of them would escape this nightmare unharmed.

Twenty minutes later they bumped off the main road and onto what was little more than a cow path.

Samantha's gaze shot to the GPS.

Caleb reached up and popped the device off of the dash. He dropped it onto the floor. "This road isn't on here."

"But the address..."

"What address? The one that druggie told you?"

Sensing she was about to fall into a trap, Samantha pressed her lips closed.

"Were you going to say this isn't the road to get

there? How would you know? You haven't entered it into the GPS, have you?" He reached down and picked the device back up, started flicking through screens with his thumb. "No, don't see it saved. Of course, that doesn't mean you hadn't already checked out where this zombie sighting was located.

"But wait…" He twisted his neck as if an idea had just occurred to him. "You couldn't have, could you? Because you just learned of it twenty minutes ago back at that gas station and you've been sitting here next to me ever since. I would have seen you." He dropped the GPS again. It landed with a *thunk* on the floor.

Then he threw the car into Park, twisted in his seat and pinned her against the door. His breath hot on her neck, he muttered, "Where'd you get the address, Samantha? And why exactly do you want me to go there?"

Samantha licked her suddenly dry lips. "If you don't want to do this—".

"Don't want to do what?" He lowered his face, so his nose was close to her skin. He inhaled, held the breath for a second then inhaled again. "I know I shouldn't, but I want to do way more than we are doing right now. How about you?"

Samantha's chest was tight; her breasts ached. A strange combination of stark fear and pure lust twisted through her. One hand was balled at her side, the other open, ready to touch him, coax him into coming even closer.

She closed her eyes, thinking if she couldn't see him, one emotion—fear or desire—would win out over the other. But both continued to grow, began to morph into something she'd never felt before. Her hands shook; her breath came out in huffs.

"Tell me who you are and what you are, so I can understand this pull you have on me," he muttered.

Then he kissed her.

His lips were hard and punishing, but his body was tight and wary, as if he was as afraid of her as she was of him.

But that was impossible. He was the hunter. He'd battled monsters most could never imagine facing.

Why would he fear her?

His hand moved to her neck, his thumb tipping up her chin while his fingers danced over her nape. He murmured against her lips, "Everyone has one. Why did you have to be mine?"

His what? She wanted to ask, but again was afraid. Everything about Caleb seemed to intimidate and excite her. She stayed silent, lifted her lips back to his instead.

And he took them. His tongue plunged into her mouth. The hand holding her neck tensed and the other moved under her body, pulling her down in the seat.

He was on top of her now and his hands were inside her coat, under her blouse. The buttons she hated popped free. She wiggled lower and jerked his shirt up, out of his pants.

His sides were firm, sinewy. She remembered what they looked like when he was naked and standing before her. A moan left her lips. She shifted her body so his sex rubbed against hers through their clothes.

She wanted him to hold her, wanted him inside her.

It was at that moment all she wanted, all she could think of. Her coat was bunched against the door where she had shoved it after taking it off earlier. His hand fell on it. He grabbed it to toss it out of the way.

She tilted her head and kissed his neck. Absorbed his scent, and the rough feel of the stubble on his chin. Tasted him and murmured to him—words of need and want, words she'd never said or felt before.

Her heart was soaring. Her fear was gone.

And then she realized he hadn't moved, not since placing his hand on her coat.

She closed her mouth and her eyes, and lay there, knowing she had been found out.

Chapter 12

Desire raged through Caleb, so much that it squashed aside all feelings of doubt, all concerns, fears and questions he'd had regarding Samantha, even those brought on by the address she'd claimed to get from the drugged-out kid.

His entire being was focused on her, wanting her, having her...loving her.

Then his hand felt the cylinder hidden in her coat. It could have been a lipstick, but he'd never seen her apply any. It could have been a lighter or a flash drive or any number of innocuous things, but he knew as soon as his hand felt the object hidden in the lining of her coat that it was none of those things.

None of those things had to be hidden, not from him or anyone. It brought back reality like a slap to the face.

Slowly, he straightened his arm and lifted his body off of hers.

Her eyes were closed and guilt was written all over her face.

He wrapped his fingers around the object and ripped it from the coat, tearing a hole the size of his fist in the lining.

Then he shoved his body off hers and stared at the object in his hand—a small silver cylinder. It looked innocuous, but he knew it wasn't.

"Who are you working for and what do you want from me?" he asked, his voice cold...dead. Dead as one of the zombies he hunted. It was how he felt inside.

He had known better than to trust her, to let her get close, but despite himself he had, and now there was no avoiding the pain her betrayal would bring with it. His only hope was that he could believe whatever story she told him and that he wouldn't have to kill her because of it.

She didn't reply at first. She pushed herself upright and pulled her shirt closed. A number of the buttons were missing, and her breasts seemed to want to break through the material. She hadn't worn a bra today; he'd noticed that when she was lying beneath him. She looked vulnerable, sitting there, her shirt barely held together over her bare skin, her face flushed and her hair wild around her face. Her lips were swollen, and her neck was red where his constant stubble had rubbed against her much more sensitive skin.

She looked sad, sexy and scared. And all he wanted to do was pull her to his chest and tell her everything would be okay, but he couldn't because it wasn't and he wasn't her savior. He was her biggest threat.

"Do you even have a friend?" he asked.

She bristled. "Yes, I have a friend. Allison. Everything I told you about her is true."

But everything she had told him wasn't.

"What is this?" He held up the cylinder, praying she'd tell him it was a camera, that she worked for a blog or tabloid as he'd originally suspected.

"I…" Her eyes locked onto the silver tube. He could see her deliberating, deciding what to tell him, how to lie.

He closed his fingers over the object, cutting off her view. Her eyes shifted to his face.

What she saw there must have scared her. Her lips parted and she sucked in a breath. "I don't know. Not really."

"Okay. Let's try something easier. Where did you get it?"

The pause was longer this time. Then finally she replied, "The doctor."

Iron ran through his veins. "The zombie doctor?"

Her pulse jumped at her throat. "Yes."

"You know him. You're working with him." The words fell cold and flat between them. She didn't know it, but she'd just given him everything he'd ever wanted. Someone within arm's reach on whom he could pin to the creation and control of zombies. Someone he could kill.

He looked at her, waited for the bloodlust to hit. This close to the full moon it should be bubbling inside him, be barely contained by the steel cage he kept it restrained in when not in his wolf form.

But it didn't strike.

Despite his anger, he had no desire to hurt her. In fact, the mere thought of it caused him to cringe and shake.

Hurting her, he realized, would be as painful as hurting himself. Even more so.

He needed her. His wolf needed her and the damned beast wasn't going to let a little thing like her betrayal allow him to hurt her.

She leaned forward and replied, "I'm not working for him willingly. He has Allison." She swallowed. "When I hadn't heard from her in a week, I started trying to find the lab. I didn't find it, but I didn't have to. He called me." The fear she must have felt at the time shone from her eyes now. "He sent me to the Internet, to the videos, and told me he'd call back after I'd seen them. Then he told me what I had to do if I wanted to see her again. He told me about you." Her gaze was earnest, almost pleading. "After seeing those images, I couldn't leave her with him. I'd have agreed to do anything and all he said he wanted was for me to meet you and tell you about the lab."

She wanted him to believe her, but could he?

Not if he was smart.

He steeled his mind, concentrated on her deception, not her soft curves or alluring scent. "He kidnapped her. Why not go to the police?"

"I did, but—" She bit down on her cheek.

"What?"

"I couldn't tell them about the zombies. They wouldn't have believed me. Then Allison called them and told them she was okay."

He raised a brow. "She talked to the police?"

"According to the police, she did. Whoever they talked to knew all her private information and even e-mailed them a picture with that day's newspaper in the photo. They quit talking to me after that."

Caleb tapped his finger against the gearshift. If Allison had talked to a detective, she wasn't a zombie, or hadn't been at that time anyway. He'd never met a zombie who could carry on a conversation.... His finger stilled. Except last night. That zombie had been amazingly vocal. But the creature's skill had to have been an illusion. One that wouldn't have held up to a one-on-one conversation like the police would have had with Allison.

"So, what are you supposed to be doing for this doctor? Why the new address?"

Samantha's lower lip disappeared into her mouth. "I don't know."

Maybe not, but she knew something. He grabbed her by the wrist and jerked her toward him, forced his wolf to believe the action was for her own good. "What do you know?"

She glanced from her wrist trapped in his fingers to his eyes. He didn't blink, and he didn't lower his gaze. "The lab isn't in Waco. That was a lie. The doctor told me to tell you that, to get you away from the real location. Wisconsin."

He dropped her wrist as if it were wrapped in white-hot silver. "I was right. I knew there was too much activity there." He muttered the words, more to himself than her. He'd been close, so close, and he'd let Samantha with her big eyes and sad stories lure him away.

She placed her fingers around the wrist he had just held. She didn't rub the skin, but he could tell from the gesture she wanted to.

He had hurt her. His wolf rumbled.

He turned in his seat to face the windshield, wished he could get out of the car and walk away for a few minutes. This close to her, enclosed in the small space filled with her scent, it was impossible to concentrate on the facts of what she had done, what she knew.

His mind was too full of her, his body too aware of her. And his wolf too damned protective of her.

He had spent the last twenty years fighting the beast inside himself, but that beast had never wanted anything as badly as it wanted Samantha.

He gritted his teeth and tried to force the feelings aside. "Do you know where the lab is?" If she did, if she told him, would he believe her? Or was all of this a convoluted con designed to suck him into a trap?

"No," she answered, and then turned to him. "I'm sorry I tried to use you, but you have to understand Allison needs me. I'm all she has."

Her tone was so damned earnest, it hurt him to hear it.

Torn and confused, Caleb turned away and stared out into the trees. "Why the new address?" he asked again, this time to himself. The address Samantha had pretended to get from the kids at the gas station had significance, but nothing involving zombies.

However, if she got it from the doctor...

"What were you supposed to do when I took you to this new address?" he asked.

She shook her head. "I don't know. He just said to get you there."

"Well, then, we should go."

Samantha hadn't known what to say when Caleb had agreed so readily to take her to the address. She had thought once she admitted the truth he would boot her out of his car and leave her stranded in the woods. The only thing she hadn't been sure of was if she would be breathing at the time.

But he had simply jerked the car into Reverse, backed out of the cow path and got back on the road.

They had driven maybe ten miles when he put on his blinker again.

They were at a camp, the kind you expected to be filled with hormone-filled tweens making pottery and going on nature hikes. There were cabins, two community buildings and a giant field. And the entire place was surrounded by trees.

There were also signs posted everywhere warning that this was private property and no hunting was allowed.

As they pulled onto the property, Samantha noticed a glint from the roof of one of the common buildings. She squinted, then reached for Caleb.

"There's someone—"

"With a gun? We passed another outside, hidden in a tree. Trust me, guns are the least of your worries here."

His words chilled her, but not as much as his tone.

Apparently, she wasn't the only one in the car with a secret. Caleb knew something about this place. She pulled her hand back toward her body, but kept her eyes on the roof where she had seen the glint.

Caleb stared out the window at the camp. It was empty now, but in a day's time it would begin to fill. Anticipation of the full moon would bring the pack weres and those who hoped to be chosen to join the exclusive group.

The buildings had aged since he'd been here last. Paint peeled off the trim and rot was apparent on some of the logs, but still the place was in decent condition.

He wondered if the woman who ran it had aged, as well.

He didn't have to wonder long.

Anita Barnes stepped out of the cafeteria/kitchen building and into the full sun. Her hair was glossy-black, not a gray hair in sight, and her skin though tanned was wrinkle free. She didn't look a day over thirty. But she was at least two decades older.

That's when Caleb had seen her last, when she had chosen him and turned him into a werewolf like herself.

When she saw him, she lifted her lips in what others might have taken as a smile, but not Caleb. He knew he wasn't in her good graces. She might be happy to see him, be hoping he had finally decided to give up his rogue ways and join the pack, but she wouldn't let him in easily.

No, he had done the unthinkable—turned his back on her offer of standing by her side as she led.

Even after twenty years, she wouldn't have forgotten that.

He parked the car and motioned for Samantha to wait inside with the windows up. He didn't want her to hear the ensuing conversation. Then he stepped onto pack ground as a rogue, a were that Anita, if she so chose, had every right to destroy.

"Long time, Caleb. You look…good." She angled her head and let her gaze roam his body. Then she lifted her gaze and met his, ordered him with her eyes to submit and lower his eyes.

He did. He wasn't here to make trouble. He wasn't sure why he was here, but the coincidence was too great. No one but weres and those sponsored to become weres knew this address.

How had the zombie doctor?

He waited for the pack alpha to give him a signal before lifting his gaze. She turned to the side, telling him she accepted his show of subordination.

"So do you, Anita. And the camp. You've kept it up."

She turned back to him, her shoulders squared. "We've changed in twenty years. Our weres are more established. We learned taking in desperate kids who begged for our help wasn't the way to grow strong."

"I didn't realize the pack had a goal of world domination."

"Financial security is far from world domination," she retorted.

"Far from what I was told the weres stood for, too." He crossed his arms over his chest and glanced around the camp. There were subtle signs of changes that he hadn't noticed at first—satellite dishes, an addition on the back of the main rec building and an expensive roadster parked next to the cabin he knew belonged to Anita.

Anita lowered her head, but kept her gaze on him. "Are you judging us, rogue?"

He lifted his lips in the imitation of a smile. "This isn't my pack. Who am I to judge?"

"Exactly." She twisted her lips and took a step back. "So, why are you here? Are you thinking after all this time you can change that? Join the pack? As I said, things have changed. We're more selective now."

Like the two drugged-out kids he'd seen at the gas station. Yeah, the pack was selective now.

"No, I haven't come to join."

She didn't reply. Her gaze had moved from him to his car and the redhead staring out the windshield at them. "You brought someone with you."

Her voice was hard, like flint. She turned on the ball of her foot and her hand darted out to grab him by the front of his shirt. He outweighed her by thirty pounds, but she jerked him against her as if he weighed no more than a newborn pup.

But then he let her, and she knew that, too.

"Admission to the camp is invitation only. You know that."

"Then why didn't you have us shot when we entered?" She wasn't stupid or sloppy. She'd seen both of them in the vehicle. And even if she hadn't, she would have smelled the nonwere Samantha even shut inside the vehicle.

Her fingers loosened, but her face stayed tense. "I was curious. I didn't expect to ever see you back here, not after so long."

"Really?" He gestured at Samantha, told her to get out, but lowered his voice so she wouldn't hear his conversation with the alpha. "Then how did she know to bring me here?"

Anita's brows lowered. She dropped her hold on Caleb completely and took a step toward Samantha. Caleb lifted his arm, blocking her approach. The wolf in him snarled and he couldn't hide the reaction, not surrounded by other werewolves. His lip rose and an angry rumble escaped his lips.

Anita stared at the arm cutting across her path. "You've forgotten your place, rogue."

"No, you've forgotten. You didn't make me a rogue… you didn't beat me, and neither did any of the lapdogs you sent after me. I chose to leave. Don't force me to do something now you will regret."

She laughed. "A threat. Surrounded by my wolves and you give me a threat. For what? That?" She tossed her head toward Samantha. "Has the lost little boy found himself a special toy after all these years?"

"Don't worry about what I've found. Worry about what she has to say, and what would happen if you challenged me here in front of your wolves. I've played along, given you the respect you are owed as alpha, but I won't be pushed."

She glanced at Samantha, laughed again, but the edge was gone. Her eyes darted to the sides, checking for which of her wolves were watching, estimating what they could see.

Caleb didn't move. He'd spoken the truth. He didn't want to challenge her, didn't want to beat her. He wanted nothing to do with the pack; he never had.

"Talk," she bit out, her gaze on Samantha.

Caleb lowered his arm. "Tell her what brought us here," he told her.

"The kids—?" Samantha started.

"The truth." His tone was as harsh as Anita's had been. This wasn't the time for games.

Samantha's hand slid over the top of the open passenger door. "Someone gave me this address. He told me to get Caleb to bring me here."

Anita shrugged and turned her attention back to Caleb. "A wannabe. We still get them." She angled her head and studied Samantha. "What's your story? You look to be healthy and attractive enough. What are you looking for, eternal youth? Revenge on some guy? Despite what Caleb may have told you, this isn't a one-way deal. We give you the change then you're one of us. No exchange, no backing out, no exceptions." She glanced at Caleb. "Not anymore."

"Samantha isn't here to join," he replied. "She's here to get me killed. At least, that's my guess. I came to see if you knew who was supposed to be doing the killing."

Surprise rounded Anita's eyes. "You think I sent some piece of ass after you, to lure you back here so I could get rid of you?" She shook her head and glanced over her shoulder as if checking to see if anyone else was enjoying the joke. "You've developed quite the big head, zombie hunter. As I said, we aren't making the mistake we made with you, not anymore, but that doesn't mean I'm twisting my tail into a knot worrying about what you're doing. Truth is, until you pulled in here today I hadn't given you a thought, not for over a decade. Make that two."

It was a lie. He could see it in how carefully she held her body, but not all of it was a lie. She hadn't sent for him; he could see that much, too. But she had thought about him more than once. And quite likely wouldn't cry a tear if someone did shoot him square in the head with a round of silver right here and now.

But that was a long way from setting him up. Which meant Samantha wasn't working for Anita. That left the doctor. But how had the doctor known about the camp?

A new suspicion tickled the back of his mind.

"So, things have changed. You've upgraded." He turned as if seeing and admiring the camp for the first time. "How'd you manage all this?" He gestured toward the luxury roadster he'd noticed on arrival.

"I told you. We don't just let anyone in, not anymore."

He nodded as if that explained it, but of course, it didn't. The pack wasn't a cult. They didn't take every dollar a were earned. Yes, the members were expected to donate to the pack, but it was, at least when Caleb had been here, voluntary. "You must have some generous wolves now."

Something flickered behind Anita's eyes. "We do."

"You wouldn't be charging for membership, would you?"

Her complexion darkened. "You can't buy your way into the pack. Is that what your friend thinks?" She tossed an angry look at Samantha. Then throwing up her arms, she took a step back. "Look, I don't know why you're here and honestly, I've lost interest in finding out. The full moon is tomorrow. I have work to do." Gravel crunched under her boot as she turned.

Samantha stepped out from behind the car door, and Anita leaped. She wrapped her hand around Samantha's throat and squeezed. "Time for you to leave."

Samantha's hand moved to her side, where if she'd been wearing her coat, her pocket and perhaps her gun would have been. But her gun, with its mundane bullets, wouldn't stop the alpha, not with the power of the pack behind her.

Caleb hadn't wanted to challenge Anita, but she left him no choice, left his wolf no choice. He thrust his body between the two females.

Shocked, Anita dropped her hold.

With Samantha shielded behind him, he faced the alpha.

"Someone knows about this camp. Someone I very much want dead. As I said, you've upgraded. How are you making that money, Anita?"

The alpha's eyes blazed. Caleb could see she wanted to change, but this close to the full moon when the entire pack would descend on the camp and she'd need to be her strongest, she wouldn't. She would want that change to be fast. She would hold her shifts until her body exploded with the need, until it almost changed on its own. Then she could give the gathered weres the performance they all expected, and present herself as the strongest and fastest of them all.

Caleb, however, had no such concerns. He snapped his teeth to remind her of that fact.

She growled; her body vibrated with the need to dominate him.

But she wouldn't. She couldn't. She'd tried before when he was weaker, when he had nothing but revenge to drive him, and she'd failed. Now he had something else, something stronger—Samantha and his wolf's determination to protect her. To love her.

"I don't want your pack, Anita. I don't want your rank. But I do want the person you're working with. Either give him to me, or I'll take everything you value. You'll be the rogue on the outside, not me. Think about that," he added.

She lifted her lips to show him her teeth.

He stepped in close. "And if you touch her..." He jerked his head to where Samantha still stood, silent and tense. "I'll not only dominate you, I'll kill you." His gaze moved to the sniper now standing fully visible on the rec hall's metal roof. "That goes for your minions, too. You might want to warn them."

He gestured for Samantha to get in the car and moved back with one smooth slide of his foot. "Full moon, Anita. I'll be here. You've got until then to make up your mind."

Then he got in the car, slammed it into Reverse and spun out toward the road.

A gun fired as they roared through the camp's pillars.

But the bullet didn't hit them. The shot was no more than a weak attempt at saving face.

He'd allow her that.

For now.

Chapter 13

Samantha bit down on her cheek as the bullet pinged into their bumper. Her fingers scraped over the velour seats.

The woman and Caleb had spoken low. She had missed most of what they had said, but she had heard one thing.

Wolves. There had been a lot of talk of wolves.

She touched the bruised skin on her throat.

"I don't know what caused her to do that," Caleb ground out. He stared into the rearview mirror as if the woman, Anita, might be driving behind them.

Samantha resisted the need to do the same. The woman had unsettled her. She had been powerful and not just physically. She had exuded rank and confidence. But by all appearances she simply ran some kind of primitive camp.

"What kind of camp was that?" she asked, her hand still touching her throat and her voice rough.

Caleb screwed the steering wheel to the right. Samantha's body jerked to the side. She grabbed hold of the door handle and waited.

"Anita's camp. She runs it."

"You've been there before." It was an obvious truth, but all Samantha could think to say. Anita, the camp, how Caleb had acted around the woman—none of it added up.

But Caleb had definitely known the woman before and she had certainly remembered him.

"She was jealous," she murmured.

"Who?"

"Anita. The reason she grabbed me. She was jealous." It was the one thing Samantha did understand. When she'd seen the athletic but still curvaceous Anita sidle up to Caleb, seen how close he let her stand to him, she'd known they'd had a past. And it had eaten at her. Devoured her.

Her fingers tightened around the cold metal of the door handle.

She shouldn't be thinking like this, feeling like this. She had no right, and worst of all she had no claim.

She wasn't Caleb's girlfriend. She was his betrayer.

Anita jealous?

Caleb snorted.

Anita wasn't jealous. At least not in the "I love him" way Samantha thought.

No, to Anita, he was property. A werewolf she'd pegged early on as making a strong companion, a mate to add strength to her position as alpha. Kind of an "if you can't beat them, join with them" mentality.

Except he hadn't been willing to play.

He hadn't even bothered to turn her down. He'd just left. The ultimate insult, but also the smart move for survival. No alpha left another werewolf as strong or stronger than them alive. If he'd been female, Anita would have killed him or tried to on sight. As a male, she'd seen him as another way to strengthen her own position.

Which was why he'd suspected she was behind Samantha's knowledge of the camp...or the address of the camp at least.

He still suspected Anita was up to something. Unlike the other werewolves in her pack, Anita's one and only job was being alpha. She ran the camp and lived off the money the werewolves under her sent for pack expenses. She had never been too flush when he had known her. For that matter, neither had the camp.

Something had changed and it wasn't just the higher-class weres she took in now.

No, the pack was getting money from somewhere else, too.

And Caleb smelled something rotten. Zombie rotten.

He glanced at Samantha.

"We're taking a break."

She'd been studying the barren trees as they drove. She jerked when he spoke. "A break?"

"From our trip."

"Oh." Confusion and a shade of fear clouded her eyes.

"I have business here. Once it's resolved, you can—"

Her gaze dropped to the cylinder he'd left lying on the console between the seats. Her eyes darted back up, a question in their depths.

He stared at the cylinder, too, but noticed nothing strange about it. Then he placed his hand over it and felt a constant, but almost imperceptible beat.

"You don't hear it," she murmured.

His fingers closed more tightly over the metal. She was right. He heard nothing.

"It's moaning, super low like a broken speaker," she explained.

Her description intrigued him, matched the steady pulsing inside his palm.

But he couldn't hear a sound.

And she could.

"This happened before," he said. "Didn't it?"

She nodded. "At the motel. It's how I got the address." She held out her hand.

He was reluctant to let the device go, as if holding on to it would somehow give him the ability to hear what he couldn't. But after a second he rolled the cylinder onto her open palm.

She flipped it over, showed him a tiny strip of black. "A number shone here before, a phone number."

There was nothing there now, but then if Samantha was telling the truth, she already had the number.

"He expects to hear from you," he said.

She dropped the cylinder back onto his palm and pulled her hand away, tucked it under her arm.

"We need a phone, and not my cell." He put his foot back on the gas and continued to the destination he'd already been heading toward. Another dive motel. This one made up of little cabins tucked into the woods.

The place that specialized in werewolves had been around for fifty years. It was owned by a husband and wife, both wolves. Caleb had met the man the night of his turn. He hadn't been kind, but he hadn't tried to kill Caleb in those first confusing hours, either. Caleb trusted him as much as he trusted any were.

"You want me to call?" Samantha pulled her coat around her body as if it offered some kind of protection. From him or from the zombie doctor, he wondered.

"It's what he expects, right?"

She nodded.

"Then I want you to call."

And Caleb wanted to know what was said, wanted to know which of the multitude of suspicions he'd had in the past few days were correct. And who besides the zombie doctor he needed to kill.

Standing in the tiny office of the 1950s-style motel Caleb had driven them to, Samantha held the black rotary dial phone to her ear. With every ring, more tension ran up her back.

Caleb was sitting a few feet away. His gaze was on the fire crackling in the small stone fireplace, but she knew his inattention was deceptive. He was listening and she suspected he'd know if she tried to hide anything. With the receiver pressed against her ear, he should only be able to hear her side of the conversation, but despite the fact that he couldn't hear the buzzing cylinder, something told her he would hear every word of this conversation. Both sides of it.

The doctor came on the line with no preamble. "Are you at the camp?" he asked.

Her gaze cut to Caleb. He didn't look at her, gave her no guidance as to how to reply. Without it, she did what came naturally. She told the truth. "No, not any longer."

"Why not?" The words were terse, laced with impatience.

"Caleb..." Samantha stumbled. She looked at Caleb. He still gazed at the fire. "The woman who runs the place... I don't think she and Caleb get along." Or at least not how the aggressive female wanted them to get along, but Samantha kept that clarification to herself.

"But he knew her?"

"Yes." Samantha could feel the smile at the other end of the line.

"And the cylinder? Was he close when I rang?"

Without glancing at Caleb this time, Samantha replied, "Yes."

"And?"

She knew what he was asking. She just didn't know what the answer meant. "He didn't hear it."

"Good. Perfect. As I thought."

The doctor went quiet. Afraid she was about to lose him and her chance to see Allison, Samantha jumped back into the conversation. "What now? I did as you asked and I haven't seen Allison. Where is she? Is she close?" Her voice rose as she asked the questions. She hadn't realized how tense she was until then. She bit off her next words and forced her emotion back under control.

"You did and she is. Tell me. Where are you? I'll send her to you."

Panic fluttered inside Samantha's chest like a giant black moth coming to life, but before she could answer and say the wrong thing, Caleb was beside her shoving a note into her hand.

"Right now I'm at a motel, but we won't be staying here. They're booked. There's some kind of...festival or something going on this weekend."

"Yes, yes. I know. Where will you be?"

"There's a cabin about a mile from here. The owner agreed to let us stay there, but there's no phone so I told Caleb I had to call home first."

"Very smart. Give me the address."

Samantha read the directions written on the slip of paper. According to what she read, there was no road to the place; she and Caleb would be walking in.

"Be there at midnight tomorrow night," the doctor told her. "Allison will be, too."

"But—" Realizing she'd been about to blurt that Allison should meet her here instead, Samantha slammed her lips together.

"But what?" The impatience was back in his voice, and perhaps a shadow of suspicion.

Samantha glanced at the zombie hunter. His gaze was level, his demeanor soothing. She took a breath. "Caleb. What about Caleb? He'll be there, too."

The doctor laughed. "Don't worry about that. It will be the full moon. The hunter will be occupied. Very occupied." The line clicked and the phone went dead.

She could only stare at the phone, shocked and unsure. Allison was coming to a cabin tomorrow night. A cabin she wouldn't be at.

Someone pulled the receiver from her fingers—Caleb taking it and lowering it to the phone.

Caleb. Remembering the doctor's closing words, she stared at him. *Occupied*. What had the doctor meant by that?

There were lines around Caleb's mouth, tiny ones that told Samantha without a doubt that the hunter had heard the doctor and that he hadn't like the doctor's words any more than she had.

But what did they mean?

The zombie doctor knew Caleb was a werewolf.

Caleb had no doubt of that now.

The cylinder must have been set to some frequency weres couldn't hear. Caleb had had no idea such a weakness existed. He wondered if Anita did. If so, she had hidden it from everyone else. Weakness wasn't part of the werewolf recruitment materials; it wouldn't have played well.

And the camp. Samantha hadn't been given the address by chance. The doctor, however, must not have known of Caleb's past with Anita. He must have expected Caleb to be welcomed along with the others, to have been sitting at the camp tonight unaware and too caught up in moon madness to fight back.

But what Caleb still didn't know was whether Anita was working with the doctor. If she was, surely she would have known of his plan. She wouldn't have sent Caleb away. She would have put up the act Caleb expected of her and then pretended to come around, forgive him and invite him back into the camp.

And she certainly hadn't done that.

Maybe he had misjudged her. Maybe the car and new satellite dishes were indeed funded by rich werewolves.

Maybe he wasn't the only werewolf the doctor wanted. Maybe he'd heard of Caleb, figured out where his hunting abilities came from and planned on taking out any potential future hunters along with the one he already knew existed.

There was one last night before the full moon. One last night of sleep before the wolf inside him clawed to escape, and before the zombie doctor had said to expect Allison.

Caleb and Samantha were in their cabin now. Not the cabin Samantha had told the doctor about. Caleb's plan was to settle Samantha here, where she would be safe, then visit the old cabin Mike, the owner of the motel, had said was vacant.

Assuming there was some kind of tracker on the cylinder, he would take it with him.

And in case the doctor had spies, too, Caleb would be seen coming and going tonight. He would stay there. Then tomorrow he would visit the werewolf camp again and see if he could learn more about their new source of revenue.

What he learned would help him decide his move for tomorrow night.

Go to the cabin to greet Samantha's "friend" or go to the camp to be trapped by the doctor?

He glanced at Samantha. Maybe he would do both.

He hoped to God her friend was still that—a friend—and not a flesh-hungry monster. But deep in his gut he knew the odds were huge that after the full moon she wouldn't exist at all.

And that Samantha would hate him more than she had ever hated anyone or anything before.

* * *

Samantha waited in silence as Caleb roamed the tiny one-room cabin. The place was dark and ice-cold. Based on the motel's outside appearance, she was afraid to wander far from the door. She'd flicked the light switch and had been rewarded with no more than an empty clicking noise, but Caleb had strode into the space as if it had been ablaze with light.

Whatever his hearing lacked his sight obviously made up for.

He rummaged with something on the other side of the room. Within seconds she heard the distinct sound of a match being struck and the crackle of something catching blaze. Caleb bent over a small fireplace and blew the flame to life.

The fire and his position next to it made the space seem less small and more intimate. She pulled her hand from the wall, unsure whether to step farther into the space or not.

Caleb stood; the fire cast him in silhouette.

"I'll leave a gun and a knife. Remember, aiming is more important than firing."

"You're leaving?" She took the step she'd questioned only seconds earlier.

He didn't answer, just turned to poke the fire again, then stood to leave.

She stopped him by moving into his path. "What's going on? Why did the doctor want us to go to that camp?"

He looked down at her, his expression hard to read and not just because of the dim light. "I won't be back tonight. Don't leave the room for anything." He took a step to move past her.

She grabbed him by the arm. "Don't." The word was soft, barely more than a whisper. "I don't want to be alone." She didn't know if she could be. The thought of being stuck in this room, waiting all night with no idea what was going on... She edged closer, until her breasts touched his arm.

She looked up at him. "Stay with me. Please."

She wasn't sure what she was asking him—to stay tonight...or forever. Did it matter? she asked herself. Right now she knew that she couldn't fathom facing a night without Caleb by her side, her body tucked against his, his warmth making her feel safe, human, normal... just for a while.

He turned his body as if to ignore her touch, but under her fingers, his arm trembled.

He wanted to stay with her as much as she wanted him to stay. Confident of that, if of nothing else between them, she rose on her toes and pressed her lips against his.

"Please," she murmured against his mouth.

He sucked in a breath and his gaze flickered, a flash of wild, out-of-control hunger, so intense she should have been afraid, but she wasn't. A tremor ran through her, too—excitement and expectation.

Tomorrow night she would know if the doctor had told the truth, if Allison was okay.

If she was, Samantha would leave with her, run as fast and far as she and her friend could. She'd leave Caleb and zombies behind. She would have to. Allison would need her, and that was all that mattered.

But tonight she and Caleb were still a team. As false though that might be.

His hands cupped her backside and he pulled

her against his hard form. She could feel his desire against her stomach. He muttered curses and words of admiration against her lips.

Wrapping her hands around his neck, she pulled his mouth down to hers.

Curses or compliments, neither mattered.

Being here with Caleb did.

He kneaded the muscles of her butt, pulled her up so she rubbed over the hardened length hidden by his jeans. She ran her hands down his chest, felt the ungiving planes of his pecs, the rocklike ripples of his abs, marveled again at how any man could be built like him, especially one who didn't live in a gym.

And Caleb didn't. He roamed the roads, wild and free, hunting monsters, killing monsters, never settling, never giving up.

She had never met anyone like him.

He spun, twirling her with him, and fell back onto the bed. Less than six feet away, the fire crackled. The room smelled of wood smoke, and warmth flowed over her.

Her palms pressed onto his chest, she rose up and stared down at him. Without speaking, he pulled free the band she'd used to tie back her hair. It fell over her shoulder.

He wove his fingers in its length, gathered it into a bunch and brushed it against her cheek. He seemed fascinated by the locks, as fascinated as she was by him.

She moved her hands to the waist of his jeans and shoved his tight-fitting T-shirt up, baring his skin. With his free hand, he grabbed the material from her and ripped the shirt from his own body.

Then he flipped them over, so he was on top and she was pressed into the mattress beneath him. "I buy them by the gross," he murmured.

She smiled because she knew she was supposed to, because she knew he'd been trying to lighten the mood, but it was a wasted effort. Her focus on him was too strong, her need to touch him and be touched by him too overwhelming.

She trailed her lips down his neck, to his chest. The smell of the smoke mixed with his natural scent, creating something new and so alluring she could hardly form a rational thought.

His hands, cool against her fevered skin, brought her back to where they were. He slipped her shirt off her body, his touch gentle as if afraid she would bruise just from the brush of his fingers.

"But you...you have a much more limited wardrobe," he murmured before bending lower and nuzzling her between her breasts. The fire had warmed the room now, but still Samantha shivered. Her nipples hardened and she arched her back, hoping his tongue, which darted out to taste her skin, would find them.

With a groan, he grabbed the stretchy bra and shoved it over her head. "I hate this thing," he muttered.

And Samantha did, too. Uncomfortable with her breasts free under Anita's gaze, she had put it on earlier. But now she swore she would never wear another bra that was so difficult to remove—not while Caleb was near.

A chill passed through her at the reminder of their future, or lack of one.

Caleb seemed to sense the change. He tensed above her.

"Don't. Don't think. Not now. We can't afford to. If we do..." He shook his head, the stubble on his chin scraping over the recently freed mounds of her breasts.

He looked down at her. "Don't. Not now."

His eyes glowed. It was the fire reflected in them, of course, but at that moment it looked as if the fire were within Caleb, and she felt it, too, burning inside her.

She needed him more than she needed anything and she wasn't going to let a silly little thing like thinking, knowing what was to come, stop her from having him.

She shoved her hands into his hair and yanked his mouth down to hers. "Love me," she said.

She regretted the words as soon as they left her lips, but there was no taking them back. The truth of the matter was she wouldn't have even if she could. She wanted him to love her. Wanted to love him in return. This wasn't just a meaningless way to pass a night, sex between strangers.

Somehow, inexplicably, this was much, much more.

"I will," he whispered. "I do."

Was her mind, her desire, playing tricks? She grappled with the thought, wanted to ask him to say it again, but then his tongue thrust into her mouth and his hands moved to the waist of her pants and all thought of asking him to repeat anything except the delicious feel of his tongue stroking hers or of his fingers rubbing her thigh fled from her brain.

Chapter 14

He'd said it. He'd told Samantha he loved her. No, he hadn't used the word, but he'd said it all the same.

He hadn't said that to anyone, not for years…a lifetime.

And now he couldn't take it back. Yes, he could deny it, pretend it hadn't happened, but his wolf would know. His wolf wouldn't forget, and the beast wouldn't let Caleb forget, either.

The damned creature wanted Samantha and he wouldn't let Caleb rest until he wanted her just as badly, until he would give up his soul to have her.

Or worse, his plans for revenge.

Caleb stiffened at the thought. He couldn't. But then maybe he wouldn't have to. Maybe after tomorrow all of it would be over; maybe he would be free.

And maybe he would have killed Samantha's best friend.

Would she want him to love her then?

"Caleb?" Samantha called to him, a question in her voice and her eyes.

He'd stopped kissing her, grown cold deep inside with the thought of losing her.

Her eyes were soft, confused. Pain was only a few seconds away. She thought he was going to reject her.

He laughed at himself. Reject her? No, that wasn't the way this was going to play out.

"Caleb?" Her fingers brushed his cheek, soft, caring…worried.

He turned his head and captured her thumb between his teeth, bit down playfully, like a wolf would play with its mate. "I'm fine…except this." He jerked his belt from his pants and shoved the clothing off his body.

Naked, he moved onto his side and pulled Samantha along with him. He ran his hand down the length of her body, admired the warm glow of her skin in the firelight. "Lithe," he said. "Like a dancer." Or a wolf, but he didn't say that, didn't voice the obvious comparison of her lean, muscular beauty to that of the creature that ran wild through the forest. "Do you dance?"

He didn't look at her for a reply. The question was more for himself than her, more to keep his desire in check so he didn't rush things, throw her onto her back and thrust deep inside her in one fevered, out of control plunge.

"Not—" she began, but he silenced her with a kiss, pulled her body flush against his and inhaled her scent, let his wolf revel in being so close to her.

The beast deserved this moment. Caleb deserved this moment.

Her fingers tiptoed down his skin until she found his hip. She stroked him, her thumb dipping lower toward his sex, but not quite there. She teased and tantalized him with that tiny distance. She made tiny circles, moving lower with each, until he was hard as steel and throbbing with need.

The backs of her fingers skimmed over him.

Desire clutched him, like a fist closing around him. His body tightened. He pressed his face into the crook of her neck and inhaled again. There was a spice to her, alluring and exotic, something he couldn't identify and knew if he ever smelled it again he would only think of her.

Her bare foot slid up his calf, then her thigh inched higher over his. She was open for him. His sex touched hers and he could feel the heat of her core.

She scraped her nails over his hips now. Pain and pleasure mixed together; breaths puffed from his lips.

Her hand dipped lower again till finally her fingers wrapped around him. She slid the skin up and down over his hard shaft, swirled her thumb over the tip.

He groaned and edged his thigh farther between hers until she was riding it. She slipped his sex into her folds, moved it back and forth until her breaths too came in puffs and sweat covered both of them.

They paused and stared at each other.

Tomorrow things would change. Caleb knew that, and based on the sad shades of hope and desire in Samantha's eyes, he suspected she did, too.

Unable to wait any longer, afraid she would pull out

of the fog that had settled around them, he angled his hips and thrust inside her.

Her eyes closed and her hands moved to his shoulders. As he pulled in and out, as tension and desire continued to build, she clung to him. He nibbled on her neck. Then he flipped onto his back so she was astride him.

With her staring down at him, her hair free around her face and brushing the tops of her breasts, he slipped his hands under her buttocks and lifted her. Her head fell back, her breasts rose and he lowered her, lifting his hips as he did and plunging into her fast, hard and completely.

Her fingers curled, her nails scraping his arms.

More pain, more pleasure.

He lifted her again and again. Repeated the movement until his heart threatened to fly from his chest.

He moved his hands from her butt to her breasts, massaged them as they continued to move. Her lips opened, pants of air escaping. She stared into his eyes and murmured something he couldn't hear…or wouldn't let himself hear.

Words of love he knew she wouldn't repeat after tomorrow.

Then her body tightened around his. Her eyes closed and her fingernails dug into his skin. He let himself go, too, let his wolf free. He forgot who and what he was, just spiraled up and back down, until they both lay exhausted, Samantha crumpled on top of him, her still rapid breaths puffing warm over his skin.

With one hand, he pulled her hair to one side, baring her neck, then he caught the skin between his teeth, marking her one last time as his.

* * *

Samantha lay beside Caleb, staring at the wooden beams that divided the cabin's ceiling into three wide stripes. They were both naked, neither feeling the need to even reach for a sheet to cover themselves after their bout of lovemaking was over.

Caleb, she assumed, because he was so comfortable being naked. Samantha because she was afraid any move on her part, even reaching for a sheet, would break the mood, end the moment…and cause Caleb to leave.

She didn't want him to leave…not ever.

The fire had begun to die down, but its warmth still floated over their bodies. Samantha's leg was draped over Caleb's. She could feel the tiny hairs that covered his skin.

Caleb moved and she tensed, afraid he would push her away. But he merely reached for her hair and brushed a lock from her face. "I need to go to the other cabin, in case your doctor is watching. Make it look as if we are staying there."

Her fingers, spread wide on his chest, stiffened. She stared at them, pale against his skin. He was tan everywhere. She was pale everywhere. A symptom of their so very different lives.

"I should go, too, then. He'll be looking for me." It made sense, but even as she spoke she knew Caleb wouldn't agree.

"There just needs to be activity. I'll give him that." He moved as if to sit up. Her hand slipped from his stomach and her thigh landed on the cold sheet beneath them.

A chill shot through her.

This was it. He was leaving.

"Will you be back?" she asked, trying to sound unconcerned. Concern would mean she was weak, afraid. She wasn't. She'd faced down zombies; she could face anything.

Including life without Caleb.

He swung his legs over the side of the bed and sat with his back to her. "Just stay here. I've talked to the owner. He'll see you get food."

"Food?" She could survive a few hours without food.

He glanced at her over his shoulder. "Stay here until it's over."

"Over?" Forgetting her nudity, she swung her body around and knelt on the bed. "I can't stay here. I have to meet Allison."

"No. You don't." There was steel in his eyes.

She pressed her fingers onto the tops of her thighs. "I do. She's why I'm here."

He took a breath. "You don't think you can trust the doctor to do as he said, do you?"

Did she? She shook her head. "No, but if there's a chance…" She scrambled from the bed and searched for her clothes.

Caleb stood, too. He pulled the clothing from her fingers. "I can't let you leave."

"You can't stop me."

He wadded up her clothes and tossed them into the fire.

She watched in horror as they melted into nothingness. Her hands fisting at her sides, she took a step back "I have others."

"In the car. I didn't bring them in. I'm not going to."

It didn't matter. She had other options: the sheets, the

blankets, the shower curtain. She wouldn't let modesty keep her from saving her friend.

But she wouldn't let Caleb know that. She kept her gaze from wandering to the blanket, prayed he didn't throw it into the fire, too.

Instead, he pulled on his own clothes and walked to the door.

Her arms crossed over her chest, she watched him. She had dreaded Caleb leaving; now she couldn't wait for him to go so she could put together her plan and follow him.

He opened the door.

The motel owner stood on the other side.

Samantha cut off her gasp and her need to grab the blanket off the bed to cover herself. She stared him down and bore holes of anger into Caleb's back.

Caleb took a step back. For a second she thought the other man was going to come in. Her fingers twitched, moved toward the blanket, but a smaller dark shape moved past the two men.

A dog or—this time Samantha's gasp couldn't be hidden—a wolf padded into the room.

"Mike raises husky/wolf mixes. He trains them as guard dogs. Linda is yours for the night, and for as long as you need her."

The canine wandered around the room then walked up to Samantha and sniffed. Apparently satisfied, it turned and stalked to a place near the fire to sit. Its golden-brown eyes flitted over Samantha, then back at the two men. The expression in the creature's eyes was easy to read—bored, annoyed, resolved.

"Linda?" Samantha asked, her gaze shifting from the animal to Caleb. "I'm... I don't need her."

His hand on the door, Caleb stared at her. "But I do. The dog is well trained. She won't let anyone enter or leave, not until Mike or I release her." Then he strode out the door.

Samantha used her heels to push herself upright in the bed. Somehow she'd managed to sleep. Not at first. Right after Caleb left, she'd tried following.

The dog, Linda, however, hadn't seemed to approve of the idea. The creature hadn't even seemed to be watching Samantha as she pulled the sheet from the bed and fashioned a toga-style dress from it, hadn't cracked an eyelid as Samantha had stared at it, looking for some sign the animal was awake.

Assured it wasn't, she'd stepped toward the door and without warning, the creature had leaped forward, its hair bristling around its neck and its teeth flashing.

Samantha had tried to maintain control, to appear unshaken, but there was something about facing down the snarling animal that had rattled her far worse than any of the zombies she'd had a hand in killing.

Still, she had reached out a shaking hand, and almost got bitten for her efforts. She could swear she'd felt the canine's teeth brush her skin as she yanked her hand toward her chest. But there had been no mark and when she looked back at the creature it stood exactly where it had been before—as if it hadn't moved at all.

Still, Samantha had been shaken. She'd stepped onto the bed and walked backward until reaching the headboard. There she had collapsed and eventually fallen asleep. When she'd awakened, it had been to the sound of the motel owner delivering lunch. Apparently, she'd slept through breakfast.

Mike was in the room now. He dropped a white paper bag of what smelled like burgers on the table. "Brought you lunch. I'll take Linda for a while. Give you a chance to get up and stretch your legs."

Unlike Caleb, he wasn't even pretending the dog was there to protect her.

Samantha gathered the blanket around her body and stared at a blank spot on the wall. It was probably a mistake. You were supposed to talk to your captors, make them see you as a person, but Samantha had no words in her. She was too angry, too desperate to leave.

She'd gone through so much, put others through so much, all to save Allison, and now that she had been promised a visit Caleb and this strange man with his stranger dog were keeping Samantha from her.

He grunted and motioned to the animal, which trotted past him without a glance Samantha's way.

"I'll give you a few minutes," Mike said. "Make use of it."

Then like Caleb, he left.

Samantha wasted three seconds frozen on the bed, unsure if she could trust that he was actually gone. Then she was on her feet, her nudity forgotten. She raced to one of the small windows that flanked the door. The lower ledge hit her right above the breasts. It was small, maybe two feet wide, but big enough for Samantha to shimmy through.

Of course, anyone watching the door would see her escape through the window.

She cursed and glanced around the room. Her gaze went to the bathroom. She scurried toward it.

The space was barely big enough to turn around in.

A prefab shower filled one end. The door opened almost into the toilet, and the sink was right beside both. She stared at the tile-topped cabinet, wondering...

As the idea formed, she hurried back out to where the motel owner had left the burgers, grabbed them and moved just as quickly back into the bathroom. After ripping open the bag and tossing its contents into the shower, she crouched on the sink and waited.

Five minutes later the door to the room opened.

"I'm in the bathroom," she called.

There was a grunt, then the door closed again.

Samantha reached down and turned the knob, inched the bathroom door open just a bit. The dog, Linda, lay six feet away, its tail covering its nose.

"Linda?" Samantha called. "You hungry? Come here, girl." She used the same voice her neighbor, who seemed to constantly be misplacing his golden retrievers, used when trying to locate his pets.

The dog's ears twitched. Her tail slowly uncurled from around her face and she moved to a sit. She didn't, however, come.

Samantha called again, this time tossing a bit of the hamburger out into the room.

Linda stood, sniffed the burger, then gulped it down.

Her confidence building, Samantha called again and again, repeated the steps until Linda was halfway into the bathroom.

Then she tossed what remained in her hand into the shower. As the dog trotted after the meat, she leaped, grabbing the top of the door to swing out.

She made it into the main room and landed on her feet. With a sigh of relief she turned, ready to jerk the door closed behind her and trap the canine inside the bathroom.

But the dog wasn't in the bathroom.

The dog was standing right in front of her. Teeth bared, it jumped up, placed both front paws on Samantha's shoulders and knocked her to the ground.

Her heart heavy in her chest, Samantha stared up at the snarling, angry beast.

She'd taken a chance and she'd lost.

It was over. Everything was over. She could only pray now that somehow Caleb found Allison and saved her. Without Samantha's help.

She closed her eyes and waited for the pain of razor-sharp teeth piercing her flesh.

She felt nothing.

She opened her eyes. The dog was still there, and its teeth were still exposed, but there was something off about the expression in its eyes.

Bored. The dog looked bored.

Sure she was going mad, Samantha blinked and raised her body a smidge, enough so she could pull her elbows beneath her. The dog closed its mouth and took a step back.

Samantha stared at it, insanely sure the animal understood far more of what was happening than could be possible. Sure, too, that the dog had no more interest in watching her than she had in being watched.

As if on cue, the animal twisted its neck to glance at the window. The sun was still high; a sliver of light shone through the slightly parted drapes. The noise of cars coming and going, and people talking seemed suddenly much louder than Samantha had noticed before.

If she could hear them…

Samantha opened her mouth to scream.

The dog looked back at her, its expression this time saying, "Go ahead."

"They won't help me, will they?" she asked, her voice soft.

She was talking to a dog; she couldn't bring herself to put much volume behind the words.

But the dog seemed to agree with her. It backed off another foot, into a sit.

Samantha pushed herself more upright, too. She was naked again, and strangely, talking to the dog made her aware of the state, more so even than when the motel owner had been in the room. She gestured toward the bed and its coverings. "Do you mind?"

The dog tilted its head back to the window. Taking that as a no, Samantha pulled the sheet from the bed and tied it around her body in its earlier toga-party style.

Feeling more comfortable, she studied the dog. People said having a pet made old people live longer; something about the companionship and having someone to talk to. The hospital where she trained had dogs come in once a week and the patients did seem to respond.

So, talking to the dog wasn't crazy. It might not get her out of this room, but it could make her feel better about being trapped here. And who knew, maybe talking to the dog would have the same effect on the animal. Maybe the creature would relax, perhaps even come to trust her.

It certainly couldn't hurt.

With that in mind, Samantha started talking.

She told the creature everything: how she'd met Allison, what they'd been through together, how Allison had disappeared and how she had found her. She told it about meeting Caleb, how he looked when he killed those zombies the first night, how scared and excited she had been watching him. She told it about their trip and how she'd known all along she was betraying him, how she regretted it even as she was doing it, but how she had seen no way out. How even now knowing it would cost her Caleb, she couldn't turn her back on her friend.

She told the dog everything, even things she hadn't until that moment admitted to herself.

When she'd emptied her soul, she looked up.

The dog was watching her, staring at her as if it had never seen her before.

Samantha clutched her toga, pulled it away from her legs so she could leap away from the animal if it decided to lunge.

The dog shifted its gaze to the window, then back at Samantha. It stared at her some more, and then it seemed to make a decision. It stood and padded to the door. There it stopped and turned to face her. With its nose, it gestured.

Sure now she had lost her mind, Samantha took two steps toward the dog. "Are you… Will you…" She shook her head, then took another step. The dog moved back.

Then it turned away and padded into the bathroom.

Samantha stared after it, but only for a second. Then she sprinted through the door.

Chapter 15

Caleb stood at the edge of the woods. He'd gone to the cabin, entered, made noises as if Samantha were with him hidden inside, and then he'd exited, leaving the metal cylinder behind. He'd slipped out the door in his wolf form and roamed the forest, hunting for any sign or scent of zombies or anyone else....

He'd found nothing.

He had spent a night away from Samantha, a night when she still wanted him...or would have if he hadn't trapped her in that motel cabin with Linda, a werewolf, sitting guard.

If there had been any possibility that he could keep what he was from Samantha, keep her believing that she loved him, he had blown it last night.

He picked up a rock and tossed it from one hand to the other. It was over now.

The night had fallen. The camp was crawling with both werewolves ready for their monthly change and humans hoping to be chosen to join them.

Caleb had seen no sign of the doctor or his zombies last night, but tonight was the appointed night, when the doctor had told Samantha he would send Allison to the cabin.

But the cabin would be empty. Linda would keep Samantha trapped at Mike's motel, safe. If Allison did show at the cabin, if she wasn't a zombie already...well, she would just have to wait.

But Caleb knew the doctor's promise was only a diversion. He knew the doctor was after him, at his most vulnerable when the moon was full and he was caught in its fever.

It was why the werewolves gathered together these nights. There was safety in numbers. Werewolves had enemies, and always had. But the pack protected its own.

Of course, Caleb wasn't part of that pack. And, he guessed, the doctor knew that now.

He scanned the crowd for Anita. If his guess was right, she'd be watching for him, expecting him and ready with some trap.

It had taken Samantha hours to find the cabin. First she'd had to find clothing. She'd broken into another room and rummaged through suitcases. She'd found a woman's jeans, T-shirt and undergarments. Everything was a couple of sizes too big, but it beat being naked.

Then she'd considered stealing one of the cars parked in the motel's lot, but she was afraid to spend any more time in the area, afraid the dog would decide to sound the alarm.

She still wasn't sure how to interpret what had happened. It had felt as if the creature understood her, sympathized with her and made a conscious choice to let her escape.

But that was ludicrous.

More ludicrous than zombies? a part of her asked.

She shook the question from her brain, along with any remaining doubts. She was at the cabin now and it was dark. She didn't know the time, hadn't wanted to ask the man who gave her a ride when she claimed to have had a fight with her boyfriend and stumbled off alone.

He had pressured her to go to the police, said the area wasn't safe at night, especially right now, but she had insisted her family was staying in a cabin and she had to get to them before midnight.

After that, he'd stayed quiet, had inched a bit farther away from her actually, until his left shoulder was pressed against the driver's side door.

And when he'd stopped and she had hopped out, he hadn't said goodbye, hadn't offered her any other warning, just clutched the silver cross hanging from his neck and smashed his foot onto the gas pedal.

She stared after him for a second, confused. But so many things had happened to confuse her, that his behavior soon faded from her mind and she'd set off on foot down the path she'd hoped led to the cabin.

Now she stood in front of it.

Made of logs with a metal roof, the cabin would have been quaint, if it weren't for the noises in the woods. The sounds of scurrying animals and squawking birds combining with the chill of coming winter had her on edge.

Or maybe it was knowing her quest was almost over. For whatever reason, she was trembling from head to toe. Her teeth clattered against each other and any sense of beauty the cabin might have provided was completely lost.

Hoping she would feel better once inside, she wrapped her arms around her body and stepped onto the front porch. The corners were covered in moss and the once-red door was streaked with peeled paint.

The cabin obviously wasn't rented out a lot. Still, it was where she had told the doctor she would be. She turned the knob and walked inside.

She could tell immediately Caleb had been there. The small space was filled with his scent. A calm settled over her. Just smelling him made her feel safe.

She walked around the room, inventorying the contents: one full-size bed with a moldy mattress, a couch with a permanent indentation in the middle cushion and a completely unstocked kitchen. There was, however, a bag of half-eaten beef jerky lying on the counter.

She stared at it, wishing it was anything else. She hadn't eaten since yesterday and her stomach, despite the stress, reminded her of it by growling.

She pressed her hand against her abdomen as if that might solve the problem and sat on a wobbly wooden chair next to a water-stained table.

Then she waited.

Midnight couldn't be that much longer.

The camp was filling up. Someone had lit a bonfire and a few people had gathered around it, most of them naked.

Werewolves looked good naked. The virus raised the human metabolism, increasing the body's natural ability to build muscle. Previously flabby female converts found themselves with twenty-inch waists and ten-inch biceps while chowing down on processed potato chips and pounds of butter.

If Anita had truly wanted to get rich, she could have sold the bite as a get-thin scam.

Come to think of it, she probably already did. Caleb watched as a woman with perfect highlights and manicure motioned down her slightly chubby form while talking animatedly with another female. The second was obviously a were. As Caleb observed them, the second pulled off her clothes and twirled for the first. Then both rose on their toes, obviously searching the crowd for someone.

Anita.

And knowing the alpha and her desire to grow her pack, Caleb guessed they would have a much easier time finding her than he would.

Staying in the shadows, he stalked closer.

Within minutes his quarry arrived. Barefoot and wearing only a simple T-shirt dress, the alpha padded forward. There was confidence in her gait.

With her pack gathered around her, she was at her strongest and it showed. She made sure it showed.

He let her talk to the pair for a few minutes, admiring Anita's style as she played the woman, acting bored, reluctant. Finally, when it looked as if Anita was going to walk away, the woman said something, something that turned Anita back around to face her. She smiled at the were who had been talking to the recruit when she arrived and motioned for both of them to head to her cabin. As they walked off, Caleb approached.

"How much did that one promise?" he asked, not really interested, but knowing the question would annoy the alpha.

She stiffened, but didn't let her surprise at seeing him show on her face.

"Caleb. I thought you were gone."

"Did you? Really?"

"Of course. Why would I expect you to stay? You made it clear in the past that you don't need us." She took a step after the other females.

He touched her arm. "Aren't you going to order me away now?"

She twisted so his hand dropped from her skin. "I have other things to concern myself with. Besides, you will do as you do. Won't you?"

"Well, that's very live-and-let-live of you, Anita. I'm impressed or would be if I didn't already know you had sold me out."

Already moving, she jerked to a halt. "Got a big head, zombie hunter, haven't you?"

He closed the distance between them. "Funny you should mention zombies. Where are they?"

Light from the fire reflected in her eyes. "Zombies are your obsession, not mine."

He stepped into her space, didn't touch her, but came up next to her so their chests almost brushed. "Where are your rejects?" While he'd been watching the camp, he'd noticed none of the kids he and Samantha had met at the gas station were present and none like them, either.

"Rejects?" she parried.

"You're selling them, aren't you?" The fire he'd seen in her eyes seemed to flow into him. He could feel it in his belly, swelling, threatening to explode.

She stared him down. "Selling humans? That would be illegal, not to mention wrong."

"So, not selling them. What then?"

She made another move to walk past him; he blocked her.

She bared her teeth.

He leaned in and whispered, "It would be a shame if all these new high-powered, rich recruits were here to witness your downfall."

Her back straight, she muttered through her teeth, "Are you forgetting what night it is? Look around you. See my wolves? You can't beat me. Not tonight."

"Are you willing to take that gamble? I am."

The female werewolf who had led the pudgier woman away stepped out of Anita's cabin and stared at them.

Anita lifted her hand, telling the wolf to go back inside. When she had disappeared, the alpha shifted her eyes toward Caleb. "Your melodrama amazes me. I'm not selling anyone. People come here for a variety of reasons, hoping for a variety of things. If I can't help them, they are happy to be given another option. Dr. Allen gives them that."

Dr. Allen.

"And does Dr. Allen pay for that choice or do these people?" Caleb laughed and shook his head. "Excuse me—who gives you the money? I know who is really paying the price. I've seen Dr. Allen's work."

"Oh, Caleb the perfect, returning to judge me. You ever think those people got what they asked for, what they begged for? You remember that, don't you? Wanting what you don't have so much you would get down on your knees and beg for it? Promise anything to get it?" Her eyes glimmered, but this time it wasn't from the fire. It was from anger, pure and simple.

Her barb hit, too. He had begged; he had been desperate. And then he had broken every promise he had made to her, walked away from the pack without so much as a backward glance.

But it had been necessary. And those promises he broke were nothing compared to finding his family's killers. Nothing.

"And what about these 'monsters' you've been so busy killing? How different do you think they are from us? How do you know they don't still have families? Friends? People who are just happy to see them no matter what they may look like to others?"

He snorted at her ignorance. "It isn't that simple. Zombies don't just look like monsters, they are monsters. People may think they want whatever empty promises this doctor gives them, but they don't know what else comes with the package."

"So, they deserve to be destroyed?" Anita asked. "And their families... You think they see you any differently than you saw your family's killers?" She narrowed her eyes. "Who do you think they see as the monster?"

Caleb walked away after that. He'd heard what he'd wanted to hear. He knew Anita was working with this Allen, the zombie doctor. He also knew somewhere in the camp there was a group of rejected werewolf wannabes getting the sales pitch on becoming zombies. He just had to find them.

It didn't take long. He went back to the parking area

and walked around until he found the most rusted-out vehicle in the lot. Then he followed the scent.

The trail didn't even go into the main camp. It stopped at the front gate then cut to the left. There was a path tramped into the grass. As Caleb followed it, the scent grew stronger. There were noises up ahead, too. Voices. He emerged into a small clearing.

There was no fire here, but then zombies didn't like fire. And there were no cabins, just a metal and plastic structure. There was a light on inside, casting shadows through the plastic walls. He saw bodies standing, but not moving.

Caleb had retrieved his shotgun before leaving the parking area. Now he held it at his side as he walked into the space.

The building was packed with society's misfits and rejects. Some were old, some were young, but they all had a lost air about them.

When he walked in, they all looked at him.

He must have stood out. As they turned, he heard them take a collective breath, eager, ready to become monsters.

How bad could their lives be?

The gun was heavy in his hand. They weren't zombies yet, but they were here with that intention. Humans were easier to kill than zombies. It wouldn't be murder. More like extermination. He'd be saving them from becoming what any sane human would rather die than become.

He lifted the gun.

One woman, older and clutching her side, stumbled toward him. "Are you the doctor? They told us you'd meet us here. I have cancer. It's spread. There's no hope—or there wasn't. I can't afford…" She glanced behind her. "My friend told me about these parties, but I don't have the money. They said you could help me for free. Can you? Just a few more years. That's all I want. Long enough to see my daughters settled. Their lives…they aren't good, either." She dropped her gaze, but then seemed to gather herself and raised her face back to his. "You are my last hope. This month is my last chance. I won't be here much longer."

Behind him the door he'd walked through clicked. He spun, lifted his gun and fired. The shot pinged off the metal. People around him rushed to the other side of the building as if he had just shifted. And there was a possibility of that, too. His skin itched. He fought the urge to claw at it.

His palms were wet and slippery, the gun difficult to hold.

The moon was fully up.

He opened his mouth and felt his teeth expand, felt his snout pop out.

The older woman who had been begging him for his help just seconds earlier pressed her hand to her mouth and staggered backward.

There was horror in her eyes. He'd seen it before.

But he never got used to it.

Now wasn't the time to worry about how others saw him. He needed to stay focused, and under control. If his wolf took over, his rational mind would retreat, especially now under the full moon's influence.

He couldn't let that happen.

He snapped his jaws and struggled against the moon's pull. He had tried fighting the moon before, but he had never succeeded. But then it had never truly been important before. He had just wanted to prove that he could.

But now his life might depend on it. Samantha's life, too, along with her friend's life and that of all the humans trapped in this building with him. All of their lives depended on him not giving in this time.

His arms and legs shook. His fingers curved. He could feel his nails hardening, growing.

A curse exploded from his lips. No, not a curse, a howl.

Chapter 16

Samantha hadn't moved from the chair for what felt like hours. It had to be midnight. She rocked forward a bit and gripped the wooden seat.

Allison should be here soon...if the doctor hadn't been lying.

And Samantha was unarmed, she now realized. She had been too focused on leaving the motel and her canine guard to think of searching for any weapon Caleb might have left behind.

But as the minutes ticked down, she was coming back to herself and realized how foolish it was to be sitting here without a weapon.

She wasn't afraid of Allison. She could never be afraid of her friend, but she couldn't trust that the doctor would actually send Allison, that zombies wouldn't tromp through the door of the remote cabin instead.

Adrenaline zipped through her. With a harried glance at the door, she raced to the kitchen and began jerking open drawers. The first four were empty. The last stuck.

There was a noise outside. The wind...or a car? Couldn't be the latter; there was no road. Unless it was an off-road vehicle. Samantha hadn't considered that before now.

Panicked, she yanked on the drawer. It flew open. At first she thought it was empty, too. Then she saw what she was seeking in the back, a rusty filet knife, the tip of the blade stuck in the side of the drawer. She pulled the implement out and turned, just as the door to the cabin creaked opened.

The world exploded around Caleb, the moon punishing him for fighting back. He fell to his knees; his body convulsed. The older woman who had begged for his assistance ran toward the other humans. She groped at the group blindly as if someone would step forward and explain what she was seeing.

So, they hadn't been told what to expect, Caleb thought. Just heard the sales job, not the dirty details that came with being a werewolf.

He grunted as another shock of pain lanced through him.

Caleb hadn't been told, either, but it wouldn't have mattered. He would have walked through hell to get werewolf powers and immunity to a zombie's bite.

He did walk through hell, every time he thought of his family devoured by those zombies.

Caught up in his own drama, he missed the change in the room. The air seemed to thicken, as if someone had started a fog machine. Still convulsing, he sucked in a lungful and coughed.

It tasted…rotten, like sulphur.

Half-shifted, he twirled.

The older woman was still staring at him, but her eyes were sightless. She fell forward onto her knees, then forward again until she was facedown on the dirt floor. Around the room others fell, too, until Caleb was the last being standing.

His wolf took advantage of his loss of concentration and shoved his way forward. Caleb fell, too, but not victim of the gas—victim of his wolf half.

On the ground, hair sprouted from his skin and his bones bent. Thrashing, he tried to regain control, but it was too late. He'd lost. He shifted.

As a wolf, he leaped to his feet and swirled. His first instinct was to run…not away, just run. It was what weres did under the moon. Ran, hunted, made love, embraced life.

But the smell in the building stopped him. It wasn't the smell of life; it was the stench of death. His muscles tensed and his fur rose.

He trotted to the right. Bodies lay strewn around the space. He nuzzled the first—a woman, her mouth and eyes open, her skin slack. Beside her lay a man, also dead.

He sniffed them both, judging his hunger. Wolves hunted their own kills, but they weren't above taking carrion when hungry.

And Caleb was hungry. Starving, he suddenly realized. He opened his jaws ready to snack on the female. As his teeth touched her flesh, something inside him objected, some part of him—buried, hidden—yelled this was wrong. He wasn't a wolf, didn't live as a wolf lived, didn't let his instincts rule him.

Confused, he hesitated and growled.

The wolf didn't like to be controlled, not ever, but especially not tonight. It was hungry, the moon was full and a banquet had been spread out before him.

Why shouldn't he eat? Caleb reached for an arm.

A noise rumbled from the woman's throat and her hand twitched. She opened her eyes and stared into the wolf's face.

He steeled himself for the scream.

She tilted her head to the side, reached out her arm and jammed her fingers into his fur. Then, mouth open, she jerked him toward her.

The wolf and the man both snarled.

She was a zombie. The gas, whatever it was, had turned her into a zombie.

Which meant... Caleb's gaze darted around the space.

There were more groans and more hands clawing at the air.

Every human in the place had been turned into a zombie, and Caleb was trapped inside the locked building with them.

His wolf snapped at the leash Caleb had managed to keep slipped around him. And with a scream that came out a roar, Caleb let it go.

As the door continued to creak open, Samantha couldn't move. Her palm, which clutched the knife, was sweaty. Her heart was beating loud and fast.

She dropped her hand to her side, hiding the blade,

then positioned herself so she would see whoever entered the cabin before he, she…or it…saw her first.

"Samantha? Are. You. Here?" The words were stilted, but the accent was pure Tennessee. Samantha dropped the knife and jumped toward her friend. The heavy scent of some musky perfume caused her to hesitate, but only for a second. Allison had never worn perfumes before, but then she'd never been held captive by a zombie-making doctor before, either. Samantha had smelled the rot of zombies firsthand. She could understand why her friend might need some weapon to keep the stench of the doctor's patients at bay.

She pushed her way through the cloud of cologne and pulled her friend into a hug.

For minutes she couldn't move, not even to wipe at the tears that leaked from the corners of her eyes. She squeezed Allison again.

She couldn't believe it had been this simple. Couldn't believe the doctor had kept his word. She stroked her friend's hair. It clung to her fingers as if filled with static. Samantha laughed, thinking how she would take Allison to the salon, spend crazy money on getting her hair conditioned, her body massaged and her mind purged of whatever hell she had endured.

As she stood next to her friend all her worries evaporated. She knew everything would be okay now; it would all work out, somehow. Caleb would forgive her for lying to him; Samantha could even forgive him for locking her in the motel with the guard dog.

There was no problem too big for them to work out.

Once he met Allison, he'd see that, too; understand why Samantha had had to work for the doctor.

Samantha straightened her elbows and held her friend at arm's length to look at her. She still couldn't believe the doctor had kept his part of the bargain, couldn't believe it had all been this simple.

But it had. She was holding the proof in her hands.

"You look…" Tired, drained, out of sorts. All of those were true, but not what you said to someone who needed your support. "Great." That was true, too. There was no way Allison couldn't look great to Samantha. She was alive; that was all Samantha had prayed for.

Allison turned her head side to side, obviously searching the room for something. "Are you alone?" she asked.

Surprised her friend didn't fall back into her arms and start babbling about everything she had been through, Samantha dropped her hands. "You mean Caleb?"

Allison returned her gaze to Samantha. Her normally sparkling eyes were flat; her voice was, too. "Yes, Caleb Locke, the hunter. Dr. Allen wants to meet him."

"But Dr. Allen isn't here, is he?" Samantha's gaze darted behind her friend to the still partially open door as she whispered the question.

Allison didn't reply.

Samantha slipped her fingers into her friend's hand. Allison's skin was cold and her fingers seemed reluctant to bend. Ignoring both, Samantha made their secret sign in her palm, then stared into Allison's eyes.

But instead of returning the sign, Allison just tilted her head and said, "The doctor wants Caleb Locke. You can take me to him." Then her fingers tightened around Samantha's.

A cry of pain rushed to Samantha's lips. She bit it

back and tried to jerk her fingers free, but Allison's grip was unyielding.

"You can take me to him," she repeated.

The biting pain in Samantha's fingers increased until she couldn't feel them at all. She quit jerking, quit moving. She stared at her friend. "Allison, when did you start wearing perfume?"

"Take me to him."

Her record was broken, stuck on the one line.

Samantha closed her eyes. New tears burned at the backs of her eyes, but these weren't the product of joy. They were propelled by a much darker emotion. Still, she couldn't bring herself to face the truth. "I don't like it, Allison. I don't like it at all," she murmured. "When we get home, back to Tennessee, you'll give it up, won't you? Go back to unscented soap and oatmeal facials? I'll take you to a spa, make sure everything is one-hundred-percent natural. You'll like that, won't you?"

And Allison would have. She would have squawked about the money, but she would have loved being pampered. Allison was all natural, but she was also all girl.

Samantha opened her eyes and stared at the dead, flat eyes that watched her.

But this person…this body…an animated corpse really…wasn't Allison.

She wasn't at all.

The truth shot through Samantha like a spear, burned as it sank in, hurt more the longer she held on to it, accepted it.

She wanted to double over and retch on the floor, but her dead friend, the zombie, still held her fingers, still gripped them tight enough Samantha wondered if she had already broken them.

Samantha was that numb, body and soul. She wouldn't have felt it if the body that had been Allison's had picked up a spear and jammed it into her heart.

"The doctor…" The recording started again.

Samantha couldn't listen to it again. "Yes, of course. I can take you to him. I want to take you to him. It's what I planned all along."

Allison's lips closed over the rest of her words. She smiled, not the crooked, quirky smile Samantha remembered, but a perfectly orchestrated half-moon of her lips.

It made what Samantha had to do easier.

She took a breath and tugged lightly on her fingers. Slowly Allison's hands opened.

Samantha straightened her fingers, then curled them closed again. They weren't broken. They were bruised and numb, but would still do what had to be done, if Samantha could do the same.

"I need to get my purse," she mumbled and gestured toward the kitchen where she had left the knife. She touched her friend's elbow, pushing her slightly toward the chair she had occupied earlier. "Here. You're tired. You've been through a lot. Sit and I'll get everything together."

With her record stopped, Allison seemed easy to lead. She sat, her feet flat on the floor, her back and legs pressed against the chair like every kindergarten teacher's dream pupil.

Like a zombie, doing as it was told.

Feeling cold, inside and out, Samantha forced a brittle smile on her own lips and scurried into the kitchen.

Confident Allison wasn't watching her, she picked up the knife and hid it behind her arm.

The blade was cold, too, like an icicle resting against her skin. Allison was just sitting there, waiting. Samantha could sneak up behind her and pith her. She'd pithed zombies before, and death was what Allison would have wanted, would have asked Samantha to do if she still could. Her friend wouldn't want to exist like this, wouldn't want to become what Samantha knew she would become, perhaps already was.

The zombie she was staring at seemed calm and controlled, but for how long? How long until Allison was like the others, stumbling around alleys, attacking people, eating their brains?

Samantha clutched the knife in her suddenly sweaty palm and shivered.

All thoughts of what the creatures around had been just seconds earlier fled from Caleb's brain. His teeth flashing, he twirled, biting and tearing as he spun.

Someone grabbed him from behind, around his hind legs, and jerked at him. He curved his body and chomped onto a hand, bit through flesh down to bone. He ripped and tore, sawed his jaws over the hand until there was no muscle or skin left, just bone. Then he bit through that, too.

A new sound built around him, echoed through the building. A hungry sound. Zombies smelling blood, facing their first hunger. They moved in toward him, formed a circle that grew smaller and tighter.

He continued his frenzied attack with no thought of how he would escape, if he would escape.

Escape didn't matter. Killing the creatures did.

A man dressed in worn carpenter jeans grabbed the bloody arm of a woman who had already got in Caleb's path. He stared at the gory stump, then jammed it into his mouth.

She screamed and smacked at him with her remaining hand. He placed a palm on her forehead and kept eating. Others followed his lead, dining on the fallen and even those who hadn't, until the zombies formed one squirming mass…teeth latched on to anything that landed in their path.

Another hand grabbed Caleb, this one catching him by the fur ruff around his neck. As he turned, a face moved into view. The girl who had spoken to Samantha outside the gas station. Her mouth was open. It was obvious she meant to bite into Caleb's neck.

He bit hers first, got lost in blood and moon lust. Was only aware of the smell and taste of blood, of the stickiness of his paws and the way his coat clumped together, grew heavy…

Something bit him on the tail. On autopilot now, he twirled, his teeth ready.

Linda, in her wolf form, barked at him, then grabbed him by the tail again and tugged him backward.

Linda. He knew her. Trusted her and Mike as much as he trusted any weres.

Not long ago he'd given her a job, an important job, he remembered. But he couldn't recall what.

She jerked again. "Get out. Mike is outside. We're going to torch the place." A wolf himself, he understood her.

As she barked the last, a zombie lumbered toward her. It lifted its arm and smacked the female werewolf in the side of the head. Her toenails scratching, she slid across the concrete floor.

Caleb watched the wolf, his brain still processing why her appearance here was important.

Samantha.

Linda was supposed to be guarding Samantha.

The gears in his brain shifted, fell into new, sane slots. His wolf took a step back and allowed the man to think.

If Linda was here, Samantha wasn't at the motel, and she wasn't safe.

He had to leave.

He jumped over a pile of zombies that writhed like worms on the floor, each trying to devour the others. He made it to the door before he looked back and saw Linda lying unconscious ten feet away. A zombie was bending over her.

With a growl, Caleb leaped and landed on the creature's back. He snapped his jaws around the back of its neck. He bit and tore, harder and more violent than when he was lost in his wolf. This time he was fully aware of what he was doing and why. This time he wasn't just killing a zombie, he was saving a friend. A friend who could tell him about his mate.

The zombie's neck half gone, it dropped to the ground like the dead carcass it was. The other zombies, smelling the kill, mumbled noises and stumbled closer.

Caleb ignored them. They didn't matter; not now. He sank his teeth into Linda's neck and jerked her backward to the closed door. His backside bumped against it; he growled his frustration. He had gained control of his wolf, but with the moon still high and the bloodlust so recent, he didn't think he could get his body to shift... not quickly enough.

He growled and slammed his hindquarters against the door again.

A hand grabbed him by the scruff and both he and Linda were jerked through the suddenly open doorway.

Caleb jumped to his feet and spun. Mike slammed the door closed behind them and thrust a metal rod through the handle.

"Get back," he yelled as he scooped up his unconscious wife and sprinted past Caleb.

Torch the place. He remembered Linda's words.

With a curse, Caleb broke into a run, too.

Behind him, the building erupted into flames.

Chapter 17

Samantha stared at her friend's back, her fingers opening and closing around the knife's handle. Allison's hair covered her neck completely, covered the spot where Samantha would have to shove the blade.

Her hand trembling, she took a step forward.

She could do this. It was like shooting a rabid dog. Her father had done that once. He said it hadn't been hard, not once he focused on the disease and not the dog.

Samantha could do it, too.

Focus on the zombie, not Allison, she told herself.

She turned the knife so the serrated edge would be down when she struck.

Thrust and twist, she told herself. Then twist again.

Three seconds and it would be over…forever.

Three feet from her friend's turned back she stopped.

Her hand was shaking so badly the knife waved back and forth in the air. She shoved her empty fist into her mouth to keep from crying out.

Her father said it hadn't been hard.

But then her father was a liar.

She turned and padded as quickly and quietly from the cabin as she could.

Outside, she jammed a wooden lawn chair under the doorknob then stumbled down the steps into the yard.

The knife was still in her hand. She shook her arm, tried to dislodge it. Her fingers wouldn't loosen. She knelt and slammed the blade into the frozen ground. The tip caught; she jerked it out and slammed the knife down again. The blade sank into the earth halfway now. Another jerk, another slam, and the blade broke off and flew up into the air, spun off into the darkness.

But still Samantha couldn't stop. She lifted the handle and smashed it again and again against the hard ground until her arm ached and finally her fingers let go.

And even that didn't help. She folded her body down until her head rested on her knees and cried.

The knob on the cabin door rattled and then something—a body—smashed against it from the inside.

Samantha sprang to her feet. Her gaze shot to the knife she had just dismantled.

Then she ran.

Fire. Yet another way to kill a zombie Caleb hadn't considered before. Of course, in most cases it would be impractical, but for a space packed with fifty or so freshly made zombies it really was the perfect solution.

He was in his human form again. Something about

the fire—maybe the light overpowering the moon—made it easy for him to shift.

Fifty yards behind him, Linda was unconscious. Caleb had tried to awaken her, but Mike had pulled him away and pointed at the collapsing building. As the roof fell so did the walls, and zombies poured out of the place like ants out of a flooded anthill.

Caleb could feel Mike's worry. He knew the other wolf wanted to check on his mate as badly as Caleb wanted to race to find Samantha, but Mike didn't. He stood his ground, did his part to protect a pack that had never treated him with anything but disdain.

Caleb was the zombie hunter, not Mike, and he couldn't leave him here to fight alone. Besides, until Linda awoke, he didn't know where Samantha was.

So, he shouldered the shotgun Mike had provided and strode toward the zombies, shoved the muzzle into one head after another, firing and repositioning as quickly as he could. A few yards away, Mike did the same. At one point, Mike's aim was too close. Shot peppered Caleb's bare foot and calf. He winced, but kept going.

The quicker this batch of zombies was down, the quicker he could find Samantha.

When the last one fell, he dropped the shotgun and strode back toward Linda. Mike was already there, holding her against his chest.

"She came to tell you she'd let your female go," he said. "She wanted you to know she couldn't keep her, not after hearing her story. But Linda wanted Samantha to be safe, too. She wanted you to give the girl a chance to face her past and her future on her own."

"Her future?" Caleb's brows furrowed.

Mike rubbed his cheek across the wolf Linda's fur

and murmured against her neck. "She's a romantic and a bit of a women's libber." He laughed. "She wasn't happy when I asked her to keep your female trapped anyway. I should have known she'd let her go."

"You're the dominant." There was a pack alpha, but there were dominants and submissive wolves, too. And there could only be one dominant in any relationship.

Mike cocked one brow. "When she lets me be."

Then he turned and carried his mate toward the camp.

"She'll be fine," Caleb called.

Mike looked at him over his shoulder. "If I had any doubt of that, I'd kill you for getting her into this." He stared at the charred mess of building and zombies, then stalked off.

Caleb watched them leave. They were headed back to the camp. Caleb should be headed there, too. He glanced at the black spot that had been the building, and more than that, what had been humans, too. People tricked into thinking what the doctor offered them would be better than whatever future they faced on their own.

The doctor had to be close. Those people hadn't turned into zombies by themselves. Someone had pumped something into the building that killed and turned them in one or two easy breaths. And Caleb had been lured there, too. The doctor had planned on him dying, being torn apart by the doctor's newly created monsters.

And the doctor would want to be nearby to witness his victory.

Caleb should go to the camp, look for the doctor and find Anita. The doctor had to be stopped, and it was past time for Anita to answer for what she was doing.

Alpha or not, she didn't have the right to unleash zombies on humanity, and despite her arguments, she was responsible for every person taken in and every person killed.

But Caleb's mind was on Samantha. Where she was, how she was. He couldn't pursue the doctor or Anita, not until he knew Samantha was safe.

His wolf growled in agreement.

He stared at the smoldering remains of the building, not really seeing any of it.

According to what Mike had said, Samantha had left the motel on her own; that was good. He'd been afraid the doctor had found her and somehow gotten past Linda.

With that worry alleviated, he thought about Samantha and where she would choose to go on her own.

There was really only one answer—the one place he had made it clear he didn't want her to go.

The cabin where the doctor had said her friend Allison would be. The friend he was sure was already a zombie.

Panic wrapped around him, but he shook it off. Fear was his enemy. He had to put aside any personal attachments he thought he might have for Samantha and be nothing but the hunter.

He lifted his chin so the moon's light streamed over his face. Its pull tore at him. He didn't try to control it, didn't try to slow what was happening to his body or to avoid any bit of the pain. He embraced it. Unrestrained, his bones crunched, his skin stretched and guttural noises escaped from his throat. Then in one violent second it was over and he was standing on four legs. A wolf.

Ash drifted over him and clung to his fur. The ground felt dry and cracked under his paws. As all of this registered, he was off, running toward the cabin, one thought, one goal, pounding in his brain.

To get to the cabin and destroy the zombie.

He had to kill Allison.

Branches slapped Samantha in the face. Briars tore at her clothes. Her foot hit a rock and she stumbled, fell onto her hands and knees.

She jumped back up. Blood bubbled on her palms.

She stared at it in horror, remembering the zombie in the video attracted by his companion's blood…attacking, devouring…

She grabbed leaves from the ground and scrubbed them over her skin then threw them in the opposite direction she meant to go. They floated back down at her feet. She kicked at them.

"Sa-man-tha."

Allison was behind her.

Samantha broke back into a run, heading she didn't know where.

Caleb charged through the trees. The ground was icy and slick, but in his wolf form the semifrozen earth didn't even slow his steps.

He was close now. He recognized the terrain.

He broke through the trees into the clearing, stopping long enough to scan the area before moving toward the cabin.

The door was hanging open, as if something had been rammed against the wood.

He didn't bother to go inside. He spun instead, his nose on the ground, and searched for the scent of Samantha, or zombie.

He found both, and both were headed in the same direction.

His body stretched to its full length, he sprinted again.

Samantha's feet and fingers were numb, but her heart was pumping hard. Allison was growing closer. She hadn't yelled again, but Samantha could hear her smashing through the brush. She wasn't bothering with stealth. But then zombies didn't.

She…it…not she…not Allison…it… Samantha had to think of the body behind her that way. If she didn't, she wouldn't be able to do what she would have to do to survive.

Her stomach clenched. She had no weapon and even if she did, she had no idea how she would bring herself to look at the body that had been Allison and kill her.

Her concentration thinned, she didn't see the log stretched across her path. Her shins rammed into it, then her body pitched forward and she somersaulted onto the ground.

Pain shot through her back. She tried to stand, but the ground was slick. She couldn't get her feet back under her.

"Sa-man-tha." Allison's upside-down face filled her view.

Her hands digging under dead leaves, Samantha clawed at the ground beside her.

A weapon. She needed a weapon.

Her fingers touched the sharp edge of a rock.

Allison leaned down as if to help her up. Samantha rolled forward, head between her legs, and landed on her butt three feet away. Her feet sliding on ice and leaves, she scrambled to a stand.

Allison stared at her with hollow, empty eyes. "Caleb Locke. The doctor wants him."

Back to the recording.

Samantha tightened her hold on the rock. Having it should have made her feel better, more in control, but the nausea was back. "Leave, Allison. Go back to the doctor. Tell him Caleb isn't here." *So I don't have to do this,* she added silently.

Allison tilted her head side to side, then stepped over the log. "Must get Caleb Locke or get Samantha."

She held out her arms like a damned movie zombie and took a giant step forward. Her fingers wrapped around Samantha's neck.

She inhaled loudly and looked down. "Sa-man-tha. You are bleeding."

The scent left by Samantha and Allison was erratic, following no set path, as if the person in the lead had been running wild, panicked.

At each twist Caleb slowed, circled until he was sure of the new direction. Then he would break into a run again, go as long as he could before another unpredictable turn.

He'd made it past three when he saw them. Allison with her hands wrapped around Samantha's neck. The zombie pulled Samantha toward her then stopped. She seemed to say something. Her mouth opened, her teeth flashed and she jerked Samantha again, this time her jaws descending toward her friend's bare neck.

Caleb leaped.

He hit the pair hard. His body shot between them like a shim, pushing them apart. Samantha fell to the ground, but Allison only staggered.

He yelled at Samantha, told her to run, but in his wolf form it came out as a growl. Frustrated, he spun toward the zombie—Samantha's friend, the reason Samantha had come to him, the woman she had begged him to save.

She reeked of rot. The stench was covered by some musky cologne, but the smell of death was impossible to hide, at least from a wolf. The body standing before him might look human, but it wasn't. Probably hadn't been since the video Samantha had shown him had been made.

Samantha was trying to save the dead. And that, Caleb knew all too well, was impossible.

The zombie swiveled, looking from him to Samantha. She frowned.

Caleb didn't wait for her to sort out what had happened. He lunged. His teeth pierced the flesh of Allison's arm. He could tell by the taste of her blood what he'd already guessed was true. She wasn't alive and hadn't been for weeks.

Samantha yelled and scrambled to her feet. She had a rock in her hand. She held it up as if ready to strike.

Caleb didn't wait to see which one of them. He jerked the zombie to the ground, levered his jaws around its neck and tore his way through muscle, tendon and bone.

He kept tearing until its head disengaged from its spine and rolled to the side.

When he looked up, Samantha was gone.

Samantha felt as if she had been running for hours... days...a lifetime. She had thought she was cold before, but that was nothing compared to the icy sheath that covered her inside and out now.

Her body kept moving, stumbling along as fast as her feet would carry her, but her brain was dead, stuck on the image of that wolf or dog, she wasn't sure which, standing over Allison, ripping out her throat, of it looking up at her, its muzzle covered in blood.

Allison's blood.

A shiver ripped through her, but the shiver was a lie. She couldn't deny that she had let the beast complete its attack, that she hadn't done a thing to save her friend, that she had, in fact, been ready to do the same herself.

Her hand was empty. She had dropped the rock over a mile back, but she could still feel it pressed against her palm. She still knew exactly which sharp edge would be best to plunge into her friend's skull. Could still feel the surge of fear and adrenaline and the need to strike that had rushed over her right before the wolf had interceded.

She would have killed Allison. She had thought she wouldn't be able to, but she had been wrong. When it came to her life or her friend's, she would have used that damned rock. She would have forgotten every promise she had ever made in order to survive.

Didn't that make her a monster, too? Even more so? She still had full function of her brain, still remembered every secret she had shared with her friend, every soda they'd split, every afternoon they'd wasted shopping.

And still she would have killed her.

Samantha dropped to her knees and retched. Her stomach was empty, but it didn't matter. She continued to gag and cough until her throat and lungs burned. Then, her palms and knees pressed into the dirt, she let her head hang between her shoulders and took deep, heaving breaths.

Finally empty, body and soul, she was able to think again.

It was over. There was no going back. She had to move on, think of where she was now, what she wanted now.

She knew the answer immediately.

Caleb. She had to find Caleb.

She forced her body to uncurl and her legs to hold her weight. Then she squared her shoulders and started walking. It was a cold, rough walk, but the added challenge of avoiding rocks and hidden holes gave her something on which to concentrate.

Ten minutes later she hit a paved road—the county highway that led to the camp. It looked different tonight. Cars and trucks were parked on both sides, some off in ditches, some partially blocking one lane.

It looked as if Anita was throwing a party.

The moon was full overhead, round and silvery. The extra light it cast should have been reassuring, but instead another shiver threatened. Samantha rubbed her hands over her arms and willed her unease away.

She had just seen her best friend torn to bits.

If she wasn't shivering, suffering some symptoms

of shock, she'd be worried that she was turning into a zombie herself.

Right now pain, whether physical or emotional, was her friend.

A howl ripped through the night. Before Samantha could register the sound, assure herself the cry didn't mean the wolf or dog she'd seen attack Allison was near, another animal joined in, then another and another until the howls formed a chorus.

Something moved in the trees to her right, bodies racing through the underbrush. Her heart beating loudly in her chest, she darted behind a truck and ducked down.

A growl or a snarl and then the bodies were gone.

Samantha stood with her hands on the truck's bed. She glanced to the side, recognized the vehicle from the motel parking lot. The motel owner's.

Mike would know where Caleb was.

With no more thoughts of roaming wolf packs, she cut through the trees toward the camp.

There were noises in the woods, strange noises. She'd grown up in the country, had gone hunting with more than one boyfriend in the dead of night and early morning. She was used to the uneasy feeling of being in the woods in the small hours. She was used to the sounds of tree frogs and angry raccoons, too.

But these noises and the feeling that crept over her were different.

For one thing the noise was more a lack of noise. There were a few stirrings here and there, but no frogs or other creatures called. Of course, frogs wouldn't be out in the cold—even if they had tree frogs in this part of the country. Samantha had no idea.

But she knew the stillness couldn't be normal. Every forest had nocturnal animals. It was as if the trees were watching her…or something hiding in the trees was.

She could see the camp now. A bonfire burned in a stone circle. She hurried toward it, both for the warmth and to get out from under the shadow of the trees.

But near the fire, the uneasy feeling only grew. Despite the multitude of vehicles parked along the road, she was alone. She stood on one of the stones that formed the fire's circle, her hands held over the dying flames, and glanced around. There were no lights on in the cabins. Everyone could be asleep.

Needing to know, she crept toward one of the buildings and pushed open the door. It swung inward on silent hinges.

There were rows of beds, like at a summer camp, but all were empty.

She walked from building to building and found not a single bed was occupied, and there was no sign of anyone in the kitchen or baths, either.

The camp was deserted.

She glanced back at the now almost dead fire.

Should she pull a Goldilocks and settle herself into some bed, hoping people returned soon and someone offered her a ride? Should she go back to the motel owner's truck and wait for him, hope Caleb came with him?

Maybe it was just shock catching up with her, but neither seemed like a safe choice.

She opted instead to wedge her body into a dark corner of the cafeteria, a heated space, but next to a window where she would have the opportunity to see whoever or whatever approached before they saw her.

Sitting on the concrete with her knees drawn up to her chest, she stared into the darkness and waited. Minutes later her head nodded forward. When it hit her knee she jerked back awake. The process repeated awhile later. After the third time, she quit fighting, laid her cheek on her knees and drifted off to sleep.

Chapter 18

Caleb's first instinct had been to follow Samantha, but he had to make sure Allison was dead first. Truly dead. Even with her head missing, her body could still operate if the brain stem wasn't destroyed. It took another few minutes to be one hundred percent certain.

By then Samantha had a good start on him, not that he couldn't catch up. She would be stumbling blindly through the woods. In his wolf form, catching her would be no challenge at all.

He glanced at her best friend's corpse. Her head had rolled three feet away from her body. Her eyes and mouth were open.

She had been going to bite Samantha. He had no doubt of that, no regret for ending Allison's zombie existence, but how would Samantha feel?

He doubted she would see things the same way.

How did you face a woman after killing her best friend?

Except she didn't know he was the killer. She'd seen a wolf take her friend down. She'd run from that wolf, not Caleb. He could get cleaned up and never let her know. He could live a double life. Other werewolves did. Caleb had never had to because he never let anyone get that close.

But now he had.

He had accepted what his wolf knew all along.

He had to have her.

But he also couldn't live a lie.

If he and Samantha were to be together it could only be with her knowing he was a werewolf, which meant her knowing he had killed her friend.

It was unlikely she could accept the first fact. Impossible that she could accept the second.

He lifted his chin, stared at the moon and howled.

Then, weary to the marrow of his bones, he lowered his nose and trailed after her.

Laughter sounded close by. Samantha jerked, her head knocking against the wooden wall behind her. Blinking, she rubbed the back of her skull and struggled to remember where she was.

She'd awakened so many unexpected places lately she'd forgotten where she should be. But she knew wherever that was, it wasn't here.

The room was dark and smelled of cleaning products and bacon. She wrinkled her nose. A cafeteria.

At the sound of more laughter she moved onto her knees and wiggled forward, until she could see out the window. The gray skies of dawn greeted her.

There was a group around the now blazing fire.

They were men and women ranging in age from twenty to eighty and each was naked. One man, broad shouldered and obviously good friends with his local gym, strode into a cabin and came back with an armful of clothes. He tossed pants to two other men of the same general description. A few seconds later, two of the women wandered into a cabin, too.

But most of the group stayed as they were, naked and laughing. They seemed happy, more than happy…fired up.

Samantha scanned the circle for signs of empty beer cans. One man was taking sips from a plastic water bottle, but that was it. None were staggering or even leaning to the side. They all seemed sober, just hyped up on adrenaline.

What kind of camp was Anita running?

And how exactly did Caleb know her? Know the group? He obviously shared their lack of modesty. Samantha had to think he had something else in common with them, too.

Her gaze went back to the fire, wondering if she should leave her hiding place. She couldn't stay crouched inside the building forever, and while it was strange most of the people gathered here chose to be and stay naked, none of them looked anything except human.

More specifically, none looked like a zombie.

So, perhaps Caleb and Anita were part of some nudist group. There was nothing supernatural about that. She could handle a little nudity.

As she glanced back over her shoulder for one more secret look at the group before joining them, five wolves/dogs bounded into the clearing. She clutched the doorknob, her mind telling her to rush out and yell a warning to the people gathered around the fire, but her legs refused to move.

Then something strange happened. The wolves rose onto their hind legs like poodles trained to dance, and their bodies began to shake. Their fur disappeared, seemed to be sucked back into their bodies. Their muzzles shortened, their ears shortened, everything about them changed until they weren't wolves at all, but humans. Three men and two women, naked and looking every bit as exhilarated as the rest of the group.

Samantha's hand lay on the handle; she couldn't move it, couldn't move at all.

Werewolves.

It wasn't possible.

But then neither were zombies.

She took a step back, glancing around the room as she did. Panic grabbed her. She needed to find a weapon. Her mind racing, she jogged through the cafeteria and into the kitchen. She jerked open a drawer and shuffled through it, slammed that one shut and tried another, kept moving until she found a set of knives, then she stared at it stupidly.

Silver. Wasn't silver required to kill a werewolf?

Or was that just myth?

She grabbed the knife anyway.

God, she wished Caleb was here. He would know. Her mind stuttered.

Caleb…his own comfort with being naked…his strange conversation with Anita about wolves…the dog Linda… Piece after piece fell into place and all of them added to the same picture, the same disturbingly obvious picture.

Caleb was a werewolf. Her fingers went limp. She stared blindly at the open drawer in front of her, couldn't see the knives, couldn't see anything. The man she had made love to, loved, wasn't the action hero in her fantasy. He was one of the monsters.

She had jumped out of one fire and into the arms of an inferno.

Somewhere along the way, Caleb had lost track of time. The sun was already edging up over the horizon when he approached the camp. The pack had returned. They were gathered around the bonfire, soaking in the warmth radiating off the embers and reliving their time running under the moon.

Still in his wolf form and still hidden from their sight by the trees, he watched them. None seemed aware that the building filled with humans had burned, that every person inside it was gone. He wondered how many of the werewolves knew what Anita was doing. Wondered how many of them would care.

Those people had heard about the pack and what it offered from somewhere. Caleb guessed at least some, if not most, had been brought here by the werewolves gathered around the fire. Perhaps the entire pack was in on Anita's moneymaking scheme. Perhaps they purposely invited the weak with the bait of becoming a werewolf, knowing those invitees would be switched to zombie.

Two men dressed only in jeans walked past him with coolers. Three others placed metal racks around the edges of the fire. They were preparing for the monthly pack breakfast, a tradition almost as sacred as the run itself.

After a night in wolf form, running through the trees, the group would be famished. They would tear through at least three sides of beef, and most of a hog.

A woman stirred the fire, testing the coals, then lined steaks up on one of the grills. Caleb's stomach rumbled.

He ignored his body's demand.

He was here to find both Anita and Samantha.

Samantha first. He lowered his nose to the ground. Her scent headed toward the fire. If he wanted to find her, he would have to reveal himself. And since the others had already shifted back to their human forms, he needed to also.

Already mourning the loss of his fur in the cold temperatures, he bowed his head and concentrated on changing. Going from wolf to human was less painful, but that didn't mean it was easy. Some basic part of him fought the shift each time. He'd heard other werewolves speak of the feeling, too, but they were all part of a pack. That kept their wolf happy. For a rogue like Caleb, it was harder. His wolf resented the lack of a pack, and each time Caleb shifted to wolf, his animal nature objected shifting back. If he couldn't find a human pack to join with, his wolf wanted him to go wolf, stay wolf.

It was a struggle Caleb was used to, and one he might someday lose. But not today. He shoved aside his wolf's objections by concentrating on Samantha. He couldn't approach her as a wolf; not without her seeing him as a killer.

His wolf seemed to accept his reasoning, and released its hold on him with relative ease.

In seconds he was standing on two feet, naked in the woods. He strode forward into the open clearing. The werewolves didn't react, but he knew they all realized he didn't belong.

He didn't have the scent of the pack on him. In their eyes he was an interloper, a threat to the pack. It spoke to his reputation and how he carried himself that they didn't jump on him and try to tear him to bits.

He stopped a few feet from the circle and waited for the most dominant of them to address him. A man, one of the two who had carried the cooler, walked closer.

"You have business here, rogue?"

Caleb caught the inside of his cheek between his teeth. "It's none of yours. Where's Anita?" He was more interested in finding Samantha, but the easiest way to defuse this guy's testosterone boner was to make it clear he wasn't afraid to stare down the alpha.

As he suspected, at his question the guy lifted his chin and grunted. After a quick slide of his eyes to the other weres who watched them from the fire, he replied, "She isn't back yet."

Caleb let his gaze wander over the camp. "Guess I'll just have to wait then."

The male puffed out his chest and took a step closer. "Don't get comfortable." Then he stalked back to his now sizzling breakfast.

His arms loose at his sides, Caleb made his disinterest clear. Anita's absence had given him a perfect excuse to stay at the camp until he could find Samantha. He also, however, had to wonder why the alpha wasn't with her pack. Leaving them alone with an obviously weak second-in-command was, well, stupid.

But then Anita had been displaying a lot of stupid lately.

After a few minutes the pack's attention returned to

their festivities. Caleb waited a few more moments until he was positive they wouldn't notice him wandering around, and then continued his search for Samantha. He moved slowly, as if he had no agenda, and was just killing time while he waited for the alpha. The second-in-command didn't even glance at him, and the few others who did dropped their gazes when he turned his attention on them.

Anita's pack might be wealthy, but they were weak.

In Caleb's book, strength of mind, body and spirit was what made a werewolf, not a thick wallet. But then the pack's strength was not his concern. In fact, their weakness worked to his advantage. He should have been praising Anita's failings, but he couldn't help but feel this new pack somehow reflected poorly on him, too. He couldn't help letting it annoy him.

Vexed with himself that he was so conflicted, he shoved his thoughts of the pack aside and concentrated on splitting Samantha's scent off from the multitude of others that had traveled through the camp in the last few hours.

It didn't take him long to realize where she had gone. The cafeteria.

She was lucky the weather was nice enough the pack had opted to cook outside this morning.

He glanced at the group. Their meat was done and they were all engaged in stuffing as much as they could into their mouths.

If no one had noticed Caleb moving closer to the cafeteria before now, he was clear to do as he pleased for at least the next ten minutes. It would take them that long to reduce the pile of meat to nothing but gnawed bones.

He would only need two.

He strode toward the cafeteria's closed door.

Samantha had searched the kitchen, pulled out drawers and dumped them on the floor. She hadn't found as much as a silver thimble.

But then she wouldn't, would she? Not here in a werewolf camp.

Werewolf… She found it hard to accept, but she had to believe the impossible. Hadn't she already accepted zombies? But this…

There was a thump in the front room, in the seating area of the cafeteria. Someone had opened the door.

Her gaze shot around the kitchen. There was a window over the sink, facing the woods not the camp where she had last seen the werewolves gathered. She raced toward it.

"Samantha."

The voice stopped her. *Caleb.* She was almost to the sink, almost to the window and freedom. She stared at the square of glass. While she had been hidden in the cafeteria, it had grown light outside. She could see the pines behind the building.

"Samantha?"

The question in his voice made her pause. She had to be wrong. He couldn't be a werewolf. If she gave him a chance, he could explain everything she'd seen.

She turned to him.

He was naked, and blood stained his chest.

Her stomach cramped and she stepped back, closer to the window. Her foot hit something…a knife. She could feel the blade under her shoe.

She hadn't been able to use such a weapon on Allison.

Could she use it on Caleb? Even if she could, would it stop him? Slow him, even?

Her eyelids fluttered, but she didn't let them close. She wanted to shut them, to block out the swirl of emotion threatening to engulf her.

Caleb had raised his hand, but as she moved he lowered it.

She took another step backward. Her butt hit the edge of the sink.

He didn't move. His face paled; his jaw hardened.

"Allison is dead," she murmured, although she knew in her gut he already knew it. Her gaze locked onto his chest.

He glanced down and touched the ruddy stains on his skin.

When he looked back, she could see the truth in his eyes.

She twirled back toward the sink, boosted her body up onto the counter and escaped through the window.

Caleb didn't try to stop her. He didn't even move.

Chapter 19

Wind blew through the open window over the kitchen sink. A chill shot through Caleb.

Samantha knew. She knew he was a werewolf, knew he had killed Allison.

He didn't know how, but he could guess. She had been hiding in the cafeteria where windows looked out onto the fire. She had to have seen something that told her the camp's purpose. After that the rest would have fallen neatly and quickly into place.

He took in the state of the kitchen. Knives were scattered over the floor.

Yes, she had known.

And she had been afraid of him.

How could he blame her?

The overhead lights buzzed to life.

Anita stepped into the room. "You're an idiot."

At that moment, feeling the way he did, he couldn't argue the fact.

Sensing his weakness like a piranha sniffing blood, the alpha sashayed forward. "Jake said you were looking for me." She glanced around the kitchen. "But I'm guessing you were looking for someone else. Someone not so interested in being found, at least by you."

A growl rose in Caleb's throat.

Anita either missed the sound or was too caught up in her moment to pay it any mind. "Weres and humans don't mix. I thought you at least accepted that. You choose to be a were, you leave everything human behind, and you don't look back."

"Everything? How about those high-paying jobs you're so proud of your pack holding?" Caleb jerked his head toward the cafeteria and the circle of werewolves gathered around the fire beyond it.

She snorted. "You know what I mean. Involvement, commitments."

"But not money. You need that human money, don't you, Anita?" The annoyance he'd felt earlier toward the alpha and what she was doing to her pack returned with the kick of two mules.

Her teeth flashed. "Yes, I do."

No apology. No explanation.

Her arrogance was just one of the reasons she was alpha, but it could also be her downfall.

"Well, you're going to have to survive with less of it." He had lost Samantha. No, he corrected himself, he'd never had Samantha…not really. She hadn't known what he was. She hadn't made love to a werewolf. She had made love to a myth.

So, he hadn't lost her. He had never had her to lose.

But the man creating zombies… The man responsible if not for his parents' death, then the deaths of many other people's parents, brothers and sisters…Caleb wouldn't lose him.

Which meant Anita was about to take a big cut in income.

Nothing but good in that, Caleb thought. He crossed his arms over his chest and leaned against a counter in a deceptively casual pose.

"I saw the building. You were supposed to be inside it," she said.

He opened his mouth in a mockery of shock. "What? No 'I'm so glad you are safe'? No claims of relief?"

She grunted. "You have no use to the pack, and the pack has no use for you."

He didn't care how she felt about him. He didn't care that she wanted him dead.

Right now the feeling was mutual.

The anger he'd been holding inside exploded. He rushed toward her, his hands wrapping around her throat before she could step to the side.

She bared her teeth and did her best to use her status of alpha and the magnetic power holding the position gave her to force him to cower.

But her supposed superiority held no influence on him. It never had.

He shook her like a cat shaking a mouse. Her feet swung side to side before she gained control of them and started kicking, aiming for his gut, his groin, any part within her reach. He felt the blows, but they were like a rap with a ruler—annoying but no deterrent from his goal.

This battle had been a long time coming. He'd avoided

it for one simple reason: He knew when it happened he would kill her.

Her fingernails dug into his arms, drawing blood. She lashed out, swiping at him, dragging her nails across his cheek.

He shook her harder.

She symbolized everything that had been taken from him, every lie he had believed…chosen to believe.

"Alpha!"

Anita's second-in-command, the broad-chested, simple-minded lout who had confronted Caleb outside, stood in the doorway between the cafeteria and kitchen, his face drawn in shock.

Caleb glanced down at the female in his hands, saw what the other male saw. Anita had turned blue. Her eyes bulged and her hands had stopped swiping at Caleb; they hung limply at her sides instead.

Caleb stared from the male to the woman hanging like a broken toy from his hands.

She had lied to him, but he'd known it at the time. He had chosen to believe being a werewolf would solve all his problems. He had come to her, blocked out all the truths he didn't want to see or hear.

Anita wasn't his enemy. He was.

He glanced to the side, stared at the window that Samantha had escaped through. Then he opened his hands and let Anita fall to the ground.

He moved to step over her, but she rolled onto her back and grabbed him around the calf. He lifted his foot with every intention of smashing her in the face.

Her eyes begged him to do it. He'd beaten her. Even now she grappled for air. And, worse than that, her second-in-command had witnessed her defeat. Her role as alpha was over. As far as Anita was concerned her life was over.

Slowly he pulled his foot back and set it down on the floor, inches from her face. He could feel her exhale. Sorrow and acceptance flowed from her.

The power in the room shifted. It was his now, if he wanted it. All he had to do was claim it, claim the pack, claim everything Anita held dear.

Her second stood as he had when he'd entered the room. As Caleb lowered his boot, the other man looked up. His gaze lit on Caleb for a moment only, then dropped to the floor, recognizing Caleb as his superior.

Annoyed that he'd let himself get pulled into the center of werewolf politics, Caleb snapped his head toward the male.

The werewolf held out a note. "This came for…" His gaze darted toward Anita, but he pulled back short of actually looking at her.

Caleb didn't bother glancing down, either. If Anita was conscious, she was doing her best to act as if she wasn't.

Annoyed anew, he grabbed the note from the man's outstretched hand.

The sealed envelope had Anita's name scrawled on the outside. Without sparing her a glance, Caleb ripped it open.

I found one. You owe me 49.

It took a second for him to read the note, less for rage to boil up inside him.

The doctor had Samantha. She was the only "one" the doctor could be referring to. He must have grabbed her as she ran from the camp while trying to escape Caleb.

Caleb grabbed the alpha by the front of her shirt. With a growl, he jerked her to her feet. Her knees bent; only his hold kept her from collapsing back onto the floor.

He held the note up to her face, inches from her nose. "Where?" he demanded.

Her eyes rolled side to side, from him to the male who still stood watching them.

Caleb jerked around to face him. "Leave. And no word to anyone what you saw here. Understand?"

With a nod, the male scurried from the building.

After the door had closed behind him, Caleb dropped Anita onto a countertop. She lay on her side, rubbing her throat and licking her dry lips.

"You should have killed me," she muttered.

"I still can," he replied. If she didn't talk soon, he would. He wouldn't be able to stop his wolf from completing the act. He could already feel the beast snapping at his subconscious.

She laid her hands to the side as if telling him to go ahead.

He cursed and shoved the note back into her face. "I don't want you dead. I don't want your pack. Take me to where he is."

She pushed herself to a slumping sit. "It doesn't matter. After what Jake saw, it's over for me."

"Maybe my time's up. Maybe you'll get lucky and this doctor will be my downfall."

"I'm not that lucky," she scoffed, then shook her head. "And it doesn't matter. Even if you die, it won't regain what I lost." She squared her gaze on him. "Not unless I kill you." She laughed again. "But we both know I won't…I can't."

She had never admitted that truth openly before.

Caleb felt sorry for her. Almost.

"Maybe you can," he replied.

She lifted one brow. "Maybe I misjudged you. Maybe you are more insane than I even guessed."

He dropped the note onto the counter beside her. "Like I said, I don't want you dead and I don't want your pack. I definitely don't want to be alpha. But I do want him."

She dropped her attention to the note. "And what he has? This 'one'—it isn't a were. I would know if it was."

Caleb's lips thinned. "Dead, he will have nothing."

Anita twisted her lips, but didn't push him. "And you'll let me kill you to get him?" Her voice was both skeptical and hopeful. "I don't believe you."

"I'll let you capture me. I'll let you trade me for one or all of the forty-nine he says you owe. Wouldn't that be close enough?"

Looking more alive now, she frowned. "Maybe, but the capture would have to be good."

He shrugged. "Of course."

There was a spark in her eyes. He could see he had her. Then she pulled back. "What's the catch? How are you going to escape?"

He stared at the window where he had last seen Samantha. "No catch. We are doing exactly what the doctor wants, giving him exactly what he wants. Me."

Staging Anita's comeback over Caleb really wasn't that hard. At least not after she regained enough strength to stay upright.

Caleb had stormed out of the cafeteria building as if

something inside had angered him beyond control. Anita followed, throwing herself on his back as he moved. She'd grabbed him around the neck, bitten and clawed at him.

He'd made an act of jerking at her and falling, allowing her to land on top. Then he'd let her punch him full in the face. He'd heard the cartilage in his nose snap, smelled and felt the warm blood stream down his cheeks, and then as she jumped to a stand above him, he had closed his eyes and pretended to lose consciousness.

There was silence for a moment. Then the pack erupted into yells and howls.

Their alpha had defeated an interloper. It was cause for celebration.

After a few minutes, Caleb was grabbed under the arms and hoisted to his feet. He kept his head hanging down and his eyes closed.

Frigid water, laced with ice cubes slammed into his chest. He jerked his head up. The two wolves baring the now empty cooler took a step back.

Anita raised one hand. "Don't be concerned. He has no bite left." She stepped forward and poked him in the chest with one finger. "Isn't that right, rogue?"

The wolf inside Caleb raised his lip. Caleb's body mirrored the action. One of the men holding him loosened his grip and stepped back.

Anita whirled on him. "I said not to be concerned."

She stared the male down, her second, the man who had witnessed what had happened between Caleb and the alpha inside the kitchen.

Caleb bent his knees again, let his body sag. The man had no choice but to tighten his grip.

Anita shoved her fingers up into the hair on the top of Caleb's head and forced his face up to hers. "We take him to the cave."

The cave. Caleb should have known. Where else would a werewolf and a zombie doctor do business?

Chapter 20

Samantha moved her fingers over the ropes that were wrapped around her wrists. She was bound ankle to ankle and wrist to wrist. A cloth had been shoved into her mouth, as well.

Something had hit her in the back of the head as she'd fled the kitchen. Caught up in her discovery, she had been oblivious to what had been going on around her. So oblivious she had apparently missed the stench of zombie.

But lying on the cold floor of this cave, there was no missing it now.

A dozen of the creatures lined up against the wall. There might be more, but bound as she was, her view was limited.

They stood like statues, not breathing, not moving…at

least not their bodies. Only their gazes moved, roaming over her.

Her skin crawled under their attention. *Lust.* It was the only word she could think to describe what she saw in their eyes. But their attention wasn't sexual. It was hungry, starving, like she was a buffet of delicacies each and every one of them died to dive into.

If their brains had still worked, she would have thought they were dividing her up, carving her into pieces with their minds, choosing which select tidbit they would dive for when the feast began.

But their brains didn't work, not like hers.

And right now, she wished hers didn't work quite so well. She wished she wasn't capable of envisioning exactly what the creatures could do to her.

Pain shot through her hip where it pressed against the cold, hard-packed earth beneath her. Her head ached, too, but the physical pain she was feeling was nothing compared to the anguish of her thoughts.

She closed her eyes to the sight of the zombies and forced her mind to other things. But there was nothing pleasant to focus on—not with reality pressing down around her.

The worst had happened; what Caleb had warned her of had happened. She'd been caught by zombies, and tied as she was, she couldn't do what she should have done for Allison.

She couldn't end her own life.

Allison and Caleb. Thinking of them only increased her pain.

Samantha squeezed her eyelids more tightly together. She had let them down. She had in some way deserted them both.

And now she couldn't make it up to either of them.

There was a shuffling noise. Despite the suspicion that it would be better not to know what was happening, or about to happen, Samantha opened her eyes.

Something white flickered in the corner of her range of vision. She didn't turn her head; she didn't have to. She could tell by the way the zombies turned theirs and watched with rapt attention that the doctor had joined them.

He was different than she had expected, with strawberry-blond hair and a ruddy complexion. His eyes were brown and his features even. He was as normal-looking as a hundred men she had passed in the mall and never glanced at twice.

He padded forward until his crepe-soled shoes were inches from Samantha's face. Then he knelt and patted her on the back. She stiffened.

"So, Allison is dead, truly dead. The hunter fixed it so even *I* can't bring her back." He removed his hand and glanced over his shoulder at the zombies. He pointed at two of them. "Go outside...hide as best you can. When the werewolves come, present yourselves. Defend yourselves if attacked."

When they had shuffled out of the cave, the doctor looked at Samantha. "I hate to risk losing two more, but it's the easiest way to know when the wolves arrive and if they are working with me or against me. Your hunter is in the mix now, you know. He wouldn't be able to resist killing a zombie, even if it alerted me to his arrival. Do you think?"

He paused as if waiting for her reply, but with the wad of cloth still shoved between her lips the best she could offer was a grunt and she didn't even do that.

He leaned closer and whispered in her ear. "I'm not giving away any secrets now, am I? It's why you ran, isn't it? Of course I'm not. You were there when it happened, weren't you? When the hunter destroyed our Allison?"

Samantha flinched at his use of the word *our*. Allison wasn't his. No matter what he did to her friend's body after she had died, Allison would never be his.

"Oh, but I forgot. He didn't kill her with a gun or a knife. He used his teeth. Is that why you ran? Because you realized he and the others are werewolves?" The doctor leaned back on his heels and studied her. "Which bothered you more, friend of Allison? Seeing her die or realizing monsters are real?"

Samantha glared at him, wishing she could tell him she already knew monsters were real, had realized it when she'd first seen him on the video online.

He patted her again. "Don't worry. I want to stop the hunter as much as you do, and guess what? You get to help me." He reached into the pocket of his lab coat and pulled out a knife. "Did he grow fond of you while you were together? Just a little? I'm hoping so. I'm hoping once he knows I have someone close to him, he'll see the wisdom in working with me instead of against me. He lost people close to him once before. I don't think he will want to do it again, do you?"

His questions didn't really seem to be directed at Samantha. They were more like mindless prattle; the kind of words people said to their pets knowing the creatures didn't understand them.

Except Samantha did understand them, all too well. She wouldn't, however, give him a reaction, and she wouldn't be used as a tool against Caleb.

She lifted her chin. If the doctor drove the blade into her heart, he wouldn't be able to make her into one of his monsters like he had Allison and he wouldn't be able to use Samantha against Caleb. If she wanted to make up for the mistakes she had made, it was her only option. Not pausing to allow herself to think more, she thrust her body forward and rammed the doctor with her head.

Tied as she was, she had no hope of injuring him, but that wasn't her goal. Her goal was to get him to use that knife, to take her life instead of whatever else he had planned for her.

He fell onto his back. The knife rattled onto the ground. Seeing an opportunity, Samantha dove on the weapon and managed to grasp it between her hands.

The blade was pointed toward her. All she had to do was bend her elbows and plunge the knife's tip into her own throat, or, easier, fall onto it.

She took a breath and prepared to collapse forward.

A hand sank into her hair. She jerked and the knife tumbled from her fingers.

"Get it," the doctor told one of his zombies.

His fingers still wrapped in her hair, he pulled her backward so he could once again mutter in her ear.

"What would that solve? You have your whole life ahead of you. Maim yourself and you still have life ahead of you. I will see to that."

Hot tears of frustration leaked from Samantha's eyes.

Of course. Death wouldn't solve her problem. Even it couldn't save her from the zombie doctor.

What could?

"I'm here to make a deal."

Samantha's heart jumped, and despite the doctor's tight hold on her hair, she managed to twist her head enough to see who had spoken.

Anita, the bitch who ran the camp, stood in the opening of the cave. The zombies the doctor had sent to stand guard stood on each side of her, but Samantha's attention didn't go to them. Her eyes locked instead on the man being towed behind Anita.

Caleb.

He was naked from the waist up, and dressed only in his fatigues. Wrapped around his wrists, ankles, chest and throat was a thin chain of silver-colored metal.

No, Samantha corrected herself, not silver-colored metal. Silver. The kryptonite of a werewolf.

Anita had Caleb under her control and she was about to turn him over to the zombie doctor.

Breath passing his teeth in an inward hiss, the doctor inhaled. He stood, dragging Samantha with him.

As soon as he was on his feet, he seemed to forget her. He dropped his hold of her hair and took a step forward.

He didn't, however, forget the knife. He motioned to the zombie whom he'd asked to retrieve it, and then slipped the weapon back into his pocket.

"A deal?" He stood with his hands in his pockets and his back to Samantha. He was excited; he practically hummed with anticipation.

She clenched her hands into fists. This couldn't be happening. Caleb couldn't be standing beside Anita helpless.

"What type of deal do you think to take? You already owe me for the clients I lost...or the return of the money

I gave you. What could you possibly have that would compensate me for fifty eager volunteers?" The doctor asked the question, but Samantha could hear the hunger in his voice. He was just like his zombies, lusting after Caleb as his creations had lusted after her.

She glanced at Caleb. He was looking at her. She didn't know what she expected to see in his face, but she knew what she wanted to see: regret, love or some message that everything would be all right. But none of those feelings were there, only cold disregard.

She flinched as if struck. Then she dropped her head.

She had turned away from him, run from him when he had done nothing she hadn't wished for the strength to do herself. Run from him because he was, what—a werewolf? Did that change who she knew him to be? Did that make the man she made love to…loved…a monster? She lifted her gaze and stared him full in the face.

No. That was impossible. She had been a fool.

She willed him to look at her again, to see her remorse, to give her a chance to let him know how wrong she had been, how much she regretted her actions. But it was as if he knew she was watching him and refused to give her that little bit of relief. He kept his attention locked onto the doctor.

"Don't be cute," Anita said. "We both know what you want, and I'm here to give it to you—at the right price." She flicked her gaze at Caleb and then back onto the doctor.

"Me? Be cute?" He laughed. "We both know I already paid, and if I had to guess, you've already spent my money." He wiggled his thumbs over the tops of his lab coat's pockets. "Am I to guess you want me to accept one werewolf for fifty—" He glanced at Samantha. "Forty-nine willing patients? The math just doesn't seem to add up."

Despite his words, Samantha couldn't miss his excitement. He moved back and forth in a swaying motion, shifting his weight from one foot to the other.

Anita didn't miss it, either. She started to turn, grabbing Caleb by the bicep as she did. "Fine. I'll get your money."

"Wait!" The doctor's body moved forward a foot with his exclamation. As Anita rotated back toward him, he pulled in a breath and settled into his calm facade. "Money means nothing to me. I need subjects, and a werewolf…that would offer a new line of study. You have a deal." He strode forward, made it two steps before Anita held out a hand to stop him.

"Don't jerk my tail. We both know he's more important to you than a thousand of the pathetics you feed on. I'll give him to you, but I want another ten thousand…" Anita scanned the space as if looking for something else to demand. Her gaze landed on Samantha. "And her."

If there was any doubt of the werewolf's intentions, the slide of her lips over her teeth and the glimmering stare she directed at Samantha ended it.

If the doctor looked excited at the possibility of getting Caleb, Anita looked ecstatic over the same chance to get Samantha.

A line formed between the doctor's brows as he stared at Samantha. After glancing back at Anita, he smiled. "No more cash, but I am happy to transfer possession of my…guest."

Of course he was. He didn't need her, not with Anita handing him Caleb draped in silver. Rage tore through Samantha. She jerked at her binds and chomped at the cloth between her teeth. "Bitch," she screamed, but it came out muffled, indecipherable to anyone except herself.

Or maybe not. Anita's eyes glittered. Her hand still on Caleb's arm, she gestured to the doctor. "You have the numbers. Hand her over first and I'll leave him behind."

The doctor glanced around the room as if surprised to find her words to be true. For a second, Samantha thought he would back out of the bargain, claim Caleb and her, have his zombies attack the female werewolf, but he only smiled. Then he grabbed Samantha by her bound wrists and tugged her forward. "It is so nice to deal with someone intelligent. I would have hated to lose our working relationship. Perhaps next month you can make up for the clientele I lost. Shall we say one hundred recruits?"

Anita scowled. "That's impossible. We had to span out to Oklahoma to get fifty."

"Go to Mexico, Guatemala, the South Pole. There's an entire world for us to recruit from. Why limit ourselves?"

The way he said it made it sound as if they were a team. Samantha looked at the female werewolf, a new loathing building inside her.

Anita glanced at her, too. She seemed to read the hatred in Samantha's eyes. Scowling, she grabbed hold of Samantha's ties and jerked her from the doctor's grip. "Fine, one hundred. We'll find them somehow."

Without even glancing at Caleb she strode from the

room, dragging Samantha behind her—or trying to. Samantha had no intention of leaving Caleb behind. She dropped to the ground and lay there, nothing but dead weight.

Anita bent over her and hissed into her face. "You don't know much about werewolves, do you? I could pick you up and twirl you over my head if I liked. Of course, I also might snap that delicate little human spine of yours into a million pieces as I did. We aren't the most careful creatures, you know. And we do so like to play with our food." She flashed her teeth. They were white and very human-looking, but somehow she made them look more sinister than a mouth filled with daggers.

Not far away, someone growled.

Without looking to see who, Anita growled, too. "Get up," she muttered. "You are ruining everything." She jerked on Samantha's arm.

Samantha stared at her, realization hitting.

It was a trick…a trap. Caleb was here to save her. The chains were fakes. Once she was out, he'd go into hunter mode, slay the zombies and kill the doctor. The nightmare would be over forever.

Hoping she hadn't already ruined everything, she let Anita pull her to a stand. She didn't object when the other female bent at the waist and levered her onto her shoulder.

Then her head dangling over Anita's back, she groped for a hold on her belt and waited for the sounds of Caleb's attack behind them.

Anita strode from the cave, walked out into the sunshine and began jogging down the uneven rock path that led away from the place. But there were still no sounds behind them and no signs of Caleb.

Her body bouncing up and down, Samantha did her best to hang on to the werewolf's belt, swearing with each jostle that if this wasn't some trick and Caleb didn't walk out of that cave leaving a pile of dead zombies behind him, she would kill the female werewolf herself somehow.

Chapter 21

Anita tossed Samantha onto the dirt. Without bothering to untie her or remove her gag, the werewolf turned to tromp toward a cabin.

Ignoring the sharp pain shooting through her back from her abrupt collision with the earth, Samantha flipped onto her stomach and inch-wormed to a stand. In their travels, the gag had loosened. Using the tips of her fingers she tugged at the bunched material. After a few seconds of twisting her neck and spitting out cloth, she managed to free her mouth.

"Where are you going? Where's Caleb?"

The werewolf halted. Midstep, Anita twisted in place, one foot still extended in front of the other.

"Excuse me?" Her voice was haughty and her expression cold. She was doing her best to let Samantha know her place.

And Samantha didn't give a damn. She hopped closer, teetered and almost fell, but regained her balance enough to grind out. "Caleb. What is the plan?"

"Plan? There's no plan. You heard what I said, what the doctor said. I gave him Caleb. He forgave me the clients I 'owed' him—the ones Caleb killed, by the way. Oh, and he threw in you." She made an annoyed sound in the back of her throat.

"You gave him Caleb." Samantha had to repeat the words; they were that ludicrous. "You didn't give him Caleb." She couldn't believe it, wouldn't believe that this female, werewolf or not, was strong enough or smart enough to capture Caleb if he didn't want to be caught.

Emotion, hot and angry, flashed behind Anita's eyes. "You saw me."

Samantha shook her head. "No, there's something else going on. I don't believe you. You couldn't beat Caleb."

Anita covered the distance between them too fast for Samantha to think of pulling back—not that she would have, tied as she was she would only have landed on her backside in the dirt.

The werewolf grabbed Samantha by the front of her torn and stained shirt. "You know nothing. I'm the alpha. Do you know what that means?" She didn't wait for Samantha's answer, just kept going, her eyes still flashing and her skin flushing. "It means I'm the strongest werewolf around. No one beats me."

Her breath was hot on Samantha's face and her fingers twisted the cloth of her shirt so tightly Samantha heard the material tear. It was important to the female werewolf that Samantha believe her and say so out loud.

Samantha lifted her chin. "Only because Caleb never challenged you." She had no idea of their history, no real knowledge if what she said was true, but she knew it in her gut.

Anita dropped her hold, then with no other warning, slapped Samantha across the face.

Samantha fell. Her face stung, but she could see as the werewolf bore down on her, that she had been lucky. An openhanded slap was nothing compared to what Anita planned to do to her now.

"You're wrong. He did," a male voice interjected.

Both Samantha and Anita froze at the words.

A man, stocky and dressed in a T-shirt and camouflage pants, stepped into view. His arms were musclebound, so much so they barely crossed over his massive chest.

He glanced at Samantha, but only for a second. Then he stared at Anita. "What is she talking about?"

Her hands curling into claws, Anita turned on him. "The full moon is over, Jake. Get back to your life."

He took a step forward. "This is my life. You aren't the only werewolf who cares about the pack, Anita. In fact, maybe you aren't a werewolf who cares about the pack. If you were you would want the strongest to lead us."

Anita widened her stance, and Samantha could see the tremor that ran through her. "The strongest does lead us."

He shook his head and looked back at Samantha. "Who is she?"

"No one."

"She talked about Caleb." He reached into his back

pocket and pulled out a pocketknife. After flipping it open, he tossed it onto the ground beside Samantha.

Using her feet to propel her, Samantha twirled in the dirt toward it, but Anita beat her and kicked the weapon out of reach.

"She's no one, and neither is Caleb. He never acknowledged the pack. He certainly didn't want to lead it." She shrugged. "Not that it matters. He's gone now, and I'm still the strongest."

"What did you do?" There was anger in the man's voice, but it was controlled. He was angry, but he was unsure, too. Samantha watched, trying to figure out what was happening, what her best move would be.

"She gave him to the zombie doctor," she told the stranger.

The man spun, his gaze shooting back to Samantha as if he'd forgotten she was there. The uncertainty was still in his eyes. He shook his head and looked at Anita. "You wouldn't. He's a were. Even if he isn't in the pack—"

"That's right. He isn't in the pack. That's all that's important here. That and that you shouldn't be here." Her hands fisted at her sides, she strode toward him. "Go home, Jake. Go back to your cushy job in the city and do your part for the pack. Collect your paycheck and your bonus, drive your overpriced tank on wheels, work out in your steel-and-glass box of a gym and stay the hell out of what doesn't concern you.

"Caleb isn't here and he isn't coming back. I'm alpha and we both know you can't change that."

Samantha belly-crawled toward the knife. Neither of the werewolves seemed to notice; neither seemed to even remember she was with them.

Her chin jutted out, Anita shoved her face into Jake's.

He was taller than her, but not by a lot. What he gained in height she made up for in attitude.

She lifted one lip and snarled.

Samantha's fingers closed over the knife's handle. She turned it around and began to saw on her binds, praying the blade wouldn't fold up on her as she did.

Jake hadn't moved. He hadn't struck the female daring him to do so, but he hadn't backed down yet, either. Desperate to be free before he did, Samantha doubled her efforts and sliced one finger open in the process. Too busy to curse, she shifted the knife so the sharp side of the blade once again ran over the rope. She bent her wrist up and down, moving the knife as she did.

The blade gnawed its way through the rope with heart-tearing slowness. Samantha concentrated and kept sawing.

"An alpha does what is best for the pack," Jake muttered, but his gaze wavered, dropped down.

"An alpha decides what is best for the pack," Anita countered. She pulled her already impressive frame taller.

Anita was battering the other werewolf down. Samantha didn't know how, but she could see the transformation. It was as if the larger male was melting, shrinking as she watched.

She didn't have time to worry about him. The blade was almost through the last of the rope. As it snapped through the final strands, her cramping fingers lost their grip on the tool. It fell from her grasp onto the dirt. She pulled her wrists apart like the Hulk bursting free from his human form.

Jake's gaze darted toward her; his stance shifted.

Samantha saw his notice, but didn't pause to analyze it. She pounced on the knife and again began sawing, this time on the ropes tying her ankles.

Jake looked up, his eyes meeting Anita's. He sucked in a breath as he did.

His actions meant something; Samantha could tell by the still that settled over the pair. More sure than ever that she needed to be free, she ignored the blisters forming on her palms, ignored the cramping in her fingers and ignored the questions forming in her brain. She didn't know what she would do when she was free. She couldn't outrun a werewolf; certainly couldn't win a battle against two of them. But she also couldn't lie here helpless and let whatever fate Anita had dealt Caleb just unroll.

The blade slid through the last of the rope.

Samantha was free. The knife still open and gripped in her hand, she staggered to her feet.

Jake didn't move his eyes from Anita's face, but Samantha sensed he knew she was free, sensed he expected something of her.

She glanced down at the knife, and then at the tapered back of the female werewolf.

He wanted her to use the blade on Anita.

Samantha had killed before, but it had been a zombie, an already dead creature. Could she kill Anita, even to save Caleb?

Jake pulled in a breath that filled his chest. "I saw Caleb defeat you. I know the truth. You aren't the strongest. You aren't the alpha...not anymore. If Caleb isn't here to claim the position, or doesn't want to claim it, it's up for grabs. Open challenge rules."

"Open challenge? And do you think to try me?"

Anita's voice was confident as ever. She tilted her head to the side and laughed. "You can't beat me. And, as you said, Caleb isn't here. He won't be here ever again. So, who's going to take me on?"

"Me." Arm held out and weapon ready, Samantha threw herself over the space that separated them.

Caleb would be here again. Samantha wouldn't let Anita win.

As Samantha moved, so did the werewolf.

Samantha slashed down with the knife. The blade tore into Anita's shirt, over the werewolf's shoulder and down her arm, leaving ripped cloth and an angry red line of blood in its wake. The blow she delivered wouldn't be fatal, at least for Anita.

Angered by Samantha's attack, it was almost guaranteed the alpha would kill her.

Anita roared and lunged, but Jake shoved her from the front.

Thrown off balance, the alpha landed on the ground. Snarling, she rose on all fours. Her back arched and her neck stretched.

There was magic in the air. The hairs on Samantha's arms crackled. She couldn't swallow. She was about to see a shift, about to be the victim of that shift.

But Anita didn't change. Blood continued to seep from her wound and animal noises continued to flow from her throat, but she stayed completely human.

Her body began to sway. She twisted to look at her wound. "Silver," she spat. "You cut me with silver."

Samantha stared at the knife in her hand, then up at Jake. He nodded.

Still shaking inside, Samantha strode forward and pressed the poisonous metal against the weakened werewolf's throat. "That's right, and if you try to stop me from saving Caleb, I'll show you how he taught me to kill a zombie. You ever kill a zombie, Anita? You know the trick?" She tapped the werewolf on the back of the neck, through her hair. "The brain stem. You pith them just like a frog in biology lab. One quick shove, a twist and voila, one dead zombie. Or in this case, alpha."

Anita growled, but she didn't move. Samantha leaned closer and wrapped her fingers into the other woman's hair, just like Anita had done to her. Then she jerked the werewolf's head back and whispered in her ear, "So, do I win the challenge?"

The alpha lowered her head.

The male werewolf moved forward and took the knife from Samantha's hand. Then he shoved Anita to the ground and pinned her there with his knee jammed into her back.

Samantha staggered to a stand, stared at the pair, but only for a second. She had to get back to Caleb.

No one followed when she ran—not to stop her and not to help her, either. She was on her own.

Chapter 22

Caleb strained his neck to one side. The silver strapped around his body burned. Anita had insisted on the chains. She'd said the doctor wouldn't buy the trade otherwise, and Caleb had agreed because it was the only way to save Samantha. He had pulled on a pair of pants then waited as Anita, her hands gloved, had looped the metal around his body.

The silver burned his skin and drained his energy, but it wouldn't kill him—not unless it was driven into his heart.

But by the looks of the way the doctor was scampering around his lab, Caleb doubted he had any plans to do away with his new prize yet.

After Anita and Samantha had left, the doctor and his zombies had vacated the cave. They had taken him maybe a hundred yards through the woods to a converted bus. Inside was a fully operational lab.

Caleb shifted his eyes side to side, taking in the expensive equipment and wondering exactly how the doctor had paid for it, how he had paid Anita, for that matter.

The doctor approached, a needle in his hand. With cool professionalism he swiped a cotton pad that reeked of alcohol across Caleb's arm, then pricked his vein with the needle. The blood flowed smoothly into a vial attached to the needle. Caleb watched, dispassionate.

Perhaps the doctor wanted to add werewolf-making to his menu of offerings.

"I am so happy you agreed to work with us," the doctor murmured as if Caleb wasn't still draped in silver and completely helpless. "I have been wanting to study the effects of werewolf blood on my LifeAfter vaccine."

LifeAfter. So, that was how he sold his zombie conversion. Bile rose in Caleb's throat. The man was sick.

"Anita had given me a few vials of her blood, but not nearly enough," he said, switching an empty vial for the full one.

The news that Anita had sold her blood to the doctor shouldn't have surprised Caleb, but it did.

"I asked her for a werewolf before, but she wouldn't agree to the exchange. She did, however, give me your name."

Caleb's teeth ground together. So her loyalty to their kind hadn't extended to him.

"I didn't realize at the time how perfect you were. Of course, once I learned more about you…" He popped the current vial off the needle and removed it from

Caleb's arm. After pressing a bandage to the wound and wrapping tape around it, he stepped back. "It was too bad about your parents. I'm afraid early experiments didn't always go as planned, but then with all advancements costs must be paid." Without another word he picked up the vials and strode from the room.

Behind him, Caleb lunged forward. His parents. The doctor knew them, of them. Rage raced through Caleb, but his body, weakened by the silver and loss of blood, fell back against the table.

He stared at the bus's white ceiling. He'd found his family's killer and he couldn't do a thing about it. He could only lie here and wait for the doctor's next move.

Caleb had been left lying on the table for hours. He had lost track of time. The doctor and a few zombies had come and gone, taken more blood, poked at him, swabbed the inside of his mouth and left him again.

The doctor had known about Caleb's family, was responsible for their deaths. In a different world, a world before Samantha, the information would have sent Caleb into a blind rage. He would have forgotten everything except his desire to see the doctor's blood on his hands. But now while he still wanted revenge, he wanted something else more—Samantha's safety.

He had sold himself for that, and as long as he thought Anita and the doctor were keeping their part of the deal, he would keep his.

The door rattled. The doctor or one of his zombies back for more blood. Caleb leaned his head against the vinyl tabletop and closed his eyes. This was his new life—for as long as his blood lasted.

Cool hands grabbed him by the arm, jerked at the needle the doctor had left jammed in his arm during his last foray for blood.

Caleb's eyes flew open. He stared into hazel eyes overflowing with worry and anger.

Samantha. She was here.

Forgetting the silver draped around him, he jerked upward. The chains scraped across bare skin. The previously untouched flesh sizzled. The stench of newly seared skin filled the room.

Samantha pulled back her hands and stared at him, horror replacing everything else.

"Get out," he rasped. The doctor had let her go once. He wouldn't do it again.

Ignoring him, she lifted the chains from his body. It was a wasted effort; they were padlocked in the back and twisted in such a way it would take hours to unwind them. He tried to tell her, but she wouldn't listen. Instead she lay on the table beside him and wedged her body under the chain. So she was pressed chest to chest to him, shielding him from the poisonous silver.

Staring down at him, she whispered, "I'm not leaving you here."

Her hair fell forward, framing her face. He wanted to reach up and brush it away, but with his arms pinned at his sides, he couldn't.

"I only agreed to go because I thought…" Her words tapered off. He could feel her heart beating against his chest, could feel her breath warm on his lips. She smelled of worry and woods, flowers and spice. She smelled of Samantha.

He lifted his head and captured her lips with his.

Her lips were soft and timid against his, making him

realize how afraid she was. Still, despite that fear she'd come here to save him.

"I won't leave you again," she murmured, her lips pressed against his.

His brain told him to send her away, to lie and tell her he didn't love her, didn't need her. That it was the only way to save her.

"I can't—" he started, but she stopped his words with a kiss.

"I know you're a werewolf. I know you killed Allison. I know both should bother me, and I'll admit they did, but neither matters. I love you. Nothing can change that."

She loved him. Despite everything he was and had done, she loved him.

Strength roared through him. As much as the chains would allow, he wrapped his arms around her and kissed her, devoured her, worshipped her.

She loved him and he loved her. Nothing else mattered.

"No!" The doctor stepped into the room. In his hand was a syringe and it was filled with a green-colored liquid.

Caleb knew immediately what it was and what the doctor planned to do with it.

His arm raised over his head, the doctor raced toward them. Caleb flipped over, taking Samantha with him. The needle plunged into Caleb's back, and the icy-cold liquid flowed from the syringe into his body.

Every muscle in his body constricted. His throat closed. He couldn't breathe, couldn't move his weight off Samantha even though he knew he had to be crushing her.

"Caleb," she yelled. Her hands were trapped against his chest, her face cradled against his neck. She clawed at him and screamed his name again.

"Stupid wolf." The doctor cursed. "Bring me more," he bellowed. Bodies shuffled into the room.

Zombies.

"Grab them, flip them over."

Hands, cold and hard like bone, gripped him by the shoulders. Still convulsing, Caleb could feel his body being flipped. The doctor turned to the side and plucked a second syringe from a tray.

Caleb gritted his teeth and fought. Fought the poison tearing through his body, fought the hands trying to flip him over.

"Hold him," the doctor ordered one of his zombies. He leaned toward Samantha, the syringe hovering, a bead of green liquid clinging to its tip.

"It's okay, Caleb. It will be okay," Samantha whispered. But Caleb knew better. He knew if he lost Samantha nothing would be okay ever again.

The twenty-year-old leash he had kept on his wolf snapped. The hold the silver had on him disappeared. In a rush he shifted—one second he was Caleb the man confined by silver chains and the next he was a snapping, snarling wolf, wiggling free of those binds.

He twisted his head toward his tail and the hand that held that syringe. His teeth sank into flesh. Fresh flesh. Living human flesh.

The doctor screamed and tried to jerk back, but Caleb didn't let go, wouldn't let go. He pulled harder, felt muscle and skin pull free from bone. The doctor screamed again. His face white and his eyes huge, he staggered backward. The syringe fell to the ground and spun across the floor, unbroken.

Caleb leaped, but three zombies threw their bodies in front of him. One grabbed him around the neck and lifted him off the ground. He flung his weight back and forth, shoved his feet into the creature's face and tore at its features.

But the monster showed no reaction. Its eyes, hollow and lifeless, stared back at Caleb.

He could hear the doctor's crepe-soled shoes squeaking over the floor and knew the man he wanted to kill—had to kill—was escaping.

Then Samantha was beside him. He could feel her, smell her. He tried to yell at her, tell her to run, but his voice came out a bark and he knew his efforts were wasted.

She picked up a tray and swung it double handed at the zombie who held him. The creature froze, but only for a second and then it returned to squeezing Caleb's neck. The other stood motionless beside it, watching Caleb's life being squeezed from his body, waiting for his corpse to fall.

"Hey, braineaters, hungry?" Samantha yelled from only a few feet away. From the corner of his eye, Caleb could see her and the scalpel she held. As he watched, she slashed down, slicing into her own skin. Blood spurted, and the zombie who held him dropped him onto the floor.

No! It was the only thought Caleb could form. He leaped again, this time making contact with the creature's neck. Frenzied, desperate to protect the woman he loved, he slashed his teeth through the zombie's rotting flesh, turned and attacked the monster beside it and then the third. He twirled, his teeth snapping, his body moving as fast as he could, never aiming, just taking out as much of the monsters as he could until their legs could no longer support them and they fell to their knees. Covered in blood, he kept moving. He couldn't bring himself to stop.

"Caleb?"

Samantha's voice pulled him out of his fog. Thinking he'd done it again, shown her how much of monster he was, he looked up.

She was standing only a few feet away, her eyes wide and her face drawn in shame…and behind her, holding the scalpel to her throat, was the doctor.

"I can't let you destroy them. They gave themselves to me, trusted me." The doctor's voice shook, but his hand was still, too still. "I promised to take care of them."

"Like you took care of Allison?" Samantha whispered.

The doctor jabbed the surgical instrument against her skin. A tiny line of blood flowed over its silver tip. "Allison was different. Allison betrayed me, betrayed all of us, but still I gave her what others pay for, beg for. Even with her betrayal, I didn't hurt her. He did." Hatred flowed from the doctor. "He hurts all of them."

Still in his wolf form, Caleb slid his feet backward, tried to position himself to leap.

The doctor noticed his movement and angled his head. "Shift. I want to see it."

Willing to do anything that would buy him time to think, Caleb complied. This change was slower and more painful than the last, but still faster than any before that. Since he had met Samantha, admitted to himself that he cared for her, each shift had been easier. His wolf was calmer and this was his payment.

Too bad he wasn't in a position to celebrate the improvement.

Naked and human, he stood there. He was unarmed, no human weapon and not a wolf, either.

The doctor seemed to recognize this. He let out a breath, seemed to relax. "Pick up the chain." He motioned to the pile of silver forgotten on the floor.

Caleb hesitated. The doctor moved as if to stab Samantha again. With a nod, Caleb walked to the chain and bent to pick it up. Samantha made a noise, but it was cut off. Not wanting her to do or say anything that would encourage the doctor to hurt her, Caleb scooped up the length of chain. It burned his skin, but the pain was tolerable. He blinked, wondering at the change.

"Now wrap it around yourself," the doctor ordered. Realizing he was risking tipping the man off to his increased tolerance, Caleb draped the chain over his shoulder, cringing as he did. Shoulders hunched, he shuffled to the side then stumbled. On his knees and less than a foot now from where the syringe filled with medicine lay, he looked up. "Let her go," he said, his voice soft and, he hoped, weak.

The doctor stared down at him, his face drawn in a caricature of concern. "I wish I could, but it's obvious you don't understand the importance of my research, don't understand how important it is that you work with—"

Caleb lunged forward, picked up the syringe and drove the needle into the other man's thigh.

The doctor froze, every muscle in his body doing as Caleb's had, constricting, but the doctor didn't recover.

There were no tremors. His muscles just quit moving, his chest quit moving. His mouth was open as if he were going to object, but no noise, not even a gurgle, came from his throat.

Caleb glanced at Samantha. "Leave," he said. He kept his gaze hard, demanding.

He knew she'd seen him kill before, both as a wolf and a man. He knew she'd said she accepted him, but he also knew when presented with the blatant evidence of what he was she would change her mind. She'd run, not just from the doctor and zombies, but from him, too. He was simply saving her the trouble of having to do it.

She took a step back, out of the doctor's reach. Then with her gaze on Caleb, she said, "Kill him."

There was no fear in her eyes, no horror. She knew what Caleb was and what she was asking him to do.

He turned to face the doctor.

Caleb didn't shift. He didn't want this death to be the product of a frenzied wolf attack. He wanted to make sure the doctor knew why he was dying and that there would be no life after for him. The poison moving through his body might be changing the man into a zombie, but it would never get the chance to fully make its transformation.

The serum would never make anyone into a zombie again, not after Caleb found whatever supplies there were and destroyed them.

But first, he had to destroy the man who had created it.

The doctor teetered in place. Halfway between life and death, he couldn't fight, couldn't even object as Caleb plucked a scalpel from a tray and spun him around. His arm wrapped around the doctor's neck, Caleb whispered in his ear.

"Now is the time to pray. Time to pray there is no life after death...not for you." Then he shoved the sharp tip into the base of the doctor's neck and twisted.

All rigidity left the man's body, now nothing more than a corpse. Caleb straightened his arm and let it fall onto the gore-covered floor of the lab.

Samantha's gaze was locked onto the body and Caleb's was locked onto her. There was disgust in her eyes. Caleb saw it, recognized it, accepted it.

Thinking she could get past what he was had been insane.

Not wanting to see that look directed at him, he took a step and turned to the side. "There's money in the car. I hid it in a slit in the upholstery. You'll find it there. Use it to get away."

He closed his eyes and waited for the sound of the door opening, of her running, but the only noises were her breaths, soft and even. Then inexplicably she moved closer until her hand brushed his bare arm.

"Are you telling me to leave? I'll understand if you do. I know I'm not what you want—not a werewolf—but..." Her hand moved away and she turned back toward the door.

Unable to believe what he had heard, Caleb lifted his gaze to her. She stood a foot away, her lower lip trembling and her eyes huge.

She looked...scared.

Scared that he didn't want her? Hope flickered in his chest. He raised his hand, then lowered it again. He'd made a choice twenty years ago, known full well what the cost of that choice would be. He didn't deserve to find a way out of it now.

She took a step toward him. "Caleb?" Then her face folding, she moved to turn away.

With a growl, he jerked her against his chest and brushed her hair away from her face. "I don't want a werewolf. I don't want anything...except you."

Her eyes glimmering, she placed her palm against his cheek. "That's funny, because that's all I have to give."

He didn't wait for her to say more, didn't need to hear more. He captured her mouth with his.

She was his, forever.

Epilogue

Caleb and Samantha returned to the camp. It was deserted, or so Caleb thought at first.

Jake, Anita's second-in-command, was sitting on one of the rocks that formed the edge of the fire pit.

"Anita?" Caleb asked.

What happened to her wasn't any of his business, but he had to ask. Samantha had filled him in on what had occurred after she had left the cave.

The pack wouldn't survive without an alpha. They depended on someone strong to lead them, to keep order. A pack of rogues could be as dangerous as the zombies.

"Gone. She's on her way to Canada. She can join a pack there, take a more submissive role without losing face."

"Will she?" Samantha asked.

Jake stared at Caleb. They both knew the answer. If she didn't, if she tried to do there what she had done here, she wouldn't be relocated. She would be exterminated.

"We need an alpha," Jake offered.

Samantha's hand tightened on Caleb's arm. She had told him Jake thought he was the wolf for the job. What she hadn't told Caleb was how she felt about that.

"Yes, you do," he replied.

"You're the likely candidate."

Caleb laughed. "You think? I doubt many others would agree."

Jake's gaze stayed steady. "They'd be afraid not to. You're the strongest. We all know it."

"Strength isn't enough. There has to be desire, too, and dedication."

"You know what will happen if we don't have an alpha."

Caleb did, but he had other concerns, too. He had Samantha now.

"What? What will happen?" she asked.

Jake's gaze slid to Caleb before answering. When Caleb didn't object, he answered. "Fights. Some will go rogue, maybe attack humans. Wolves need a leader…a leader they know no one else can beat."

Her fingers moved again, pressed briefly against Caleb's skin. "And you think Caleb can stop that?"

Jake nodded. "I know it."

She turned then, so she was staring at Caleb, as if it was just the two of them completely alone. "I'm studying to be a nurse. You know that."

Caleb stiffened. They hadn't talked about how Samantha's plans for her future might interfere with being with him.

"I wouldn't be much of a nurse if something I did endangered others, would I?"

Afraid he knew where this was going, Caleb didn't reply.

She turned to face Jake. "Which cabin is ours?"

"Which—" Caleb stared at the woman he loved. "You mean you want to stay here? You want to run the camp?"

Rising on her tiptoes, she pressed her lips against his. "I want to be with you, and you need to be here. So, I'll be here, too."

He wrapped his arms around her waist and looked over her head at Jake. "For a while, until the challenges are done. That's all I'll agree to." Samantha wasn't a werewolf and while she thought she'd be okay living like one, Caleb had his doubts. And nothing was more important than Samantha. Nothing.

With the pack business taken care of, Jake loaded his SUV and drove off. He would get word out to the pack. Before the next full moon everyone would know of the change.

"Will they miss the money?" Samantha asked.

Caleb shrugged. "I doubt it. From what I've seen Anita is the only one who really benefitted from it."

"So, no more recruits?"

Caleb shook his head. "I never understood that. Becoming a werewolf shouldn't be like joining a gym. No one should be sold on doing it."

Samantha was quiet for a moment. "How about the zombies? There are more somewhere, aren't there?"

Caleb pulled her tight against his body. "There must be. The lab is still out there."

"Maybe the pack can help with that," Samantha said.

"The pack?"

"Killing zombies. They're all werewolves."

Caleb squeezed her again and pressed a kiss to her temple. The pack, of course. He wasn't alone anymore—not as a hunter and not in life.

He would never be alone again.

And he would, with Samantha's and the pack's help, rid the world of zombies once and for all.

* * * * *

nocturne™

COMING NEXT MONTH

Available July 27, 2010

HNCNM0710

REQUEST YOUR FREE BOOKS!

2 FREE NOVELS PLUS 2 FREE GIFTS!

⬧ HARLEQUIN®

nocturne™

Dramatic and Sensual Tales of Paranormal Romance.

HN10

Five hunky Texas single fathers—five stories from Cathy Gillen Thacker's LONE STAR DADS *miniseries. Here's an excerpt from the latest, THE MOMMY PROPOSAL from Harlequin American Romance.*

"I hear you work miracles," Nate Hutchinson drawled. Brooke Mitchell had just stepped into his lavishly appointed office in downtown Fort Worth, Texas.

"Sometimes, I do." Brooke smiled and took the sexy financier's hand in hers, shook it briefly.

"Good." Nate looked her straight in the eye. "Because I'm in need of a home makeover—fast. The son of an old friend is coming to live with me."

She was still tingling from the feel of his warm palm. "Temporarily or permanently?"

"If all goes according to plan, I'll adopt Landry by summer's end."

Brooke had heard the founder of Nate Hutchinson Financial Services was eligible, wealthy and generous to a fault. She hadn't known he was in the market for a family, but she supposed she shouldn't be surprised. But Brooke had figured a man as successful and handsome as Nate would want one the old-fashioned way. *Not that this was any of her business...*

"So what's the child like?" she asked crisply, trying not to think how the marine-blue of Nate's dress shirt deepened the hue of his eyes.

"I don't know." Nate took a seat behind his massive antique mahogany desk. He relaxed against the smooth leather of the chair. "I've never met him."

"Yet you've invited this kid to live with you permanently?"

"It's complicated. But I'm sure it's going to be fine."

Obviously Nate Hutchinson knew as little about teenage

boys as he did about decorating. But that wasn't her problem. Finding a way to do the assignment without getting the least bit emotionally involved was.

Find out how a young boy brings Nate and Brooke together in THE MOMMY PROPOSAL, coming August 2010 from Harlequin American Romance.

MYSTERY CASE FILES

LOOK FOR THIS NEW AND INTRIGUING

BLACKPOOL MYSTERY

SERIES
LAUNCHING AUGUST 2010!

Follow a married couple, two amateur detectives who are keen to pursue clever killers who think they have gotten away with everything!

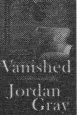

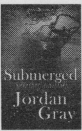

Available August 2010   Available November 2010   Available February 2011   Available May 2011

BASED ON THE BESTSELLING
RAVENHEARST **GAME**
FROM BIG FISH GAMES!